THE CASE OF THE SHIFTING SARCOPHAGUS

The Masked Man Of Cairo Book Two

SEAN MCLACHLAN

To Almudena, my wife
And Julián, my son

Cover design by Andrés Alonso-Herrero.

I

CAIRO, SPRING 1919

The sarcophagus hadn't been there the night before.

When Sir Augustus Wall walked into the main showroom of his antiquities shop, he stopped dead in his tracks and stared. The sarcophagus stood in the center of the room amid his collection of statues, engraved stones, and canopic jars. It was a large specimen made of red granite, its sides carved with a series of rectangular pillars to imitate a palace and topped with a lid showing the hide of a panther in low relief. That it wasn't a royal sarcophagus was obvious by the fact that there was no cartouche in the inscription that ran along the edge of the lid.

What was far less obvious was how a sarcophagus that must have weighed at least a ton could have appeared in his showroom without his noticing.

Augustus ran upstairs and fetched the pistol from his bedside table. Feeling better with its reassuring weight in his hand, he went back downstairs.

Hurrying to the front door, he found it locked and bolted. Then he made a thorough search of the entire house—the ground floor that he used as a shop and storeroom, the courtyard with its burbling fountain and Egyptian statuary, the first floor that he reserved for his private quarters, and the unused second floor. He even went up to the roof, finding the door locked and bolted like the one to the street, and seeing nothing up there except some dusty old ceramic pots for plants and a bare trellis.

The squawk of a neighbor woman hanging laundry reminded him why he never came up here. Cairo's roofs were women's space in the daytime, and at night were used by families, who generally put up screens to keep hidden from prying eyes.

He wanted to hide from prying eyes too, which is why he had taken a house in the old native quarter in the first place.

But now it appeared he had been subjected to an intruder—one who didn't take things but left things behind.

Ducking back downstairs without apologizing to his neighbor's wife—for to speak with her would have compounded the insult—Augustus made his way carefully through the house a second time. He found all the windows locked and secured, and no trace of a break-in.

He stopped and thought for a moment. His opium sleep of the previous night could not have been disturbed by any amount of noise, which explained why he didn't hear the sarcophagus being moved in, but what confounded him was the fact that he could find no sign of forced entry. When he had risen half an hour before, he had washed what was left of his face and put on his mask to hide his war injury, gotten dressed, and had proceeded downstairs as he usually did. Nothing had appeared out of place, he had heard no strange sounds in the house, and until he saw the sarcophagus in his showroom he had no idea that anything was amiss.

At last he returned to the sarcophagus. It was carved in the style of the Old Kingdom and was of fine craftsmanship. Besides a few chips and abrasions here and there it looked in excellent condition. It stood on four thick blocks of wood.

Augustus circled it, studying every detail. Could it be one of Suleiman Hanzade's fakes? Augustus had numerous examples of Suleiman's artistry in his shop, for sale to the more boorish of his customers who didn't deserve real Egyptian antiquities. He sold them mostly to Americans and London bankers and such people as only wanted something to boast about in their drawing room without having any true appreciation of the object's historical importance.

Augustus pulled out a Woodbine from his cigarette case, struck a match against the sarcophagus, and lit it.

Inhaling the smoke, he thought some more. It could, indeed, be Suleiman's handiwork. Not even someone of Augustus's expertise could tell for sure, but that didn't explain how it ended up here. Suleiman and his stunning wife Zehra had always treated him with kindness and would never have disturbed his desire for privacy by breaking into his home. He couldn't think of anyone else who would have either. His few friends respected him too much and his enemies ... well, his enemies would have used the opportunity to kill him in his sleep.

The doorbell rang. Augustus went to the front door and checked through the peephole. Moustafa, his hulking Nubian assistant, stood outside, waiting to start the day's work. Good, he needed another mind to help unravel this.

Augustus decided not to say anything at first. He let the man in and greeted him as usual, and they went into the showroom together to get it ready for the day's customers.

Moustafa stopped as he came into the showroom, his gaze resting on the sarcophagus.

"What an excellent specimen, Mr. Wall!"

"Isn't it? It came last night. Special delivery, you might say."

"Oh," Moustafa replied, peering at it more closely. "Is it from Mr. Hanzade?"

"No. Or at least I don't think so," Augustus replied, taking another drag from his cigarette. "It appeared here last night while I slept."

Augustus proceeded to tell his assistant everything he had discovered that morning, which was precious little. Once he finished, Moustafa looked at the sarcophagus dubiously and then said with apparent reluctance,

"We should open it."

Augustus felt a tingle of excitement. This was turning out to be a good day.

"Yes, I suppose we should. But don't you think we should wait for the police?"

Moustafa shook his head with an air of finality. "No, sir."

Augustus chuckled. It appeared the Nubian had as little regard for the abilities of the Cairo police as he did, although the fellow was too polite to say so directly.

"Very well," Augustus said. "We'll open it."

He went to one of his storerooms and fetched a pair of crowbars. Handing one to Moustafa, they stood side by side, fitting the crowbars into the seam between the lid and the body of the sarcophagus.

With a heave, they pried the lid up an inch. Just as they did so, Augustus felt a jolt of worry. What if this thing was booby trapped? Ancient booby traps had nearly done him in on more than one occasion and this thing could hide modern dangers as well.

But the lid had come up and it hadn't exploded or shot out spikes or anything. Besides, if whoever had put this thing here had murder on their minds, they could have easily dispatched him without his ever waking.

Straining their muscles, they pried the lid up further and pushed it several inches away from the case. Augustus broke out in a sweat from the effort. Even Moustafa, a mountain of a man and one of the strongest fellows Augustus had ever met, looked like he was having trouble.

Once they had moved the lid enough, the two of them dropped their crowbars with a clatter and looked inside.

While Augustus had not been prepared to find a new addition to his stock this morning, he felt doubly surprised at what he saw inside the sarcophagus.

It was an elderly European man. His features showed some refinement, as did his neatly combed gray hair and dinner jacket.

A slash across his throat, covered in coagulated blood, showed that he had been murdered.

2

Moustafa Ghani El Souwaim had a bad feeling about this sarcophagus. The whole affair was a baffling mystery, and when his boss was confronted with a mystery he did not rest until he solved it. That meant, of course, that Moustafa would get no rest either. It also generally meant that he would get shot at, chased, perhaps kidnapped, and all sorts of other unsavory experiences that would take him away from his family and studies.

With a deep sigh, Moustafa resigned himself to what God had written for him. Nur and their five children had tolerated his absences before, and they would have to do so again. As for the article he was preparing on Nubian influences on Late Period Egyptian art, that would have to wait too.

The first thing Mr. Wall did after seeing the body was check the pulse, although both of them knew what the result would be. The man was dead, and judging from the fact that the limbs were stiff but the body had not yet begun to bloat, he looked like he had been so for at least several hours but not more than two days. Mr. Wall cursed and went for the telephone to call one of his least favorite people—Sir Thomas Russell Pasha, Commandant of the Cairo Police. Mr. Wall disliked him because the policeman always forced him to go to social events. Moustafa disliked him because he had crushed the independence rallies earlier that year, killing dozens of Egyptians, injuring hundreds, and imprisoning thousands for no greater crime than wanting to be masters in their own country.

Russell Pasha arrived within half an hour with a colonial policeman dressed in a smart blue uniform and red fez, a man from the Soudan just like Moustafa. The two exchanged glances and a brief nod, but kept quiet as the Europeans talked.

"Well, well, well, what fresh trouble do you have for us this week, Sir Augustus?" the police commandant asked in English. Mr. Wall generally spoke in Arabic in mixed company. Russell Pasha did not. Just because he was in charge of the law and order of Africa's largest city did not mean that he spoke its language.

Mr. Wall pointed at the sarcophagus. "As I said on the telephone, someone has delivered a body to me in rather unique packaging."

Russell Pasha walked over to the sarcophagus, looked inside, and jerked back with surprise.

"Great Scott! I know this man!"

"Do you?" Mr. Wall asked.

"He's Alexandre Legrand, a retired policeman."

Mr. Wall perked up. "Oh, this is getting thicker."

"It will get thicker yet. He was chief of police in Paris until he retired and moved here just after the war for his health."

"It doesn't seem to have done him much good," Mr. Wall said, lighting a cigarette.

"Must you be such a misanthrope? Alexandre Legrand was a good man."

"Obviously someone didn't think so."

"Indeed. You've never met Monsieur Legrand before?"

"Never set eyes on him. I fail to see why someone would give him to me."

"You told me they snuck it into your home and there was no sign of a break in?"

"Indeed. You may look around, of course, not that you need my permission given the circumstances."

"How could you have missed this big sarcophagus here when you returned home?"

"I was already home. I was asleep upstairs."

Russell Pasha put a hand on the sarcophagus. "There's no way they could have moved such a weight without causing a devil of a racket."

Mr. Wall tensed. "I … take medication to help me sleep."

Russell Pasha gave Moustafa's boss a sympathetic look. The police commandant had been through the war too. Moustafa, thank God, had not, but he had seen what it could do to a man.

"Well, we must look around, of course," the police commandant murmured as he looked away.

Russell Pasha and the colonial policeman spent an hour searching the house and found exactly what Mr. Wall had found, and what Moustafa had found while waiting for them to come—that is to say, nothing.

"This is a damned queer business," Russell Pasha said, scratching his jaw. "Well, I'll get to work. First thing's first. Constable, take the body to the car and drive it to the morgue."

"Yes, sir," the Nubian policeman said. Moustafa moved to help.

"If you don't mind," Mr. Wall said, "could you leave the

sarcophagus here for the time being? I have a couple of experts I'd like to have take a look at it. They might give us some clue as to why Monsieur Legrand was killed and why he was delivered in such a fashion."

Moustafa resisted the urge to roll his eyes. He knew his boss would want to get involved in this. He grabbed the body under the arms and pulled him out. The policeman took his feet and together they laid him on the stone floor.

"Very well," the police commandant replied as he peered into the sarcophagus, finding nothing else inside. "It's not like we have room for it at the station. It's yours until we establish ownership. If we don't, well, I suppose it's yours. It was delivered to you, after all."

"If we cannot establish ownership, then it belongs to the National Museum," Mr. Wall said.

Russell Pasha scoffed. "Don't distract me with such petty matters when I have a murder to solve."

This time Moustafa did roll his eyes. The last time the police commandant had vowed to solve a murder, Mr. Wall and Moustafa had done it for him.

Russell Pasha bent down and searched the body's pockets. He found a billfold that had his identity papers in it but no money.

"Whoever did this robbed him too. He had a fine watch and a gold ring as well. Both of those are gone," the police commandant said.

"There's a night watchman on this street. I'll question him," Mr. Wall said.

At last Moustafa spoke up. "I know the man, boss. I can act as translator."

Mr. Wall looked about to object, but then understanding dawned on his face. Or at least half of it. Moustafa still hadn't gotten used to his boss having one half of his face covered by that strangely lifelike and yet immobile mask.

"Um, yes," Mr. Wall said. "That's a good idea, Moustafa. You know the local dialect better than I do. I still need to switch from Moroccan to Cairene Arabic. There are so many differences between the two."

His boss had caught the hint. Russell Pasha spoke no Arabic, and Karim, the watchman, would feel more comfortable being interrogated by a fellow African.

After Moustafa helped the constable load the body into the car, drawing a large crowd as he did so, the constable drove off to the station. As soon as the car left, Moustafa got assailed with questions.

"Someone has been killed in the Englishman's house again?" Bisam the water seller asked, hunched over from the large water skin he lugged around on his back.

"Yes," Moustafa replied.

"That man was born under an evil star," Youssef the barber declared. "Trouble follows him around like flies follow a dying camel."

"Has anyone seen Karim?" Moustafa asked.

"He's usually asleep at this hour," someone said.

"Well, go wake him up instead of standing here gawking!" Moustafa shouted. Didn't these people have anything better to do?

Youssef went off to fetch Karim. Part of the crowd followed him, while another part stayed in front of Mr. Wall's house hoping for more excitement. Others tired of waiting and returned to the Sultan El Moyyad Café across the street to start their tongues wagging. The owner had recently added more outside seating so that his usual clientele of idlers could get a better view of Mr. Wall's house. The street's lone European resident served as a rich source of gossip. Moustafa shook his head in frustration. Was it any wonder that Egypt was a colony of the British and not the other way around?

"What's going on?" a young voice asked behind him.

Moustafa turned and saw Faisal, one of the street urchins who always got underfoot in this neighborhood. The boy was about twelve, with a dirty and patched jellaba and filthy bare feet. His tangle of curly hair stuck out every which way.

"Oh, it's you," Moustafa grumbled. "What are you doing here?"

The boy's eyes went wide. "I heard someone was killed."

"I don't have time for you right now," Moustafa said, waving his hand at him in a dismissive gesture. "In fact, I never have time for you. Go beg somewhere else."

"I'm not begging. Is it true someone was killed in the Englishman's house?"

"It's worse than that. Go away."

"What happened?" Faisal asked.

"Go away, I'm waiting for Karim."

"What happened?"

Moustafa turned his back on him, hoping he'd take the hint. A foolish move, he knew. Faisal never took the hint.

"What happened?"

Moustafa rounded on him. "Mr. Wall woke up this morning to find a body stuffed in a sarcophagus that somehow appeared in his showroom. I don't know anything more. Now go away before I kick your backside so hard it turns into your frontside!"

Faisal did not seem phased by the threat. His eyes grew even wider. "One of those big stone tomb things appeared in his house?"

"Yes, and there was no sign of a break in. Do you see what I'm up against? I have no time to chat with lazy, dirty—"

"The jinn are back!" Faisal cried. This got several people in the crowd whispering amongst themselves.

Moustafa groaned. "How many times do I have to tell you there's no such thing as jinn?"

Faisal jumped up and down. "His house was full of them and then they, um, went away. Now they're back."

"Then you shouldn't linger around here or they'll sweep you up in one of their dust storms and take you far out into the desert and feed you to the jackals."

Faisal froze in terror.

"I meant that as a way to get you to leave," Moustafa said, shoving him.

"I can help!" Faisal protested.

"You can help by going away and not coming back!"

Faisal stuck his tongue and Moustafa lunged for him. The boy scampered away, dodged someone from the crowd who tried to grab him, gave Moustafa a crude gesture, and ran off.

"God save me from such pests!" Moustafa cried.

Just then, Youssef returned with the sleepy-eyed watchman. The fellow was a wiry old man, well past his prime but good enough to keep an eye on the neighborhood at night and call out the time.

"You wanted to see me?" Karim asked, stifling a yawn and adjusting his faded green jellaba.

"Come inside," Moustafa said. He didn't want everyone to hear their conversation, although it would no doubt become the main subject of local gossip soon enough.

Moustafa led Karim into the house and shut the door behind them. Karim started to take his sandals off but Moustafa stopped him.

"The front part is a shop and not the house," Moustafa explained, then led him into the main showroom.

Karim's eyes went wide when he saw all the antiquities gathered together. Statues of deities and pharaohs stood at various points in the room, and shelves along the walls held smaller antiquities such as swords and jewelry. Further up, the walls were covered with Coptic textiles. An arched doorway at the far end opened into a courtyard with a fountain surrounded by more statues. His eyes went wider when he saw Mr. Wall and the police commandant come over.

"Ask him if he saw anyone around the house last night," Russell Pasha ordered.

Moustafa felt like replying that he would have never thought of that himself, that he was astounded by the policeman's brilliance. In fact, he felt like saying, he didn't even realize they wanted to question the night watchman and had assumed they were inviting Karim to tea.

Of course you didn't use sarcasm on a European, so Moustafa turned to Karim and asked the question he was about to ask anyway.

Karim shrugged. "No, I saw no one, just the late delivery."

"Late delivery?"

Karim pointed at the sarcophagus. "That stone box over there."

"Who delivered it?" Moustafa asked, glancing at the large wooden portal that led directly into the room from the street. Like many old houses, the gate was more for ornamentation and was opened only to let in large crowds or a palanquin, a smaller door set into the portal being used for regular comings and goings. Whoever left the sarcophagus would have had to open the entire portal to get the thing in.

"A group of Europeans delivered it," Karim said.

"Europeans? From where?"

Karim shrugged again. "Europe."

Moustafa resisted the urge to slap him. "We've established that. Which country in Europe?"

"I don't know. I didn't speak with them."

"You blockhead! Someone was going into Mr. Wall's house in the middle of the night and you didn't stop and check on them?"

"They were European!" Karim objected.

Moustafa sighed. Yes, that was how matters stood. Europeans could do anything without suspicion. It was like they carried a placard on their chest saying, "Untouchable by Egyptian Law." There had been a case last month of an Englishman who had murdered an Egyptian in some drunken brawl. The law dictated that the killer faced trial in an English court instead of an Egyptian one. The English court, of course, had found him innocent.

"Could you tell me what's going on?" Russell Pasha demanded.

Moustafa translated for him. The police commandant then demanded the answers to several questions that anyone with half a brain would know Moustafa was going to ask next. Mr. Wall, thankfully, kept quiet. At least one European gave Moustafa credit for his abilities.

"What time was this?" Moustafa asked the watchman.

"At midnight. I had just called out that all was well."

"So what did these Europeans look like? How many were there?"

"There were five or six of them, all strong fellows. Dressed simply, not in fine suits like your boss and this policeman. Most looked fairly young. They had a couple of Egyptian workmen with them. They had the stone box on a heavy cart with wheels and rolled it off a ramp on the back of a lorry. The lorry had a little crane with a thick rope tied to the stone box."

"Who let them in?" Mr. Wall asked in Arabic.

Karim blinked. "Didn't you, sir?"

"No."

"But your door was open. They might have been able to pick the lock, but how could they have slid open the bolt?"

"I wish I knew," Mr. Wall grumbled.

"Are you sure you remembered to slide the bolt, sir?" Karim asked.

"Of course he did!" Moustafa shouted. "Do you question his intelligence?"

As Karim sputtered out an apology, Mr. Wall intervened. "It's a perfectly legitimate question. Yes, I did bolt it. I am very particular about that. Besides, the bolt was in place when I arose this morning."

Karim looked as confused as Moustafa felt. "I don't understand how this is possible, sir."

"Neither do I," Mr. Wall said.

"I'm sorry I didn't question them, sir. I assumed it was one of your deliveries. You get so many. I thought it odd that it came so late at night, but your door was open, as I said, and they were moving something in. If they had been moving something out, I would have questioned them."

"It's all right, Karim," Mr. Wall said. "You did your duty. You may go now."

As Karim bowed and started to take his leave, Mr. Wall called him back.

"Um, Karim, one last question. Did you see … me there?"

Karim blinked. "No, sir."

"Of course not," Mr. Wall was quick to say. "Silly question. Thank you for your time."

Moustafa stared at his boss, utterly baffled.

3

Faisal knew that something was amiss the moment the Englishman came up to the roof that morning.

Faisal had been sunning himself, lying out of sight of the neighbor women behind the lip of the low wall that ran around the edge of the roof. When he had heard the rattle of the key in the rooftop door lock, the boy had leaped up and bolted for the little rooftop shed he called home. He scrambled over the heap of old furniture and other junk piled against the inside of the doorway and into the shed.

He had made it out of sight just in the nick of time.

Peeking through a little peephole he'd made in the pile of old wood, he saw the Englishman burst through the door, pistol in hand. The Englishman looked all around the roof as if searching for something.

The neighbor's wife cried out in surprise and no doubt hurried downstairs to hide herself. Didn't the Englishman know how to come onto his own roof without the neighborhood women seeing? Silly Englishman.

The shout sent the Englishman on his way. He moved back to the door, took a last brief look around, and then glanced at the shed.

Faisal froze. If the Englishman found him here he'd be angry. Faisal might even lose the best home he had ever had.

But all the Englishman saw was a shed full of old junk, the same old junk that had been in there when he bought the house. What he didn't see was that Faisal had cleared out the inside to make room for a bed made of burlap sacks filled with straw covered by a tarpaulin and a blanket. It was a cozy little place, safe from stray dogs and bullies, and Faisal wanted to keep it.

The Englishman gave a nervous glance in the direction of the neighbor's house and then went back downstairs, locking and bolting the door behind him.

Faisal let out a breath of relief. That had been a close one.

Why had the Englishman come up here? He never came up here. There must be some trouble!

Time for Faisal to earn his keep. The Englishman didn't know it, but Faisal worked as his watchman. He protected the house from burglars and jinn and other dangers, and all he took in return was this secret house on the roof. Plus a little food from the pantry. Just a little.

Faisal made sure all his meager possessions were well hidden in a little nook he had made under the pile of junk, so that even if someone clambered into the shed all they'd find was a few burlap sacks. After he felt satisfied his secret was safe, Faisal hurried across the roof, peeked over the lip of the wall to make sure none of the neighborhood women were in sight, pulled himself over, and climbed down the outside of the building. He used a drainpipe and the bars on the windows as handholds and footholds.

The wall was easy enough for him to climb, and he had added a few extra holds by chipping away at the seams between the stones with a sharp piece of metal he had scrounged. Most people couldn't climb this wall even with the improvements he had made, but he was the best climber in all of Cairo, perhaps all of Egypt, and he got down the side of the wall as fast as if the wall had been a flight of stairs.

He ended up in a narrow, disused alley behind the house. From there he took a circuitous route between the closely set houses and shops to make it to Ibn al-Nafis Street. Faisal could have simply taken the alley between the Englishman's house and the neighbor's house that led directly to the street, but he didn't want people to see him coming and going through there too much. They might figure out his secret.

Once he got to the street, he strolled along as if nothing was wrong, begging for alms and being ignored as usual. Once he got across from the Englishman's house, he sat on his haunches near the café and waited.

It wasn't long before a big shiny motorcar with a colonial policeman and an Englishman inside parked in front of the house. Faisal watched as they went into the house, took a dead man out to the motorcar, and the colonial policeman drove off with it. When Moustafa came out, Faisal went up to him and asked him what was going on. He got brushed off as usual.

Moustafa was annoying. The Nubian thought he was the Englishman's assistant, but Faisal was way more useful than he ever was. Moustafa didn't live in the neighborhood so he didn't know all the dangers. Plus he didn't know how to do a lot of things that Faisal did. He didn't know how to pick pockets or even how to break into a house! Sure, he was strong and he knew how to use a gun, so he was useful in his own way. He could also read the old picture writing. Faisal didn't see any use in that, but the Englishman liked it.

The worst thing about Moustafa was that he didn't know anything about jinn. He didn't even believe in them! It looked like it was up to Faisal to save the Englishman again.

But how? When the Englishman had first moved in, there had been lots of jinn in the house. Their leader looked like a big man with a crocodile head that pretended to be a statue during the daytime. Faisal had bought a special charm that got rid of them all. Now the crocodile-headed jinn remained a statue all the time.

But what had gone wrong? How could the jinn have beaten the charm? It had been made by Khadija umm Mohammed. Everyone in the neighborhood said she knew more about magic than anyone. If she made a charm, it couldn't be beat.

But wait, hadn't she said that if the charm was removed from the house it wouldn't work anymore? He had tucked it out of sight behind the crocodile-headed statue. Maybe the Englishman had moved the statue, seen it, and thrown it away?

Faisal shook his head. He should have warned the Englishman about it, but the Englishman didn't believe in jinn either and would have thrown it away just the same. Besides, to admit the charm was there he'd have to admit that he had been inside the house.

Faisal sighed. It got really complicated trying to help someone when you couldn't tell them that you were helping them. Now what could he do?

He needed to think, and the best way to think was to eat. He had some bread and apples he had taken from the Englishman's pantry, but in his excitement he had left them up in the shed. He didn't want to risk going back up there while the police were in the house, so he decided to go to the *ful* stand up the street and get some of those wonderful beans. They always made it with extra vegetables and lemon juice, just the way he liked it. A bowl only cost half a piastre and luckily he had just that exact amount of money. The day before, some foolish man had left it on a table in a café to pay for his drinks and walked off in a hurry. Before the waiter noticed, Faisal had plucked it up for himself.

Faisal grinned. That had been a good trick. The waiter would think the man had walked off without paying! But Faisal didn't feel bad, because the man was a stranger in the neighborhood and would probably never go back to that café. No one had gotten in trouble and Faisal ended up half a piastre richer.

He gripped the coin in his pocket and hurried along. It was early morning, and Mina often helped her mother serve *ful* at this hour. If her mother wasn't looking, Mina would give Faisal an extra ladleful.

Mina was eleven, about a year younger than Faisal, so she understood how hungry children got. Adults often forgot.

She was the only child who had a home who acted nice to him. All his other friends were street children like himself. Children with homes looked down on people like him and wouldn't play with him. Their parents told them not to. But Mina's parents were nice, and so poor that they practically lived on the street themselves. They only had a little lean-to made of reed mats by the side of the street to live in. They weren't proud like other parents.

When Mina and Faisal were smaller, they had played together all the time, flying kites made from newspapers Faisal swiped from cafés, or games like jacks and mankala. Then Mina's father, who had run the *ful* stand with his wife, hurt his back and couldn't work anymore, and Mina had to take his place. That was too bad.

Mina was his only friend who didn't pester him for food. No one knew where Faisal got his food, but all the street children knew he had it, and never left him alone. He didn't mind sharing, since the Englishman had plenty and never missed a little here and a little there, but it got annoying. Mina was never annoying.

As he came up to the *ful* stand, he got the morning's second surprise. Mina was wearing a headscarf! It was a pale green and looked new, although made out of cheap cloth. Mina had never worn a headscarf before. She acted differently too. She stood behind the little metal stand that held the big cauldron and ladled *ful* into bowls for two porters who had stopped their donkeys by the road for breakfast, but instead of chattering away as she usually did, she concentrated on her work and kept her mouth shut. Her mother stood nearby stacking kindling to stoke the fire beneath the cauldron and kept looking over at Mina as if to keep an eye on her.

Faisal scratched his head, found a louse, and flicked it away. What was going on?

He went over to the stand and waited for the workmen to move off to rest their backs against the nearest building and eat in the shade. Then he stepped forward.

"Good morning, Mina."

Mina didn't look up at him.

"Good morning," she murmured.

Puzzled, Faisal handed over his coin.

"The Englishman is in trouble again. I'm going to have to help him out as usual."

Mina smiled and looked up at him briefly. "Do you really work for him?"

"Sure. He doesn't know but—"

"Mina!" her mother shouted. "Mind your work."

The girl blushed and her gaze fell down to the big cauldron of beans again. She ladled Faisal a normal-sized portion.

Mina looked like she was about to give Faisal some more, glanced at her mother, and then put the ladle down.

Faisal shrugged and took a big gulp of *ful*. "As I was saying, the Englishman doesn't know that I—"

"Go eat your food next to the porters!" Mina's mother ordered.

Faisal stared at her. She'd never complained about him talking to Mina before. It was obvious she meant it, though, so he went and ate with the porters.

He ate slowly, hoping he'd have time to speak with his friend, but her mother stayed close and Mina didn't come over to talk with him.

Just as he finished his breakfast, he spotted Mina's father walking down the street, making his way painfully, his back twisted. Next to him walked a pot-bellied middle-aged man and an old woman, neither of whom Faisal had ever seen before. The middle-aged man wore a nice jellaba and had a silver ring on one finger. His head was bare and he used grease in his hair to slick it back. As they passed the *ful* stand, the middle-aged man smiled at Mina, who kept her gaze down and nearly dropped the ladle she trembled so much. The man patted his hair to make sure it was all in place and made some comment to the old woman, who smiled and nodded. The three adults passed Faisal and went inside the little lean-to next to the *ful* stand that was Mina's family's home.

Curious, Faisal gave back his bowl, not even trying to talk with his friend, and instead lingered around the lean-to. He wanted to get close and listen to what the three were talking about in there, because it seemed to trouble Mina, but he couldn't get close without Mina's mother seeing.

So he did the only thing he could do—he wandered around that end of the street, begging as usual, getting ignored as usual, all the while keeping an eye on the reed mat that served as the front door to Mina's home.

After more than an hour, the middle-aged man and old woman came out. Mina's father did not. Faisal decided to follow the two strangers, easily falling in a few steps behind them while remaining unnoticed in the crowd.

"... I think we are close to an agreement," the old woman was saying as Faisal got within listening distance.

"Splendid!" the middle-aged man replied, slicking back his hair and rubbing his belly. "I must say you are an excellent matchmaker. I just don't understand why he is hesitating."

"No doubt it is his wife causing trouble. It is often the case when the daughter is so young."

"A wife should obey her husband in all things."

"That is so, sir, but you know how these poor families can be."

"Indeed. That is why we have to come to an agreement quickly, while she still doesn't know herself. These lower class girls dishonor themselves as soon as they begin to blossom."

"Quite right, sir, quite right," the old woman said. "Have no fear. One or two more days and we will have an agreement, and then you and Mina will celebrate your marriage."

Faisal nearly fell over with shock. He hadn't understood much of the conversation up to this point, but the final statement by the matchmaker told him all he needed to know.

Mina was getting married to that fat old fool?

⁂ 4 ⁂

Augustus preferred to be anywhere but the front terrace of Shepheard's Hotel. Despite tourists being the mainstay of his antiquities customers, he loathed them, and the terrace at Shepheard's was the epicenter of Egypt's tourism earthquake. For anyone who wished to study human vanity, superficiality, and conspicuous consumption, there was no better place.

It was Sir Thomas Russell's favorite lunch spot, and the police commandant had an annoying habit of inviting Augustus to eat with him. Avoiding such an invitation wasn't possible with one such as Sir Thomas, especially not when Augustus had just had a body delivered to his house.

So Augustus sat in one of the wicker chairs eating his kidney pie while trying to ignore the incessant chatter around him. It was all boasting and flirting and cricket results gleaned from two-week-old newspapers. Good Lord, what a bore! No one seemed the least bit interested in Egypt. The terrace faced a broad street full of motor traffic and Egyptians passing back and forth on their daily business, plus a whole line of hawkers pressed against the railing selling everything from fezzes to stuffed crocodiles. Few of the people on the terrace even looked out at the street, and the rare times anyone even mentioned Egyptology it was with a sense of resigned obligation, as if coming to Egypt wasn't about seeing its ancient wonders, but to sit here blustering about how much better England was.

And Augustus had to endure it all because one does not say no to Sir Thomas Russell Pasha.

Sir Thomas saved him from a terminal case of ennui by taking another sip of his coffee and actually saying something interesting.

"I think I might have a lead on the Monsieur Legrand case."

"Really, what's that?" Augustus asked, popping a final forkful of pie into his mouth. He was always a fast eater when faced with poor company. He had been thinking of an exit strategy when the police commandant hooked him back in by mentioning the case.

"Before the war he was instrumental in crushing the Apaches. Not the savages in America, of course, but the Parisian gang that took their name."

"I've heard of them. They caused quite a bit of trouble, a bit like latter-day Mohawks."

"Oh yes, they were a gang in Georgian London, weren't they?"

"During the reign of Queen Anne, actually."

Sir Thomas waved away the correction. "Savages, the lot of them. No wonder they take on such names. I suspect that Monsieur Legrand might have been done in by some Apaches seeking vengeance."

"But surely they were all caught? I thought the gang was crushed." While Augustus took a close interest in crime, the gang had all but disappeared by 1914. That had been a war ago, a lifetime ago. He kept memories from that time deliberately hazy.

Sir Thomas took another sip of his coffee and replied. "Crushed? Well, it was and it wasn't. Many of the thugs were killed in police raids or put in prison or sent to the penal colonies, but others escaped. A great number crossed the border into Spain, where they caused no end of trouble before the Spanish authorities woke up from their collective siesta and took care of business. From there many fled to the North African colonies."

"I suppose these Apache fellows could be a possibility, but how do you know it was them and not some other criminal gang? Surely the good Monsieur Legrand made many enemies in his line of work."

Sir Thomas pulled out a pack of Woodbines and offered it to Augustus, who took one and nodded a thank you.

"I daresay he did, but the Apaches are cut from different cloth than your typical riff-raff. They're anarchists, and like to make showy gestures such as this to thumb their noses at authority. It's quite in their style, and we've heard rumors that some members of the Apache gang have come into Egypt in recent months on freighters from Algiers and Tunis."

"Would a gang of toughs go through such trouble with the body?"

"Toughs indeed, but toughs with a political bent. Before Alexandre Legrand was a police official, he was in the army. He was instrumental in quashing the Paris Commune in 1871, making him the enemy of every socialist, anarchist, and rabble rouser in France. The French government loved him, of course, and the conservative press labeled him 'The Lion of Paris'. That would explain why they put him in a sarcophagus with a lion carved on top."

"Actually it's a panther," Augustus said.

Sir Thomas waved away this objection. "I'm not an

Egyptologist and neither are they. It looks like a lion to the untrained eye."

"Fair enough. All right, that does seem like a good line of inquiry, but why deliver him to me? And why in such a dramatic and impractical fashion?"

"I think I can answer your second question. Monsieur Legrand was a lover of ancient Egypt. He made quite a study of it and once in an interview joked that he wanted to be buried like a pharaoh. He seems to have gotten his wish. As for your first question, I have no idea why they broke into your home, or indeed how they managed it. Do you?"

Augustus felt taken aback by the question, as well as the level gaze he was being treated to. "Why would I know? Do you think I socialize with anarchists? I had quite my fill of anarchy in the war, thank you."

Sir Thomas shifted uncomfortably in his seat. "I didn't mean it that way, my good man. But you do live in an odd part of town and are frequently seen in the company of the lower orders of society."

"By which you mean Egyptians," Augustus said, his hand tightening its grip on the arm of his chair.

"More coffee, sir?" asked a waiter dressed in an immaculate red fez with matching vest and slippers, plus billowing white pantaloons. No doubt the management at Shepheard's had decided this was the European idea of how Egyptians dressed.

"No, thank you," Sir Thomas said in English, waving him away.

"I would love some, thank you," Augustus said in Arabic.

"And there you go doing it again," Sir Thomas said as the waiter poured the coffee. "This fellow speaks perfectly adequate English. Must you throw that babble about?"

"Speaking Arabic helps me with my work," Augustus explained, "and my investigations."

The waiter moved away without saying a word.

"You won't be needed for this investigation," Sir Thomas said firmly. "We have the situation well in hand and we're following several leads."

Augustus almost told him what he thought of his police skills but decided against it. It rarely paid to be rude, especially with the rude.

Instead he asked, "Have you discovered where and when he was killed?"

"We talked to his wife. The night before last he went out early in the evening to meet some friends at a café. He never made it. We have yet to find any witnesses to his disappearance."

"Quite gentlemanly of them not to attack him in his home in front of the lady."

"Quite. The Apaches fancy themselves as sort of working class cavaliers. They rarely hurt ladies except for their own low doxies, who don't count. We've put a couple of men on the house just in case."

"Good idea. Then I suppose my work with the case is done," Augustus said, having no intention of leaving the murder unsolved.

"Glad to hear it." The police commandant looked at him hesitantly. "I did have one question, though."

Augustus didn't like the sound of that. "What is it?"

"You mentioned that you cannot be awakened at night? Whatever you tell me will be kept in the strictest confidence."

Augustus tensed. He saw no way of avoiding the question, however. The man would find out one way or another.

"My physician prescribed tincture of opium to keep the dreams at bay."

Sir Thomas nodded grimly. "I'd take it as well if my work didn't force me to keep such irregular hours. Damn that war. I was at Polygon Wood, you know. Filthy business."

The was silence between them for a moment. Augustus looked at him sidelong.

"So how do you sleep?" Augustus asked.

"A couple of stiff ones before bed and hope for the best. What I mean to say is that I worry about you not being able to respond if the murderers come back."

"They could have easily killed me last night had they wanted to. I suspect I'm quite safe, and I will not be moved from my house. They must have done some investigating, however, to know that I live alone and couldn't be woken up."

"Hm, good point," Sir Thomas said, rubbing his jaw. He looked at Augustus. "Very well, we'll speak no more of it."

"Thank you," he said with gratitude. As annoying at the police commandant could be, he did understand some things.

The idea of the murderers observing him unsettled Augustus. How had they found out about the opium? He doubted his physician would reveal such a thing, so they must have seen him buy it at one of his regular trips to the chemist. He tried to recall noticing any Europeans lingering about, but since he went to one of the chemists in the wealthy part of town there had always been other foreigners in the shop. He couldn't recall anything unusual.

So what else did these people know about him, and why pick him in the first place? He had no connection with Monsieur Legrand. Was it only the fact that he was an antiquities dealer who couldn't be woken up? Was it because he lived in the native quarter and thus their movements wouldn't be challenged? There must be more to it than that, something he was missing, or hadn't discovered yet.

Sir Thomas leaned forward. "I do have one small favor to ask."

Oh dear, Augustus thought. *This doesn't sound good.*

"I am happy to be of service," Augustus said, against his better judgment.

"My youngest sister Cordelia is staying here for the season, accompanied by our aunt Pearl. They've both expressed an interest in meeting you. Would you mind showing them a few of the sights? Aunt Pearl wants to buy one or two mementoes and I've assured her that you provide the best. I've told them nothing else about you. That's just between the two of us."

Augustus couldn't have felt more trapped if Sir Thomas had slapped handcuffs on him and hauled him off to the Citadel. That casual comment about not telling the ladies anything about him was an obvious reminder that the police commandant knew he was living here under an assumed name, a crime Sir Thomas chose to overlook. Augustus had foolishly thought that was a courtesy of one gentleman and veteran to another, that the police commandant understood he wanted to cut ties with those who knew him back in England, but now he saw Sir Thomas could use it to get his way any time he liked. Not only would he have to play tour guide to a pair of silly Englishwomen, but it would take time away from investigating the murder. Augustus suspected the latter was the commandant's true motivation.

There was an insult included in all this, no doubt unintentional yet nevertheless present. Young women came down to Cairo for "the season" for only one purpose—to find a husband. Cairo had become quite the meeting place for such things, and Augustus recalled Sir Thomas mentioning on a previous occasion that his youngest sister was already twenty-two and still unmarried. The woman would need a chaperone and Sir Thomas was too busy, so who better than a mutilated ex-soldier who could be trusted to behave himself but would obviously not be a candidate for marriage?

All this flashed through Augustus's mind in an instant, as did many quite vivid fantasies of dispatching Sir Thomas by smashing the coffeepot over his head, strangling him with the tablecloth, or tossing him over the railing so that he would be impaled on that fake antique dagger one of the street vendors was holding up for sale.

None of this showed on the half of Augustus's face that remained to him.

"I'd be delighted," he said.

"Perfect. Ah, here they are now!"

Augustus and Sir Thomas stood as the ladies arrived. As Augustus sleepwalked through the meaningless introductions, which led to pointless formalities followed by insincere pleasantries, he studied the two women. Aunt Pearl was on the wrong side of fifty, plump, and fashionably dressed in a style more appropriate to a woman half her age. The effect would have been comic except for the fact that Pearl had a lively demeanor and quite obviously did not care what people thought of her. This was evidenced by two clues—the first being that she was neither accompanied by her husband nor dressed in widow's black. A spinster aunt, then. The second clue was her florid features and a slight trembling of her hands. A dipsomaniac spinster aunt, although apparently quite happy in that state.

Top marks for Aunt Pearl. The institution of matrimony was only useful for economic gain, producing children, and keeping up appearances. Augustus had all the money he needed and didn't give a damn about children or appearances. Aunt Pearl was obviously of the same mind.

Cordelia proved a bit more difficult to read. A pretty girl with blue eyes and cornflower hair, obviously educated and vivacious, there seemed no reason for her to still be unattached. She had an open, intelligent face that expressed more confidence than he was accustomed to seeing in women, and a direct manner and level gaze.

That gaze fixed on him and he did not like the expression behind it.

She was staring at his mask, of course. Many badly mutilated veterans had been given such masks. It was a project by a group of French artists. She had no doubt seen one before, so why stare for more than the usual second or two?

Because she looked at him like he was a puppy with an injured paw.

Blast, what an obnoxious emotion pity could be! He'd rather be hated than pitied. Hatred was honest; it came with a degree of respect. Pity, however, was demeaning. It automatically put the pitier on a higher plane than the pitied.

For some relief he turned to Aunt Pearl to ask some triviality about the steamer that had brought them here from London. She, too, looked at him with pity, although a pity mixed with disappointment. He had the distinct impression that he had just been crossed off a list.

That's quite all right, Aunt Pearl. I wasn't on the list in the first place.

Once they had sat down, a waiter who had been hovering nearby with a smile pasted on his face swooped in.

"How may I serve you, madams?"

Cordelia turned to him and said something that sounded like "Gone west, mine fetlock."

The waiter's smile did not falter, but a slight glaze filmed his eyes. Augustus had a stroke of insight.

"Do you want coffee?" he asked Cordelia.

"Yes," she answered with an embarrassed smile.

"Gahwa, min fadlak," he told the waiter.

Cordelia repeated the phrase and got it right this time. In fact, she got it pitch perfect.

"I'm afraid my phrase book isn't terribly accurate," she said, then gave a bright, cheery laugh.

"They never are," Augustus replied. "Monsieur Berlitz is Swiss, I think. He should have stuck to making cuckoo clocks. And what would you like, Ms. Russell?"

"Call me Aunt Pearl, everyone does. And I'll order in English. A gin and tonic, please."

"Very good madam."

Augustus snuck a look at his watch. 12:17. Well, at least she didn't drink before noon.

Cordelia leaned forward and put a hand on his arm. If he had been a whole man he would have been intrigued. Now he just felt condescended to.

"It's so kind of you to offer to take us around Cairo," the young woman said.

Oh, so Sir Thomas assumed I'd say yes and already told you, did he? Cheeky bastard.

Out loud he mumbled, "Don't mention it. Glad to be of service."

Aunt Pearl leaned forward, pressing against Cordelia's arm and forcing her to withdraw it. "I'm most interested in seeing your antiquities shop. I'd like to get one or two little things for my collection."

Sir Thomas gestured with his cigarette. "Aunt Pearl has been all over the world and has quite the collection of curiosities."

"I find travel much more invigorating than marriage," Aunt Pearl declared.

Sir Thomas laughed and turned to Augustus. "I suppose you

find it strange for a spinster aunt to be put in trust of introducing a young woman to the Cairo season, but she was the only one in the family who wanted to come. Aunt Pearl yearns to see the ancient sites."

"I wanted to come to Egypt too," Cordelia said.

"For the ancient sites or the season?" Augustus asked.

The bright smile she gave him warned him he had taken a misstep.

"Both," she replied.

Aunt Pearl saved him from having to respond. "I tried to find Ibn al-Nafis Street on the map and had a devil of a time. I needed to summon the aid of the concierge. Right in the heart of the native quarter. You must be mad to live in such a district with all the independent riots going on."

"I am mad," Augustus replied as he picked up his coffee cup. "Dead Frenchmen are regularly found in my front showroom."

Everyone at the table laughed, although Sir Thomas's laughter came out somewhat strained.

"Oh dear," Aunt Pearl tittered, "you are quite mad."

Augustus gripped his coffee cup so hard it almost broke. Yes, he was mad. The sound of gunfire brought him back to the Western Front, and anytime he closed his eyes his dreams were filled with visions of trenches and barbed wire. The opium helped, giving him blissfully blank sleep, but he worried about what happened during that sleep. He had evidence that he had become a sleepwalker. Food disappeared regularly from the pantry, and if he left a bottle of wine by his bed it would be empty by morning. A couple of times he discovered traces of wine in his sink, so he wasn't drinking it but rather pouring it out. He had stopped dissolving his opium in wine and started smoking it. He saw no point in wasting his stock of Bordeaux.

But what else did he do at night? Could he have opened the door himself, some odd part of his psychology allowing the gang to bring in the sarcophagus unimpeded while his conscious mind remained ignorant?

He couldn't dismiss the possibility. He couldn't dismiss any act of madness on his part.

5

Moustafa was working in the antiquities shop alone. Fortunately, there had been few customers and he had managed to slip out to ask around the neighborhood for more information about the mysterious group of men who had left the sarcophagus.

He had discovered little. A few people he had talked with had heard the lorry pull up, and one curious neighbor had peeked out the window in time to see the men unloading the sarcophagus, but he gave no better description of them than Karim had. No one had seen how they had broken into the house, and no one had seen them leave.

Now he was stuck here dealing with tourists while his boss tried to get to the heart of the matter by conferring with the police commandant. Mr. Wall had promised to get back as soon as possible, but something had detained him.

He had just sent an annoying group of Americans on their way. They had poked and prodded at everything, ignoring Moustafa's requests not to touch anything, and had eventually left without buying a single piece. Now they had been replaced by an Englishman in a shabby suit carrying a large briefcase. He wandered around, not asking any questions and not looking terribly interested in the antiquities. Probably a lower clerk in some ministry who had come out of idle curiosity. That happened sometimes. All sorts of people came in thinking the shop was a smaller, free version of the Egyptian Museum.

Seeing that he wasn't needed, Moustafa set to work dusting the shelves. With Cairo's dust it needed to be done every day, and the boss didn't trust the cleaning lady to do it in the showroom with proper care. Some of the objects were quite delicate, not that the tourists seemed to be aware. Moustafa shook his head. When he had first taken this job, he thought only the *crème de la crème* of the foreign community would come to such a place. How wrong he had been!

After a minute he heard a click behind him. Turning around, he saw the customer holding a camera and pointing it at the sarcophagus.

Click. He took another picture.

"Who are you? Get out of here!" Moustafa bellowed, storming over to the man, who retreated. "What are you doing?"

"My job!" the photographer said, his voice shaking a little as he sized Moustafa up. "I work for the *Egyptian Gazette*."

"Out! You have no right to come in here and take pictures! If you print them, my boss will sue you."

Moustafa was tempted to grab the camera and smash it, but the man was English and could call the police.

The journalist obviously realized that as well, because he gave Moustafa a smug grin, although he did so as he hurried for the door.

"That's all right, Fuzzy-Wuzzy, I got what I came for."

Moustafa rushed after him, but the journalist was too quick. Moustafa got the impression that he was accustomed to running away after taking pictures.

As Moustafa glared at the man retreating down the street, he noticed an English couple stuck atop a pair of donkeys led by a filthy boy. The boy waved to him. The English couple looked rather precarious and uncomfortable atop the bony animals, and gratefully climbed off once the boy stopped in front of the shop.

Moustafa took a deep breath and tried to calm himself.

The man took his wife's arm and stepped up to the open doorway where Moustafa stood. Both were dressed all in white ("to keep off the sun" as the guidebooks advised), which only highlighted how dusty they had become while riding the donkeys through the busy streets of Cairo.

"Hello, do you speak English?" the man said in a loud, clear voice, emphasizing every syllable.

"Most fluently sir," Moustafa replied in the sweetest possible tones. "I can also speak French and Arabic if you prefer. Or we can write notes to each other in Old Kingdom hieratic."

Talking back to the customers was bad for business, but Moustafa wasn't in the mood for being obsequious today.

The man only laughed. Perhaps he thought Moustafa was joking.

"I like you, boy. Come on, show us inside."

Moustafa felt the urge to grab the man and shove his head deep up the ass of the nearest ass. Instead he put on a grin and ushered them in.

The donkey boy tried to follow.

"Oh no, you don't!" Moustafa said, pushing him out.

"You'll give me a commission if they buy anything, right?"

"I'll give you a smack across your backside," Moustafa growled. These donkey boys were surly little thieves, but at least they had a semblance of a job, unlike that no-good Faisal.

Moustafa glanced both ways down the street, searching for that dirty face and shock of unruly hair. He'd been lurking about lately, hoping to get more money and food from Mr. Wall. His boss was generous to a fault.

"Hey, I led them right here!" the donkey boy whined. "There are plenty of antiquities shops, you know."

"None as good as Mr. Wall's. Yes, I'll give you a commission. Now move your filthy beasts. They're blocking the entrance."

Moustafa slammed the door in the donkey boy's face and hurried to catch up with the tourists.

"What a remarkable collection," the woman said to her husband. They had already walked through the front hall and into the main showroom as if they owned the place. Now they stood gawping at the vast array of antiquities. The room was nearly filled with ponderous stone statues and colorfully painted mummy cartonnages. Shelves along two of the walls held hundreds of smaller artifacts such as ushabtis, amulets, and weapons. Another long shelf and the floor below was cluttered with inscriptions and sculpture fragments. Coptic textiles hung on the final wall. In one corner, a tall statue of the crocodile-headed Nile god Sobek looked over the scene. At the center of the room stood the mysterious sarcophagus.

The Englishwoman went right up to it.

"What a remarkable piece! This would look stunning in our garden. We could fill it with soil and grow marigolds."

"If we could afford marigolds after the shipping fees," her husband sniffed. "Must we buy some of this old bric-a-brac?"

Moustafa eyed a crocodile mummy hanging from the ceiling

and wondered what it would feel like breaking it over the man's head. The thing would probably disintegrate, leading to another hour of dusting, but it might be worth it.

"Of course we do, Henry. We have to show everyone we've been."

Moustafa forced himself to grin. "If the good sir wishes something more portable, we have a fine collection of statuettes on this shelf."

And every one of them a forgery. I'll sell no real antiquities to the likes of you.

The forgeries had been Mr. Wall's idea, and an excellent idea it was too. Only those who displayed true knowledge and interest were sold genuine ancient artifacts.

The woman looked through the row of statuettes.

"Ah, the animal gods of ancient Egypt. Look, Henry. Here's Bastet the cat goddess, Horus the hawk god, and Anubis the baboon god."

Moustafa cleared his throat. "Actually, Anubis has the head of a jackal, madam. You are thinking of the god Babi."

The woman gave him a haughty look. "You're quite wrong. Anubis has the head of a baboon and often appears as the complete animal, as he is shown here. Your employer should train you better."

Moustafa thought of a few comparisons between his customer and baboons but bit his tongue. She stood in front of a life-sized statue of a baboon, squatting on the shelf, and it was as if she faced a mirror.

"It is an excellent example of New Kingdom sculpture, madam," Moustafa said.

The woman sniffed and looked at it. "I wouldn't say it's of terribly high quality, but at least it's genuine. There are so many fakes on the market, but I can spot them all."

"You must be quite the expert, madam."

Although Suleiman Hanzade is more expert than you. He made that just a month ago.

After much haggling, the two left with a matching pair of Bastet statues dating to circa last March. Sadly, she did not take the fake statue of Babi the baboon god. He thought she and it went well together.

The donkey boy haggled more than the tourists, and it took several minutes and two whole piastres to get rid of the brat.

Just as the boy was getting the tourists on their donkeys for a painful ride to the next place where they'd be relieved of some of their spare cash, Moustafa spotted three much more welcome visitors in a motorcar coming up the street. At the wheel was Herr Heinrich Schäfer, a friend of Mr. Wall's. He was a thin, sandy-haired older German and the world's foremost expert on Egyptian art. Schäfer honked the horn to move the crowd of vendors and camel riders out of the way. A gaggle of street boys ran laughing in the motorcar's wake. With Herr Schäfer came Suleiman and Zehra Hanzade. Suleiman, half Egyptian and half Turkish, was the shop's supplier of fake antiquities, expert forgeries crafted by his own hands. His wife Zehra was full-blooded Ottoman and the manager of the family business. Men were so captivated by her beauty that they often overlooked her brains. That combined with Suleiman's artistic talent had made the Hanzades quite wealthy.

As they parked in front of the shop, the boys caught up and surrounded the vehicle. Moustafa shooed them away, keeping an eye out for Faisal. Once the boys had cleared out to a respectable distance, Moustafa eyed the motorcar. It didn't have a scratch on it. After their previous adventure, Mr. Wall had to spend quite a lot of money to get it back into its previous condition. Moustafa couldn't even spot the bullet holes.

"Hello there, Moustafa," Heinrich Schäfer said in passable Arabic as he got out of his motorcar. He reached into the passenger's seat and pulled out a stack of books secured with a leather strap. "These are for you. I think they'll help with that paper you're writing."

Moustafa's heart fluttered as he took the books and examined their spines. They were various field reports and monographs on excavations in the Soudan. Herr Schäfer was the only European besides Mr. Wall who let him borrow books. Moustafa couldn't even get a membership to the Institut d'Egypte. Africans weren't allowed to sit in a library of African archaeology in an African city.

"Thank you so much, Herr Schäfer!" Moustafa said. After a pause to gather his courage, he asked, "What did you think of my first draft?"

"It's excellent," the scholar replied to Moustafa's profound relief. "Almost ready for publication. You do need to address some of the findings published in these works. Once you have, I believe you will have no trouble getting it published."

Moustafa's chest swelled with pride. It would be his first academic paper. Once he had put the final touches on it, he would submit it to *The Journal of Egyptian Archaeology*, based right here in Cairo. He would finally make a contribution to scientific knowledge!

"Could we stop talking about archaeology for a moment and speak of murder?" Zehra Hanzade asked, alighting from the motorcar. She wore a brilliant peach caftan interwoven with gold thread. Unlike most women, she did not cover her hair, not even with a European-style hat, and let it fall over her shoulders in rich black ringlets like a girl, despite being in her thirties.

Nothing else about her reminded him of a girl, however. No, she was very much a woman. Moustafa forced himself to look her in the eye.

"Quite right, Madam, I am glad to see you again. Good morning, Mr. Hanzade."

The skinny antiquities forger shook his hand and Moustafa was enveloped in the smell of hemp smoke. How this man could create such wonderful works of art while forever sucking on that sheesha was beyond Moustafa's understanding.

Mr. Wall hurried down the street, out of breath. His boss never missed a chance to spend time with Zehra.

"Terribly sorry to be late!" he said through gusts of air when he made it to them. "Got detained at Shepheard's. Zehra, so good to see you again!"

The Ottoman woman treated Mr. Wall to a dazzling smile. Moustafa found himself smiling too. There would be some new fake antiquities in the showroom before the day was through.

"So nice to see you again, Augustus," Zehra said, scandalously putting a hand on his arm despite her husband being present. "Spending time with you always brightens my day."

Mr. Wall looked like a kitten getting scratched under the chin.

Herr Schäfer cleared his throat.

"Oh, hello Heinrich, Suleiman," Mr. Wall said, nodding to them.

"Shall we go inside?" Zehra asked, reminding his boss why they were here.

"Oh, right. Of course."

A curious crowd had encircled them, as always happened in Cairo anytime anything occurred of the least interest. Moustafa shoved a path through.

Once inside, they stood around the unwelcome addition to Mr. Wall's collection.

"A nobleman's sarcophagus of the Old Kingdom," Herr Schäfer said, and then looked at Suleiman. "Or is it?"

Suleiman slowly circled it, his eyes bloodshot but intent. After a moment he shook his head. "No, I did not make this."

"Are you quite certain?" the German academic asked. Suleiman partook of the hookah so much it was entirely possible that he had forgotten that he had ever made such a massive object.

"I always mark my creations with certain patterns of scrapes and chips so that I can identify them later."

"What kind of patterns?" Herr Schäfer asked.

Zehra laughed. "Come now, Heinrich. You can't expect us to give away business secrets, can you?"

"As long as I don't end up putting any of your creations in my book," he replied, pulling out a pipe and filling it.

"I'll check the photos for you," Suleiman said.

"Most kind," Herr Schäfer said with a nod. "It's a nice specimen. The false doors for the *ka* to pass through on either end are well done. Pity we only have these galleries of columns on the long ends instead of more elaborate decoration. Note the graceful curve of the lid with the panther in low relief, only seen on men's sarcophagi. I have a section on this in my book. The panther skin was generally worn by high priests, but could appear on a sarcophagus of the nobility as sort of a stand in for a priest in the afterlife in order for the deceased to be assured of the correct rituals. A panther can sometimes be seen as a symbol of rebirth. The inscription is well preserved,"— Herr Schäfer turned to Moustafa—"but I'll let our expert translate that."

"I am sure you can do it as well as I can, Herr Schäfer," Moustafa said, bowing.

"Nonsense! You have the greatest knack for languages of any man I have ever met."

Moustafa smiled. Herr Schäfer and Mr. Wall were the only two Europeans he had ever met who didn't pretend they were more knowledgeable than he was in areas where they weren't. Why couldn't all Europeans be this way? Moustafa had already deciphered the hieroglyphic inscription that ran along the edge of the lid, but he walked around the sarcophagus again to read it slowly.

"'Intef, nomarch of the Khentabt nome, beloved of the pharaoh Merenre. Oh my mother Nut, spread yourself over me, so that I may be placed among the imperishable stars and may never die."

Suleiman nodded. "That last bit is from the Pyramid Texts. I use it often. It has a poetic ring to it the tourists like."

"You're incorrigible," Herr Schäfer said as he shook his head and chuckled.

"But effective," Mr. Wall added. "I've sold a number of his works with that very same passage."

"Merenre was VI Dynasty, wasn't he?" Zehra asked.

Herr Schäfer puffed on his pipe, the stem disappearing under his sandy moustache. "Indeed he was. Not a very well-known pharaoh. He has a very poorly preserved pyramid at Saqqara. Not much to see now but a heap of limestone rubble. It must have been quite grandiose at one time, but it is nothing to look at these days."

Zehra smiled. "Surely it is not the size of a man's monument that is important, but how long it endures."

Herr Schäfer nodded, paused, and flushed scarlet. Moustafa almost sank through the floor. The things this woman got away with saying! And her husband just stood there in bleary-eyed bliss.

His boss was in a bleary-eyes bliss of a very different kind. Yes, there would be quite a lot of purchases today.

Zehra clapped her hands. "Ah, I think I know where this comes from! I was having lunch with another antiquities dealer last week and he boasted how he had recently sold an Old Kingdom sarcophagus to a group of Frenchmen."

"Frenchmen? Who is this antiquities dealer?" Mr. Wall asked.

"Marcus Simaika."

"I've heard of him," Moustafa said. "A Coptic Christian. He founded the Coptic Museum. The Simaikas are quite an influential family."

"One that would not want to get mixed up in murder," Suleiman said. "Marcus is on the Coptic Council, and a supporter of the independence movement. We will have to be discreet."

Moustafa nodded grimly. Any hint of scandal attached to Simaika's family would be all the authorities needed to crack down on him. Copts and Muslims were showing a rare unity these days, and no doubt the British would love any excuse to drive a wedge between them.

This murder already involved European politics, and now it could stir up the boiling cauldron of Egyptian politics.

6

That night, Faisal had two jobs to do. He did the safer one first to delay doing the more frightening one.

He waited until long past sunset, late enough that Mina would be asleep.

Faisal walked down her street in silence and near darkness, the only light being that of the crescent moon. He saw few people. There was no café on this stretch of the road, so no reason to linger after all the shops were closed. A couple of men out for an evening stroll passed by not far off, but they paid Faisal no attention as he walked silently along the shadows next to the buildings and came to the little lean-to made of reed mats.

He squatted next to the thin wall and pressed his ear against it. If anyone saw him through the gloom, they would assume he was asleep.

For a while he didn't hear much except for the regular *clack clack clack* of a knife hitting a cutting board. No doubt Mina's mother preparing the vegetables for the next day's batch of *ful.*

Then Faisal heard a body shift, followed by a groan. Mina's father. He had been helping some workmen haul bricks to make a little extra money and had wrenched his back. Now it hurt every time he moved.

Before his injury, Mina's father had run the *ful* stand and did all sorts of extra jobs. Mina could play with him and the other children. After the injury, the man could barely walk and Mina had to take over helping her mother at the stand. Plus the extra money he had earned from odd jobs had disappeared. Mina began looking thinner and more worried. Even when business was slow and she had a bit of spare time she didn't have the energy to play jacks or mankala any more.

Faisal sat still and listened, waiting to hear what he needed to know. He could be patient when he had to.

"I just don't like it," Mina's mother said at last. The way she said it made it sound like she had said it many times.

"I don't either," Mina's father replied. "But what can we do? He isn't even asking for a dowry."

They spoke in low tones to keep from awakening their daughter. Faisal had to strain his ears to pick out the words.

"She's all we have," Mina's mother said, her voice breaking a little.

"Yes, but what does she have? She'll get a better life at Abbas Eldessouky's household. The older wives will take care of her."

"But—"

"But nothing. What choice do we have? Would it be better to say no and let her live in this misery? She'll never have another offer like this again. She'll end up marrying a street sweeper! This way she has a chance to live in a proper house and wear proper clothes. God gives with one hand and with the other He takes away. He took away my work, and then gave my only daughter the opportunity of a lifetime."

"She's so young."

"Hamid's daughter got wed at ten. Even rich people do it. If I could work, I would never consider it. But as things are …"

Mina's father let his voice trail off. Faisal imagined him giving a resigned shrug. There came another groan as Mina's father moved. The *clack clack clack* of the knife started up again. He heard a soft snuffling, as of suppressed weeping.

Faisal tiptoed away. So that was it. That pot-bellied bastard had made an offer Mina's family couldn't afford to refuse.

What could he do? If Mina got married to a rich man, she'd be stuck in his house all the time and Faisal would never see her again. This was terrible!

At least he had learned the man's name. Also, Mina's parents hadn't actually said yes yet. It sounded like they would soon, but weddings took many days to plan. Faisal had some time. Probably not much, because Abbas Eldessouky sounded like he was in a hurry.

He wasn't sure what could do about it tonight. Find Abbas Eldessouky's house? And then what? Sneak in and steal enough money for Mina to run away? No, she would end up in more danger than she was in now. Poison his tea? No, Faisal couldn't kill anyone, not even someone who wanted to steal Mina. He squatted against a wall and remained there for an hour, deep in thought, but no solution came.

Faisal realized he was delaying doing what he really needed to do, which was to go check on the jinn at the Englishman's house. That scared him almost as much as Mina going away.

Still, he had to do it. The Englishman's home was his home too, and neither of them would be safe until those jinn got taken care of.

As he snuck through the alley behind the Englishman's house, he tried to summon his courage. He needed to enter through his secret entrance on the roof and go all the way down to the ground floor of the house in order to check on the magical amulet he had placed there. If the Englishman or Moustafa had found it and thrown it away, he'd have to buy another, even if it cost another 25 piastres. He had no idea how he'd afford it. Magical amulets didn't work if you bought them with stolen money.

He scampered up the side of the house and went into his shed to find a match and a candle. There was no way he'd go into that house full of jinn without some light.

The large, square roof was open in the center, looking down on the courtyard below. Faisal peered down, searching every shadow for any strange shapes. Once his heart clenched when he thought he saw a pair of eyes looking up at him, but then he realized it was only the moonlight gleaming off the polished stone of a statue the Englishman had put near the fountain.

At least he hoped it was a statue. Jinn could turn into statues sometimes.

Faisal shuddered and looked away. He made his way to a raised area on the other side of the roof. It sloped up and had a row of windows facing the north, the direction of the prevailing winds. The wind blew through the windows to cool the main sitting room below.

The Englishman hardly ever used that room, since he didn't have a family and almost never had company over. Faisal didn't understand why he wanted to live alone, but it meant that Faisal had a free run of the house at night.

At least until the jinn had arrived.

He peeked through the window. The moon was only a thin crescent, and its pale light barely penetrated the gloom below. Faisal swore he saw the shadows move. Biting his lip, he struck a match—the Englishman had so many matches he never missed them—and lit the candle.

He raised the candle over his head and peered down into the sitting room again. All seemed still and empty down there. Then his heart flew into his mouth as one of the shadows wavered and seemed to grow arms that reached up to grab him.

Faisal almost screamed before he realized a breeze had made the candle flicker and caused the shadows to dance.

He let out a breath of relief and leaned his head against the glass.

Something caught his eye.

There were marks on the glass. They looked like paw prints. Faisal held his candle up to get a better angle. Now that he could see better, he noticed they looked a bit like paws and a bit like handprints. And on the windowsill, a few hairs were caught in a rough part of the metal. He pulled them off and examined them. They were a silver-gray.

Then it struck him. Baboons! They had hands and hair just like this. He had seen lots of baboons. Street entertainers did shows with them. They could be trained to dance and jump and take coins from people's hands. They were very clever animals, almost as clever as monkeys and a lot stronger. But they were smaller than him, and could easily get through this window and climb down. From the looks of it, more than one baboon had come through here. But there were prints only on one side of the glass. The baboons had entered this way, but they had either stayed in the house or had gone out another way.

So the jinn were turning themselves into baboons! He had to be careful. Baboons were dangerous. Not as dangerous as a giant man with a crocodile head, but bad enough.

Now came the really scary part. He had to blow out the candle. He needed both hands free to climb down the wall of the sitting room. If the baboon jinn came at him while he was doing that, he'd be in big trouble.

Summoning his courage, he blew out the candle. He stood there for a moment shivering in the warm spring night, then finally put the candle in the pocket of his jellaba and squeezed through the window. The window frame scraped at his belly and back as he wormed his way through. Once he made it, he held onto the windowsill for a moment to rest before swinging over to grab the lip of an arched doorway connecting the sitting room and the hallway. From there it was an easy climb down, his fingers and toes gripping the seams between the worn old stones along the side of the arch.

Faisal relit the candle the instant he got down. That made him feel a little better. He peered around the sitting room. A couch and low table with a few books on it were the only furnishings. The rest of this floor was empty. The Englishman only came up here to use the sitting room sometimes on hot days. Jinn liked abandoned places, so they could be lurking anywhere.

With a shudder, Faisal moved to the main hallway, starting a bit when he saw his own reflection in the inside window overlooking the courtyard. He squared his shoulders. He had to be brave and not think every little shape was a jinni coming to get him.

Faisal tiptoed down the stairs to the first floor. He could hear the Englishman snoring. Holding his hand in front of the candle so he didn't cast too much light, he peeked in on him. The Englishman lay fast asleep as usual. Nothing could wake that man once he went to bed. He noted with satisfaction when he saw no bottle of alcohol on the bedside table. Faisal hated it when people drank. His father of vile memory got drunk every night before he had disappeared one day when Faisal was eight. The Englishman used to drink before bed, and Faisal took it upon himself to pour out the bottle anytime he came in the house. The Englishman had stopped bringing bottles to bed for a couple of weeks now, although for some strange reason the room had a funny odor these days, like the Englishman had been burning something.

He glanced around the room. He didn't see any jinn in here, but of course they couldn't hurt the Englishman so they were probably hiding elsewhere. Jinn had no power over Europeans, although they could still cause lots of mischief. Faisal took care not to look at the Englishman's face. He took his mask off when he went to bed, and Faisal had seen what it hid. A German shell had taken half his face off.

Faisal shuddered. Those baboon jinn would do the same to him if he wasn't careful.

Turning away, he passed through a room full of books and to the top of the stairs leading down to the ground floor.

He crept down the stairs, his bare feet making no sound on the cold stone. The candle wavered as he moved, making the shadows dance and his heart jump.

Passing through a short hallway, he came to the main front room, where the Englishman kept most of the ancient junk he collected and sold. Why did foreigners like this stuff so much? All it did was take up space and attract spirits. If Faisal was rich, he'd never spend his money on things like this—just food, a nice place to live, good clothes, toys, and food.

He trembled as he crept between all the strange shapes, those graven faces staring at him in the dim candlelight. Some looked like men, while others had the heads of jackals and hawks.

And over there was the worst one of all—the giant jinni with the crocodile head that Faisal had defeated with a magical amulet. It looked like it was still turned to stone, but Faisal knew that jinn could be tricky. He approached with care, ready to bolt for the door if the jinni moved a muscle. He kept his ears perked and glanced behind him at every step, worried that one of these creatures would sneak up behind him.

At last he made it to the statue. He squeezed his arm between the crocodile jinni and the wall, expecting at any moment for the stone to become flesh and for the huge creature to reach down and pop him into his gaping maw.

But the crocodile jinni didn't change, and Faisal's hand grasped the amulet he had placed there a couple of months before. He pulled it out and examined it. It hadn't been defaced or broken. Its magic remained intact. So how could the jinn be up to their old tricks?

Faisal turned from the crocodile jinni and screamed. A baboon squatted on a shelf nearby, looking at him like it wanted to eat him up.

He backed away, saw an old bronze sword lying on a table, and grabbed it. The blade was bent and chipped, but it felt reassuring in his hands. The baboon still sat on the shelf, staring directly at him.

"Go away!" Faisal said, shaking all over. "This is my house."

The baboon didn't respond.

Faisal stepped forward and clonked it on the head with the sword. Metal rang out on stone, and the sword snapped in two.

Luckily for him, the baboon didn't attack. In fact, it didn't do anything. Faisal saw it was a statue just like the crocodile-headed jinni.

Faisal stared at the two stone creatures. What was going on? It looked like the spell worked to trap the jinn, but they still managed to move that stone box somehow.

Clutching the stub end of the sword in his hand, he moved over to the stone box. While Faisal never liked coming in this room in the dark, he had been here enough to know that the big stone box must be the one that had appeared. He had never seen it before.

Cautiously he examined it, even daring to peek inside the half-open lid. Nothing. Just a big stone box. He got on tiptoe and noticed something carved on the top. Setting the candle on the lip of the box, he climbed up and saw it was a carving of a lion. Could this lion jinni have transported itself and the box into the house?

Then he understood. Of course! The lion jinni picked up that European body somewhere (because jinn couldn't kill Europeans he must have already been dead), and decided to play a trick on the Englishman by putting the body in his house. But the magic charm Faisal had placed in the room took effect, and the lion jinni turned to stone, stuck on top of the very same box it had wanted leave in the house. The baboon jinni had been turned to stone the very same way.

So the house was safe from jinn after all! They could come in, but once they did they got trapped.

Sitting atop the stone box, Faisal let out three silent cheers. Then he rubbed his foot on the face of the lion, gave it a crude gesture, and hopped off.

He put the sword back where he had found it, fitting the two broken pieces together. The Englishman would never notice.

Feeling much better, he went to the pantry, grabbed a few things to resupply his stock upstairs, and headed back to the roof window.

As he clambered through the window, he wondered about those baboon prints on the glass. More than one baboon had come through that way, but he'd seen only one downstairs. Where could the others be?

The more he thought about it, the more troubled he became. Obviously if jinn could still enter the house, the charm didn't take effect immediately. That baboon jinni had managed to make it all the way downstairs before getting turned to stone. Who knows how much mischief the jinn could get into in the meantime?

No, he and the Englishman still weren't safe, he thought as he bedded down in his rooftop shed. He'd have to talk with him tomorrow.

And there remained the trouble with Mina. That troubled his dreams all night long.

7

Augustus woke up the next morning in a foul mood. He scoured the house and found no sign that the murderers had returned. That left him feeling oddly neglected. He had hoped they would leave some taunting note, some clue, as to their identity.

Moustafa had wanted to stay the night to stand guard, but Augustus forbade him. If the murderers had come back, they would have ended up in a fight with his assistant while he lay drugged and helpless.

He could, of course, have not taken opium last night, but that meant a sleepless vigil with a pot of strong coffee while awaiting the dawn. Sleep without opium was not an option.

Now Moustafa was just opening up the shop. Augustus said little to him, lost in his own thoughts. He had to babysit those women this afternoon. How on Earth was he supposed to investigate a murder while saddled with them?

His mood was not improved when the peddler who brought

him his copy of the *Egyptian Gazette* every morning made his delivery. Right there on the front page he saw a photo of his showroom, prominently displaying the sarcophagus under the headline “Deadly Delivery to Local Antiquities Shop”. Below was a long article about the murder and discovery of Monsieur Legrand’s body, recounted in lurid detail with numerous embellishments to the facts. The claim that Monsieur Legrand had been done up in full pharaonic regalia was the least creative among them, although it did paint an amusing picture. Augustus began to skim the article until one line near the end caught his eye.

“Sources at the highest level state that the police are searching for the band of Edmond Depré, a prominent leader among one of the fiercest bands of Apaches, the criminal anarchist gang that terrorized Paris before the Great War. Depré had been sentenced to twenty years at a penal colony in southern Algeria but is known to have escaped and come to Cairo, swearing revenge against the former Parisian chief of police.”

“Moustafa!” Augustus shouted.

His assistant came running. Augustus thrust the paper in his hands and waited as he read it.

“I am sorry, boss. I thought he was a customer and the minute I turned my back he pulled out a camera.”

“Now we’re going to have half the city beating a path to our door. We’re closed today.”

“Sorry,” Moustafa repeated.

“It’s not your fault. These newspapermen stick their noses in everywhere. Actually this might be a good thing. I can’t imagine Sir Thomas leaked this information to the press, and he runs a tight enough ship that no one else would have either. No, I think this journalist got his information from a different source. Let’s go pay him a visit.”

Moustafa cracked his knuckles. They sounded like a series of pistol shots.

"I would gladly shove that camera down his throat, sir, or anyplace else you feel appropriate, but I wish to accompany the Hanzades to Marcus Simaika's house today to follow up on that lead."

"Very well, I'll just have to beat the fellow to a pulp myself."

Moustafa grinned. "If you do, sir, please take a picture."

"A pity I'll miss Zehra," Augustus sighed. "But it's best to split up and cover as much ground as possible. Do give her my regards and tell her I'd like to have tea sometime soon, and let's share with each other everything we learn, no matter how trivial. One never knows what will turn out to be useful."

"Yes, boss."

"Oh, and Suleiman is sending a shipment over. You'll find the check on my desk."

"Of course, boss."

Augustus grabbed his cane and headed out.

He hadn't made it far before a street urchin started following him.

"I leave you in God's hands," Augustus muttered in Arabic, using the usual Egyptian phrase for dismissing a beggar.

"It's me!" a familiar voice said.

Augustus looked at the boy for the first time.

"Oh, hello Faisal. Not busy filching apples from the market today?"

"I heard about that big box with the body in it," Faisal said as he walked beside him.

"You and everybody else. I seemed doomed to forever be at the center of neighborhood gossip."

"I told you your house was infested with jinn. They, um, went away, but now they're back! They creep in at night to cause all sorts of mischief."

Augustus chuckled. "How many times to I have to tell you there is no such thing as jinn? By the way, did you see anyone coming into my house that night?"

"No. I was asleep, and jinn can turn themselves invisible anyway."

Augustus stopped and turned to the boy. Faisal took a step back. Despite their acquaintance, the boy was still a bit skittish with him. Unfortunately, that didn't make him go away. "Look, they were not jinn but men. Human beings. Well, human beings of a low order. Karim saw them, as did one of my neighbors. They unloaded the sarcophagus, that's the big box you were talking about, and brought it into my house."

"Really?"

To Augustus's surprise, the boy looked relieved rather than disappointed at being proven wrong. Faisal scratched his head for a moment, then scratched it more persistently. Augustus didn't want to know what he was scratching up there. Then Faisal switched to scratching his armpit. Finally, the boy looked up at him.

"How could they have opened the bolt?"

Augustus cocked his head. "How do you know my front door has a bolt?"

"Um, all front doors have bolts!"

"I suppose you're right."

Faisal brightened. "I know! The jinn opened the bolt."

Augustus groaned. "Didn't you once tell me that jinn don't associate with Europeans?"

"Yes. Everyone knows that."

"Well, the group that entered my house were from France.

That's in Europe." Augustus decided not to mention that they had two Egyptians with them. Faisal would latch onto that as proof that one of them was a sorcerer. "The body was of a Frenchman too. The murderers are from a gang called the Apaches who—"

"The Apaches!" Faisal's jaw dropped with shock. "The Apaches are here in Cairo?"

Augustus stared at him. Could Faisal actually know something useful? Living on the street, the boy came across all sorts of information and witnessed all kinds of seedy goings-on. Faisal probably knew as much about crime as the police commandant, and witnessed more. Cairo's streets were no place for a child, but no one did anything about all these homeless children.

"You know about the Apaches?" Augustus asked.

"Of course! They are very great fighters. They kill people all the time. They break into houses and kill everybody inside and take all their things. I didn't know they had come to Cairo. That's very bad."

"How do you know about them?"

"Tariq ibn Nagy told me. He knows all about them."

"Does he really?" Augustus replied, getting more and more interested. This boy offered no end of surprises. "Could you take me to him?"

A sly smile spread across Faisal's face. "Well ..."

Augustus sighed. "Yes, Faisal, I'll buy you lunch."

"And a give me a piastre."

"Lunch and half a piastre."

"Half a piastre is nothing to you!" Faisal whined.

"Taking me to this Tariq fellow is nothing to you."

"Oh, all right." Faisal moped. "This way."

Faisal led him through the labyrinthine streets of the neighborhood to a small square he had never been to before. An

Ottoman-period mosque stood to one side, its walls striped with alternating courses of red and white stone and its slim minaret gracefully covered with calligraphy in low relief. Before the mosque was an open area where several vendors sold produce. A little to one side stood a man with a short, pointed beard wearing an odd jellaba made up of a patchwork of different colors. He had a headscarf made of some glittery material more suited for a bridal dress than a man's headwear. He gestured to passersby, calling to them with words Augustus couldn't hear over the sounds of the crowd. Atop a wooden stand in front of him sat a large rectangular box. The box was painted a sky blue decorated with stars and crescent moons made of hammered tin. Along its length were several little glass windows that looked like they had been made out of the bottoms of bottles.

"That's Tariq ibn Nagy," Faisal said in hushed tones. "He knows all about the Apaches."

Augustus looked at him doubtfully. "I thought you were taking me to some criminal figure. Who is this fellow?"

"You'll see. He knows everything!"

As they approached, Augustus could hear his patter.

"Come see the wonders of the world! Come see tales of heroism and derring-do! Only a half piastre to be sent into a world of magic and mystery."

"Faisal, I don't think this man is going to be of much help."

As they came up to the man and his box, Tariq ibn Nagy turned to them.

"Ah, Faisal! My best customer. Who is this esteemed guest you bring with you?"

"This is the Englishman I told you about," Faisal said, jumping and spinning in the air.

Tariq ibn Nagy put a hand on his heart and bowed. "It is an honor to meet you, sir. Faisal talks about you all the time."

"Does he now?" Augustus felt both surprised and amused.

Tariq ibn Nagy raised a finger to the sky. "Ah yes, he says you are a man of rare bravery and education. I have been waiting for him to bring you to me, for I teach all that is hidden."

Augustus felt like leaving, but he knew from bitter experience that Faisal would only follow him all day, pestering him to return.

"The boy says you know something about the Apaches."

Faisal jumped up and down. "Are you still showing that?"

Tariq ibn Nagy smiled at him. "I am."

Faisal tugged at Augustus's sleeve. "It's only half a piastre for each of us."

"For what?" Augustus asked.

"To look in the box. Then you'll see all about them."

"Faisal, I really don't think—"

"Come *on*. I'm trying to help you!"

Visions of Faisal dogging his footsteps throughout all of Cairo rose before him. With a grunt he dug into his pocket, pulled out a one piastre coin, and gave it to Tariq ibn Nagy.

The man bowed again, set down a pair of tiny stools before two of the box's windows, cleaned one with his voluminous sleeve, and invited Augustus to sit.

Augustus glanced around. People had begun to stare. Not that this was anything new. In his neighborhood everyone stared at him because he was a foreigner. They also stared at him because of his mask. Giving them a third reason to stare wouldn't make much difference.

They sat. Faisal squirmed and fidgeted on the stool next to him, half mad with excitement. Tariq ibn Nagy lit a blue candle festooned with golden stars and moons, opened a small door at the back of the box, and put the candle inside.

"Look," he intoned.

Augustus peered through the glass and saw only darkness. Then he heard a *clack* inside the box, as of a metal barrier shifting, and suddenly the interior became illuminated.

Before him appeared an engraving of Red Indians attacking a wagon train in the American West of the previous generation. It looked like it had been cut from the cover of some American dime novel, probably scrounged from some hotel room after being left behind by a young tourist.

"Behold the fierce Apache! Terror of America. When the white men came into their land, they fought with fierceness and bravery, killing settlers and soldiers alike."

Augustus stifled a chuckle. Out of the corner of his eye he glanced at Faisal. The boy was enraptured.

"This is a story that happened many years ago, in the Great American Desert, where the Apache dwell. They are fiercer than the Bedouin, and braver than the lion."

Augustus heard another *clack* within the box, and the engraving moved away, to be replaced by another engraving. As he had suspected, the words *Beadle's Dime Library* were just visible at the top of the image. The picture showed an Indian chief with a big headdress of feathers reaching halfway down his back. He gripped a tomahawk in one hand and a dripping scalp in the other.

"Behold the bravest Apache of them all, Chief Mohammed."

At this point Augustus did chuckle. "Oh, the Apaches are Muslims now, are they?"

That earned him a bony elbow in the ribs.

"Shhh," Faisal commanded. Tariq ibn Nagy went on.

"Chief Mohammed was the terror of the desert, as strong as ten men and faster than a cheetah. He was the greatest among his people, protecting the innocent and defeating the guilty. When he grew angry, lightning flashed in the sky."

The entertainer flipped a lever back and forth and the light flickered over the image of the Indian chief.

Tariq ibn Nagy then proceeded to tell a tale of Chief Mohammed protecting his people from the evil white men. His biggest challenge, however, was a traitor in his own tribe, the wily warrior Snaketongue, who wanted to steal the Indian princess Fatima from Chief Mohammed. Princess Fatima was, of course, the most beautiful maiden in the tribe, so beautiful that birds followed her everywhere, singing about her beauty. Snaketongue, who Faisal booed every time his name was mentioned, had convinced Fatima's parents that he would be chief one day and that they should give her to him in marriage instead of to her true love Chief Mohammed. Snaketongue spread lies about Chief Mohammed, saying he was a coward. To prove Snaketongue wrong, Chief Mohammed attacked a wagon train all by himself. The picture of the wagon train reappeared, gradually turning red as Tariq ibn Nagy eased down some lever inside the box. Returning triumphant to the village with an armful of American scalps, Chief Mohammed challenged Snaketongue to a duel and suddenly the light started flashing again. Two marionettes appeared within the box, painted up like Indians. Augustus glanced up to see Tariq ibn Nagy pulling some strings that ran through the top of the box, narrating the fight as he did so. The marionettes jumped and fought, hitting each other with little wooden tomahawks. With a swing of his mighty tomahawk, accompanied by a flash of red light, Chief Mohammed cut Snaketongue's head off. The marionette's body crumpled to the bottom of the box and the head bobbed on the end of the string.

Faisal cheered and clapped. The light went dark and Tariq ibn Nagy stepped back and took a bow, putting one hand over his heart.

Augustus stood.

"Thank you for a very entertaining experience," he told Tariq ibn Nagy.

"You are most welcome to come back anytime, good sir."

As Augustus walked away, Faisal followed.

"So that is what you do with all the money you squeeze out of me?" he asked the boy.

"Only when I have a little extra. Mostly I spend it on food. Aren't you going to ask him about the Apaches?"

"Well, it was all quite amusing but it doesn't get me any closer to figuring out where these Apaches are or what they want. The Apaches I'm looking for are from a … different tribe."

"I'll find them for you."

"That's quite all right, Faisal."

"For free!"

"Nothing with you is free."

"Well, it's free until I find out something."

"Something useful this time, if you please."

"Wasn't it great how Chief Mohammed saved Princess Fatima?"

"A brave man, to be sure."

"And birds followed Princess Fatima everywhere!"

"Quite poetic."

Faisal went silent for a moment. Augustus glanced at him. Silence was a rare state of being with the boy. Faisal looked deep in thought, kicking a stone in front of him as he walked.

"Is it all right to go against the wishes of a girl's parents if you need to save her?" he asked.

"Well, like the story said, the Princess Fatima was about to be married to an evil man, so I suppose it would be all right then."

Faisal's face brightened and he leaped into the air. "Chief Mohammed is a hero!"

"Most assuredly."

Faisal put a finger to his chin. "I could never cut someone's head off, though."

"No one is asking you to, Faisal."

Faisal looked up at him, all eagerness once more. "You're right! There's more than one way to save a princess from a bad marriage. Let's get lunch while I think about it."

"What on Earth are you talking about?"

"Nothing. Don't worry, I'll help you out too."

After stuffing Faisal with shwarma and giving him his half piastre, Augustus got free of the little mite and headed to the offices of the *Egyptian Gazette*. The man at the front desk said the photographer's name was Patrick Hind, but that he wasn't available at the moment because he was in the darkroom. The receptionist seemed to anticipate that Augustus wanted to lodge a complaint and tried to fob him off to a subeditor, but Augustus shoved his way through and entered the newsroom. Englishmen and Egyptians sat hunched over rows of untidy desks, pounding furiously on typewriters. Stacks of notes and newspaper clippings were piled everywhere. One young man saw him and bounded over.

"You must be Sir Augustus Wall. Pleased to meet you," he said, extending a hand. "Would you care to comment on the murder that happened in your house the other—"

His question got cut short by the metal head of Augustus's cane being jabbed into his stomach.

A sign told Augustus where to find the darkroom. He opened the door, which elicited an immediate squawk from within, and peered inside.

By the light of a dim red bulb he saw a man bent over a row of low tubs on a table. An unpleasant chemical smell permeated the air.

"How dare you barge in here?" the photographer said. "You've ruined my negatives!"

"I'll ruin more than that," Augustus growled, closing the door behind him and jamming a chair against it.

As the photographer strode up to him, fists clenched, Augustus jabbed his cane into his stomach, grabbed him by the hair as he doubled over, and dunked his face into the nearest tub of chemicals.

He held the photographer there for a moment, letting him struggle, then pulled him up for some air.

"What was that for?" the man sputtered.

Augustus dunked him again.

When he pulled him out a second time the man pleaded. "What do you want?"

Augustus dunked him a third time. A furious knocking came at the door.

"One moment, please," Augustus said in a pleasant voice.

That caught whoever stood outside off guard. For a moment there was no sound except for the photographer's splashing, then a voice called, "Is everything all right in there?"

"Private conference about a breaking story," Augustus said. "All is well."

The photographer began to struggle more. Augustus realized

he had forgotten to bring him up for air. Augustus turned his head so one ear was above water, or above the level of whatever noxious chemicals they used to develop photographs, and whispered, "Be a good boy and don't shout when I let you up again, or next time I shan't let you up at all."

Augustus held him down for another second or two to show that he meant business before pulling him up. A photo print was stuck to the man's face. Augustus kindly peeled it off.

The photographer gasped for breath. A knock came at the door.

"Is everything all right in there?" the voice asked again.

Augustus tweaked the photographer's ear.

"Yes!" the photographer managed to call out, although his voice sounded somewhat hysterical.

"You are Patrick Hind, are you not? Perhaps I should have verified your name before meting out justice. Checking one's facts is the cornerstone of responsible journalism, after all."

"I am Patrick Hind. What do you want of me?"

"You broke into my shop."

"It's open to the public."

"Not for journalists it's not. The police commandant is a personal friend of mine, you know."

That was more than a bit of an exaggeration, but this ingrate didn't know that.

"I-I—"

"You took photographs on my property without my permission, causing me to lose a day of work to keep the gaping hordes away. I could sue you for damages. Also, you misattributed the information in your article. You didn't get Edmond Depré's name from the authorities, did you?"

"Of course I did!"

His head went back in the vat of developing liquid. The knocking started on the door again.

"Cover up the negatives, I'm coming in!"

Augustus pulled Patrick Hind back out.

"A Frenchman told you the name," Augustus said. "Tell me all you know. A man's been murdered and you're speaking with the murderers in order to sell copy. I could have you up on charges."

"I didn't speak with the murderers!"

Augustus smacked him. The doorknob rattled, but the chair jammed against the door held.

"Who did you speak with, then?"

"A man named Claude Paget. I don't know if that's his real name. He told me he wasn't an Apache and didn't know them, that he was only a messenger. When I offered him money to tell me more he refused, saying he didn't know anything more."

Someone banged on the door. Several excited voices started talking on the other side of it. Augustus paid no attention.

"Why would they do this, and why deposit Monsieur Legrand in my house?" Augustus demanded.

"Claude said they wanted to thumb their nose at authority, and show how they had gotten revenge. I don't know why they picked you. They said something about you being an executioner, but I don't know what that means. Let me go!"

Augustus smacked him. "Keep your voice down. Where can I find this Claude?"

"He's the doorman at number two Sherif Basha Street."

Augustus let him go. The door vibrated with a sharp bang, but the chair continued to hold. Augustus kicked it out of position and opened the door just as the man on the other side rammed at it with his shoulder a second time. Instead of hitting the door, he flew through the open doorway, through a curtain of prints hanging from a line, and smacked into the wall beyond.

"Thank God you've come!" Augustus cried. "Your photographer assaulted me. Call the police!"

He waved his cane in the air as if in panic, thereby clearing a path through the little crowd of journalists clustered around the door. His sudden appearance and outburst caused enough confusion for him to get through. Some of the newsmen asked what happened, others accused him of attacking the photographer, while still others asked if he might be telling the truth.

Within half a minute he made it out of the office. A couple of the more persistent members of the press followed him, demanding an explanation, but once they got to the street he rounded on them and shouted he would go to the police station to have them all up on charges. This stopped them in their tracks, and he was able to get away.

Once free, he strolled down the street whistling a contented air. He doubted the photographer would lodge a complaint, not with what Augustus had cornered him into confessing.

Now he had to pay a certain French doorman a call.

Unfortunately, he had a far more onerous task to perform first. He had to deal with those relations of Sir Thomas Russell's.

He felt a rising sense of dread that could not be accounted for by the mere obligation of wasting an afternoon with a drunken spinster and a wide-eyed young woman in search of a husband. Something about the photographer's words bothered him.

The Apaches called me an executioner. Why? Of all the cases I've solved I don't think I ever sent one of their gang to the guillotine.

A volley fired in the distance, its thunderous boom echoing through the years. Augustus staggered and the sidewalk faded for a moment, replaced with a grassy field.

He shook his head so violently his mask slipped, and he hurried to replace it.

"No," he said out loud. "That's not it. That can't be the answer."

Augustus hurried on his way, shouldering through the crowd and trying not to think.

❧ 8 ❧

Moustafa stifled a yawn as he and Herr Schäfer drove to meet Suleiman and Zehra Hanzade. He had stayed up most of the previous night working by candlelight on his paper. The monographs Herr Schäfer had lent him had proven very useful, and he had spent many enjoyable hours reading them by candlelight and adjusting the text of his paper.

"You're going to be sleepwalking all day if you keep this up," his wife Nur had told him from bed as he sat at the tiny desk in the corner of their one-room house on the edge of town.

She was right, of course, but what could he do? His boss wouldn't rest until this murder was solved, and the shop wouldn't be able to do business. If he wanted to get this paper finished, he had to sacrifice sleep. Usually the muezzin woke him up, but this morning at dawn his call to prayer had signaled the end of Moustafa's work for the night.

It had all been worth it. Those borrowed monographs told him of fascinating new discoveries from the Soudan and the southern areas of Egypt around Aswan. The pieces of the puzzle had come together, and Moustafa's paper now clearly traced how Nubian artistic styles influenced Egyptian art well before the XXV Dynasty moved north out of Nubia around 700 BC to take over Egypt and establish their capital at Thebes. It would be a groundbreaking study.

Moustafa dozed a little in the motorcar as Herr Schäfer wove around donkey carts and camels. He had vivid, fleeting dreams of fame and prestige in the Egyptological community.

The mansion of Marcus Simaika stood in the crowded old streets of the Coptic district of south Cairo. Moustafa had never been to this neighborhood before, and noted with interest that other than there being churches instead of mosques, and notably fewer beards among the men on the street, it looked just like any other neighborhood in the city.

Simaika lived in a European-style mansion enclosed by a high wall. The two doormen both had pistols in holsters on their belts. Zehra had telephoned ahead and they were immediately ushered into a fine sitting room decorated with medieval Coptic textiles and wood carvings.

Simaika was a portly man in his middle years whose most distinguishing features were his thick white moustache and his steady, piercing gaze. He dressed in a European suit that looked like it had been imported from London and spoke French with a refined accent. This was out of courtesy to Herr Schäfer, who being an educated man of course spoke excellent French. Moustafa felt flattered that the Copt assumed he spoke French as well.

After the usual introductions and pleasantries, plus the required offer of tea and a heaping plate of pastries, Simaika was quick to get down to business. To Moustafa's surprise, Simaika addressed Moustafa directly.

"I heard where that sarcophagus I sold ended up. No doubt that is why you are here."

"Yes," Moustafa said, somewhat taken aback. "How did you know I work for Mr. Wall?"

"How did I know that the city's newest antiquities dealer has an assistant fluent in hieroglyphics? You underestimate yourself, Moustafa Ghani El Souwaim. You are quite well known in our little circle of dealers and suppliers."

"I see," Moustafa replied, unsure whether to be flattered or worried. With the amount of trouble his boss regularly landed him in, it would perhaps be better to remain anonymous.

"You have a rare ability for languages, from what I hear," Simaika said, switching to Arabic. Then he switched to English. "A man like you could be quite useful to me."

"Thank you, Mr. Simaika, but I am already employed," he replied, saying the first half of the sentence in Arabic and finishing with English. He felt tempted to throw in some ancient Greek he'd picked up but decided that would be rude. On the other hand, Mr. Simaika might reply in kind and Moustafa wasn't sure he could keep up his end of the conversation.

"A pity," the Copt said, keeping that steady gaze on him for a moment before turning to the others. "Now on to the matter at hand. You are no doubt here to ask after the men who bought that Old Kingdom sarcophagus. Let me tell you all I know. Firstly, as I am sure you are aware, I spend much time rummaging through Coptic monasteries, churches, and old houses looking for antiquities for the Coptic Museum. Pope Cyril has been most gracious in allowing me access to all religious buildings. In the course of my searching I often find or am offered various pagan artifacts. If I can get a good deal, I buy them and sell them on at a profit. It helps fund my work. Well, a few months ago when in the Delta I was offered that sarcophagus at a good price."

"Who sold it to you?" Zehra Hanzade asked.

The Copt shrugged. "No one of importance. A local village headman who claimed that some of his peasants discovered it. A simple man who was glad to get paid more than he earned in six months for some stone that otherwise would have been used as a water trough for bullocks."

Zehra laughed, eliciting smiles from every man in the room. "Six month's wages for a village headman is considerably less than what that sarcophagus is worth. I commend you on your skill. Perhaps my husband and I should spend more time in the villages during our antiquities hunting expeditions."

Moustafa noted that she glanced his way when she said this, a signal that Marcus Simaika didn't know the antiquities they sold were fakes. Moustafa was the only one who had discovered their secret, and only because they had created a duplicate of a statuette that he had seen come out of the ground with his own eyes. Pure luck on his part, and it appeared that otherwise luck had always been on the Hanzades' side.

"Indeed," Simaika said. "It is time consuming but every now and then one finds a bargain. I put the sarcophagus up for sale, along with a few other objects collected in my last expedition. Only the pagan objects, mind you. I never sell my Coptic heritage. I placed a small advertisement in the *Egyptian Gazette* two weeks ago, and got a quick response."

"What did the advertisement say about the sarcophagus?" Heinrich Schäfer asked.

"The exact words were 'Old Kingdom sarcophagus with lion skin decoration.'"

Moustafa smiled. Did no one recognize a panther when they

saw one? It didn't matter. If Sir Thomas Russell's assumption was correct, the mistake had roped in the Apache gang. Marcus Simaika went on.

"A few days later I had a visit from three Frenchmen. Their appearance took me aback. Obviously working class and obviously ignorant of antiquities. They spoke such a low French that I could barely understand them. I almost threw them out, thinking they were thieves taking a look at my stock with plans for some nighttime burglary, but they showed great enthusiasm about the sarcophagus and flashed quite a lot of cash, so who was I to say no?"

"Did they have any Egyptians with them?" Moustafa asked, thinking of the two Egyptians Karim the watchman had noticed.

"No, but when they came to pick up the sarcophagus they brought two more Frenchmen. These were equally low class, although one was a clever fellow who set up quite a network of pulleys on the back of a truck to move the sarcophagus. I wish I could have better understood his method. He moved it with such ease it was as if it was made of wood rather than stone."

"Could you describe them?"

"Rough characters, all in their twenties or early thirties. One has several thin scars, as if from a razor, along the back one one hand and forearm. Two had tanned skins and had obviously lived in our part of the world for some time, while the others were sunburnt, obviously more recent arrivals. The clever one was a recent arrival. He wasn't the leader, though. All took instructions from the toughest of the lot. He was the one with the scars, and a tan, and looked the oldest."

"Did you get their names or addresses?"

"None were mentioned. I'm afraid that's all I know. Oh, two other things—they paid in French francs and my guards disarmed them when they came in. My men are quite good at spotting hidden arms."

"What did they carry?" Moustafa asked.

"Pistols and knives, each and every one of them. Except for the leader. He didn't carry anything at all."

Suleiman took another pastry from the plate on the tea table and asked, "I don't want to give offence, but I must say I'm amazed that you let such people into your house."

Marcus Simaika laughed. "After the independence demonstrations, all the foreigners go armed. The knives seemed a bit odd, of course, since most are content with pistols, but they gave up their weapons readily enough and as I said they paid the asking price. That was enough to buy several fine Coptic textiles to adorn a new room in the museum. After all these foreigners have taken from us, I was only too happy to receive something back. Oh, no offense intended, Herr Schäfer. Foreign scholars who respect our ways are always welcome in our country."

"None taken, good sir," the German said, puffing on his pipe.

The Coptic leader raised his hands to the air. "I'm afraid there's nothing else I can tell you. I haven't heard from them since. I'll be sure to get in touch if I learn more. And please, don't bring my name into the investigation."

"Of course not," Zehra said. "We understand the delicate position you are in."

They got up to leave. As they passed through the front hall, Moustafa stopped to admire some bas-reliefs mounted on the wall. One showed a pair of Christian crosses flanking an *ankh*, the ancient Egyptian symbol of life.

"Interesting, isn't it?" Simaika said. "This is quite early, perhaps 5th century. The first Christians in our country adopted the use of the *ankh* to symbolize the eternal life offered by God. Later they switched to a crucifix like the rest of the Christian world. This is a transitional piece. I have others like it, including one long frieze of alternating *ankhs* and crosses. I hang this here to remind myself that the dividing lines between the various religions aren't as clear as we tend to think. We are all, are we not, seeking the divine?"

"I saw a demonstration during the first days of the big rallies where both Copts and Muslims had linked arms to block the police from moving down the street," Moustafa said.

Simaika's face lit up. "That's what we need more of in this country—unity. It's the only way we'll be able to kick the British out."

Moustafa glanced at the others, but they had already moved down the hall to admire some intricately carved wood paneling.

"I'm not sure we're ready for independence," Moustafa said. "Most of our people are ignorant and apathetic."

"If not now, when? The very act of struggling for our freedom will prepare us for it. Wouldn't you rather work for an Egyptian?"

Moustafa blinked at the sudden change of subject.

"I am quite happy with my current job," he blurted out.

Simaika raised a calming hand. "From all I have heard, Sir Augustus Wall is one of the good ones, and I am sure working for him is most stimulating, perhaps too stimulating. But I can offer you an interesting position. There's more to our history than pharaohs and pyramids. I could teach you Coptic, and teach you all about our art. You could come on my collection trips. Wouldn't you like to explore the storage rooms of monasteries that date back a thousand years, uncovering old manuscripts that haven't been read in centuries? And I'll match what he's paying you."

Moustafa froze for a second, his body at odds with his racing heart. At last he said, "Mr. Wall has been good to me. Thank you, but I think I'll remain where I am."

Simaika inclined his head and smiled as if he had expected this response. He produced a business card and handed it to Moustafa. "If you ever change your mind, call me any time. I'm going to the Sinai next month. Have you ever seen St. Catherine's? It's one of our nation's great religious monuments. Once we have our freedom we will need trained men like you to manage our heritage. There could be a place for you in the new order."

Moustafa didn't know what to say to that, so he said nothing. Taking the card with a bow, he went to rejoin the others. He spent the car ride back in silence, deep in thought.

Moustafa managed to grab a quick nap before Mr. Wall returned. To his surprise, he did not come alone. He brought a murderer along—Sir Thomas Russell Pasha. How many innocent protestors had that man ordered shot in the streets a couple of months ago? No one knew for sure. The government claimed only one, the Wafd Party claimed two hundred, and the truth lay probably somewhere in between. Moustafa himself had seen several die. And then there were the hundreds injured, and hundreds more still languishing in tiny cells in the Citadel.

Moustafa struggled to control his anger. He couldn't touch that man and live. Oddly, the police commandant came accompanied by a woman whose resemblance and easy manner with him made Moustafa guess that she was his sister.

"Things all right at the store here today, Moustafa?" Mr. Wall asked.

Moustafa understood the message. They would reveal nothing to Russell Pasha. Moustafa suspected his boss liked showing up the police commandant. Moustafa liked it too.

"Nothing of note except a few business matters we can discuss after we've entertained our guests, boss. Would the police commandant like some tea?"

"No thank you," Russell Pasha said.

Pity, Moustafa thought. *I would have enjoyed spitting in it.*

He turned to the woman. "Madam?"

"No thank you," she answered, not looking at him but at Mr. Wall. "Will you show me around?"

"Very well," Mr. Wall said. Moustafa could tell by the curt reply that he was impatient.

The woman seemed to pick this up as well, but instead of taking the hint she smiled at Mr. Wall, took his arm, and led him over to a shelf of statuettes.

"These are the sorts of things Aunt Pearl likes to have on her mantelpiece. She has quite the collection of Indian gods and goddesses."

"Then one or two animal-headed deities would fit well with all the multi-limbed Asians," Mr. Wall said. "Perhaps Aunt Pearl should pick them herself?"

"She did want to come," Russell Pasha said, "but she felt a bit tired after her, ah, afternoon constitutional."

"If it was anything like her noon constitutional, an elephant would feel tired," Mr. Wall murmured.

"Steady!" Russell Pasha said, but his sister only laughed.

"You're wicked!" she said.

"Madam, you have no idea," Mr. Wall replied.

Moustafa busied himself with dusting and setting out some new displays sent by the Hanzades while his boss tried and failed to alienate the woman through mild rudeness and a noticeable lack of attention. For some reason, that only made her friendlier. Moustafa decided not to try and unravel that particular mystery.

Egyptian women were hard enough to understand; European women were inscrutable.

After a few minutes, his boss managed to make some excuse to come into the back room with Moustafa.

"So what have you discovered?" Mr. Wall asked.

They exchanged all the information they had learned, which sadly did not amount to much. When Mr. Wall said he would put pressure on the doorman who had delivered a message for the press, Moustafa shook his head.

"Let me go, boss. I'll follow him and see if he meets with this gang again. I can also ask around the neighborhood. Give me a bit of money to loosen some tongues and I'll see what I can learn."

"I can loosen his tongue the same way I loosened the photographer's tongue."

"I think the subtle way will be best now that we are getting closer, and …," Moustafa trailed off, unsure how to put it delicately.

His boss tapped his mask. "And I'm visible a mile off? You're quite right. Here's a bit of spending money, and you're on danger pay from now on."

"If you stop getting caught up in murder investigations, Mr. Wall, I will forgo all pay for a month."

His boss laughed, thinking he was joking. Moustafa felt tempted to correct him, but knew better than to try.

It did not take much investigation to learn something of Claude Paget, the doorman at number 2 Sherif Basha Street. Every building in that fashionable district had a doorman, most of them Egyptian. The fact that Claude's building had hired a European doorman set it apart as more fashionable than most. The building, like the others on the street, was built in the Colonial style and inhabited mostly by Europeans of the middling sort who could not afford a house. European shopkeepers and businessmen, or young professionals recently arrived in Egypt hoping to make their fortune, these were the sorts of people Moustafa brushed shoulders with in the streets. He also saw a fair number of well-off Egyptians, all hoping to raise their social status by boasting of their Greek or French or Italian neighbors.

Moustafa curled his lip in disgust. While he admired many things about Europe, he despised these Egyptians who tried to be more European than the Europeans. Didn't they understand that the Europeans would never accept them, no matter how much they pretended?

Take those two fools, for example, a pair of Egyptians who looked one generation from the farm but dressed in cheaply made imitation Western suits. There they stood, speaking loudly to each other in French even though their common language was Arabic. But why speak the local language when you can impress a street full of your neighbors by speaking French?

And bad French, at that.

"Il a dit que c'était mon faute," one said, projecting his voice as if his friend stood half a block away.

"Mais c'était pas ton faute!" the other replied.

"That's incorrect," Moustafa said as he passed by, "You don't say *'mon faute,'* you say *'ma faute'*."

The two glared at him. They were the kind of Egyptians who thought themselves automatically superior to a dark-skinned Nubian from the south. Moustafa smiled and continued on his way.

Moustafa went about his investigation in a straightforward manner. Knowing the doormen of all neighborhoods spent their days sitting at their posts observing their street and having little to do but gossip with passersby, he simply went to the building opposite number 2 and engaged the doorman in conversation.

The doorman was a watery-eyed old Nubian with a ready laugh and proved eager to share some time with a fellow southerner. Moustafa posed as someone looking for an apartment on the street. He offered the man a cigarette, sent a boy playing nearby off to fetch some tea from the nearest café, and started asking all about the neighborhood. The doorman was only too happy to sing the praises of his building and district, and, by the time he had accepted a third cigarette and a second tea, had moved on from housing prices and the social status of the neighbors to the oddity of having a Frenchman sharing his profession across the street. They could see him standing at his post, a younger man dressed in tidy livery and greeting the residents as they passed through the front entrance. Moustafa noted that one of his arms hung slack at his side and guessed the man had been injured in the war. It took only a minimum of coaxing to get his new Nubian friend to tell all.

Much of it was useless—how the man behaved in an arrogant manner with the other doormen, how he was often drunk or hung over on duty, how badly he spoke Arabic, and how he didn't understand the complicated system of bribes and favors that made life work in Cairo. Moustafa did learn that Claude Paget was his real name, which told him something else—that the man was stupid. He delivered a message for a gang of killers to the press using his real name! It wasn't until near the end of the conversation that Moustafa got what he really wanted.

"When he works the day shift he's asleep half the time. See how he's nodding off at his post? These Europeans don't know their work. It's because he spends all his nights at The Gardens of Paradise."

"What's that?"

"Ah, I can see you're a good Muslim if you have to ask that! It's a belly dancing bar. A low den of sin if there ever was one. I am ashamed to say just as many supposed Muslims go there as do unbelievers. He'll be there tonight; I'll bet a month's wages on it."

Moustafa continued to chat with the man, and even accepted a tour of a vacant apartment, asking all sorts of questions about prices and amenities. The spacious rooms and fine views over the city made him think of his little one-room house and dusty yard on the fringes of the city. Nur and the children deserved a place like this, but who had that kind of money?

After they finished the tour it was time for evening prayer, and the doorman lent him a prayer rug and together they bowed toward Mecca as the neighborhood muezzin made the call to the faithful.

Once he finished his prayers, Moustafa stood up, feeling clear-headed and calm as he always did after making his peace with God. Perhaps one day He would reward his faith by granting him a higher station in life. Then he could give the children a proper education. But it was all God's will and he must submit to whatever was ordained. He only hoped the Almighty would forgive him for going to a belly dancing bar in search of a criminal.

It didn't take long to find. The first man he asked eagerly told him the way. Moustafa felt like smacking him. He felt like smacking himself too, for asking directions to such a foul place.

Sending up a quick plea for understanding toward Heaven, Moustafa made his way through the darkening streets into a narrow side lane filled with an outdoor café. Men sat at small tables, sipping tea and smoking sheeshas. Judging from the heady smell of the smoke, not all the sheeshas were filled with tobacco.

Beyond the café, the lane grew darker, the windows all dark

and the shops all closed, until he came to a small, blank door with a single red electric light burning above it. There was no sign, but the dinginess of the place and the music coming from within told Moustafa he had found his destination.

Squaring his shoulders and taking a deep breath, he knocked on the door.

The door opened instantly, and a big brute of an Egyptian, every bit as big as Moustafa, stood blocking any view of the interior. The fast-paced music of a tablah drum, tambourine, and oud filled Moustafa's ears, and his nostrils were assailed with the combined stench of tobacco, hashish, alcohol, and sweat.

"I don't know you," the bouncer said. The words came out as both a statement and a challenge.

"I'm just a man looking for a good time," Mosutafa said, slipping him a ten piastre note.

The money disappeared into the pocket of the man's jellaba.

"Entrance fee is five piastres."

Moustafa didn't need to be told the previous ten piastres did not cover it. Luckily his boss has been generous with his expenses. He pulled out another note and handed it to him.

"Go in," the man said.

Moustafa stepped across the threshold, and into a world he had only heard about through wild tales at the café. Peering through the smoky haze, he saw a long, low room with several mirrored columns. Small round tables filled much of the space, and even though it was barely past eight o'clock most of the tables were full. Men drank liquor and laughed and smoked pipes and sheeshas. Waiters in glittering gold pantaloons and vests hurried around with trays full of bottles. At the far end of the room, three musicians kept up a lively beat for a woman on the stage.

Moustafa stopped and gaped. Having spent much time around

Westerners, drunkenness didn't shock him anymore, but what he saw on stage made him want to cover his eyes and retreat to the nearest mosque.

The woman was a light-skinned Egyptian with enticingly broad hips and generous thighs. Her costume, if such a skimpy garment could even be graced with that name, barely covered her breasts and cleft and highlighted everything else. It was made of some glittering fabric, as if sewn from gold coins, and it sparkled and shimmered in the spotlight. The fabric moved as she moved, creating a hypnotic play of motion and light that made Moustafa stop and stare, mouth agape. Her smooth calves, her ample thighs, seemed like a vision of the Hereafter. Moustafa's eyes moved up past the gyrating hips to that lovely bare belly and continued to the deep cleavage of her breasts.

There his gaze stopped and rested for a while before moving down again. He did not see her face. Her body was far too distracting.

Now he knew why they called this place The Gardens of Paradise. It was like a vision of the wonders that waited for all the faithful!

Moustafa shook his head and sent up a prayer for forgiveness. How could he think such blasphemy?

"Hey, you! Stop gawking and get out of the way!" someone shouted in English.

He turned and saw a drunken Englishman in a soldier's uniform waving at him angrily. Moustafa swallowed his contempt and stepped out of the man's view.

"Come over here, my friend!" a rosy-faced Egyptian called from another table. The man had a nearly empty bottle in front of him and treated Moustafa to a wide, stupid grin. Not knowing what else to do with himself, Moustafa joined him.

"I can see it's your first visit to this kind of place," the man said, his boozy breath wafting over Moustafa and making him want to gag.

"I suppose it is obvious," Moustafa replied.

"Here." The man slapped a glass down in front of him and started to fill it with wine. "This will get you into the spirit."

"I don't drink alcohol," Moustafa said. He was tempted to quote the Koran at this lapsed Muslim but knew he'd only be wasting his breath.

The man laughed and patted him on the shoulder. "Oh, you're one of those, eh?"

"Yes, I'm one of those," Moustafa growled.

The man took the glass he had offered Moustafa and knocked it back. Wiping his moustache with a contented sigh, he said, "It is no matter. This place has much more to offer than hangovers. The booze is overpriced anyway. You can save your money for other things."

"Other things?"

The man jutted his chin in the direction of the stage. For the first time, Moustafa noticed an open doorway to the right of it. Dark next to the bright spotlight of the stage, he couldn't see what lay inside, but the cluster of scantily clad women lounging at the entrance told him enough. He gulped.

Once again he caught himself staring, and once again he forced himself to look away.

Then something else caught his attention. Claude Paget walked through the front door.

Moustafa worried for a moment that the Frenchman would recognize him. He had been sitting across the street from him for more than an hour, after all. But like so many Europeans, he didn't really see the Africans all around him.

Except for the belly dancer on stage, that is.

Claude blew her a kiss, which the dancer answered with an extra shimmy, and Claude sit down near the front. From the glances the two kept exchanging, Moustafa guessed that he was one of her regular customers.

Moustafa's hands balled into fists. He was no innocent. While he knew that Europeans came to places like this to fornicate with Egyptian and Soudanese women, this was the first time he had ever seen it with his own eyes.

The music picked up, and once more all that bare flesh distracted him. He didn't hear the waiter by his side until the man tapped him on his shoulder.

"What do you want to drink?" the man asked, sounding like he had asked the question several times already. "You can't sit here without a drink."

"A tea," Moustafa said.

"That will be two piastres."

Moustafa stared at him. "That's ten times what it costs in a good café!"

The waiter jerked his thumb toward the stage. "Do cafés have this?"

The drunken Muslim sharing his table barked out a laugh. "They sure don't!"

Moustafa grumbled and pulled out some money. He didn't know how he was going to explain all this spending to his boss.

When he looked back at Claude's table, he saw the doorman wasn't alone. Another European had joined him, a tough looking man in a cheap suit who looked French. He looked in his early twenties and had the deep tan of someone who had spent some time in Africa. Moustafa tried to ignore the temptation on stage and the raucous applause of his table companion and focus on the two Europeans.

While he couldn't hear what was said, the two seemed in adamant conversation. Claude the doorman kept shaking his head, gesturing wildly with his one good arm, and the other European looked like he was insisting on something. They got a bottle, and after a few quick slugs, Claude seemed to soften. They bent closer to one another and began to talk, both looking eager. Moustafa tried to think of a way to get closer to them, but all the nearby seats were taken and the music had risen to a fever pitch. The whole room clapped in time. His gaze flicked back to the dancer on stage, to see that her movements had grown wild. Moustafa found himself clapping in time as well. He told himself that he only did it to blend in, that the sweat pouring from his face was only due to the heat of the room.

The tablah and oud abruptly stopped, the tambourine made a final rattle, and the room fell silent. The woman threw herself on the stage floor, panting and sweating, and gave Claude a wide grin.

The European pushed some money in Claude's direction. He grabbed it, gave his companion a quick nod, and moved toward the back room. Drunkenness and haste made him clumsy and he bumped into one of the tables, nearly knocking over a bottle. He ignored the angry words from the bottle's owner and continued to the door beside the stage. The dancer leaped up and skipped after him. After a moment, the tanned European moved that way too, hooked an arm around one of the girls waiting there, and disappeared through the entrance along with Claude and the dancer.

Moustafa shuddered. He knew he must go in there, but he feared for his honor. No real Muslim should be in a place like this. He had justified it to himself by the fact that he had to investigate a murder, but could he really enter such a den of iniquity?

As if in a dream he found himself standing and moving toward the back hallway. The fake Muslim who had invited him to his table shouted some crude encouragement.

His throat dry and his heart pounding, Moustafa approached the darkened doorway. Only the faintest light shone within and he could barely make out a hallway lined with several doors on each wall. Claude and the belly dancer entered one. He did not see the other European.

"Hello, handsome," one of the women lounging by the entrance cooed, putting a hand on his arm.

"Get off me, harlot! I'm married!" Moustafa snapped.

He passed her by, ignoring the harsh language thrown after him, and went to the door of Claude's room, sticking his foot in just before it closed.

"Hey!" Claude shouted.

Moustafa pushed the door open and grabbed the man by the collar. The belly dancer, who stood by the bed in the small, grimy room, screamed and backed away.

"Where's the Apache you were speaking with?" Moustafa demanded.

"I-I don't know. I mean, what Apache?" the man babbled, going pale.

Moustafa shook him. "Tell me what you know before I turn you into a eunuch!"

"I don't know," the doorman wailed. "I'm only a messenger."

An excited babble came from the hallway behind Moustafa. He glanced over his shoulder and saw a crowd of dancers staring. He ignored them and turned back to Claude, shaking him hard enough to make his teeth rattle.

"Tell me all you know. I don't want to spend another instant in this vile den of sin."

"One of them, Albert Bernard, was in the war with me. He approached me and offered me money. This other fellow tonight I don't know. I was told to meet him here. He was supposed to give me another message."

"What is it?"

"He never got a chance to tell me. I didn't want to have any part of it anymore. I heard about the murder and was scared. But he insisted. Then he gave me money to come back here with Fatima and said he would talk to me once I finished."

Moustafa shook him again. "This is what you're going to do. You will—"

Strong hands grabbed him from behind and yanked him away from Claude. He whirled around, fists raised, to see two burly Egyptians with truncheons, obviously the bouncers to this place.

"Get out or we'll smash your head in," one of them barked. The other shoved Moustafa down the hall toward a back door at the end of the hallway. Moustafa glared at them, but decided not to fight. He didn't want to make a scene that could bring the police. If he got charged with creating disorder in such a place his family name would be stained forever.

"Get your hands off me, I'm going," he growled.

The bouncers opened the back door and shoved him out, slamming the door in his face.

"Don't come back again!" one of them shouted through the door.

"I wouldn't come to this evil place again if you offered me a Sultan's inheritance!" Moustafa shouted, kicking the door.

A soft sound made him glance about. He stood in a darkened alley, lit only by a candle encased in a red globe above the door. On both sides of the alley rose blank walls, the windows high above all shuttered and the ground littered with orange peels and a few empty bottles.

A figure separated itself from the deeper shadow. The light from the back door of the belly dancing bar gave enough illumination for Moustafa to recognize the tanned Frenchmen. The man paced toward him, his fists up and ready.

Moustafa cracked his knuckles and grinned.

"Oh, you want to fight?" Moustafa asked. "That's fine. I was looking for you anyway."

The man said nothing. He had already taken off his jacket and rolled up his shirtsleeves, obviously expecting this encounter.

He stopped just out of reach of Moustafa and got in a fighter's stance.

Moustafa's eyes narrowed. Moustafa had been raised in a small village in the Soudan, then left at sixteen to work on the docks and boats of the Nile. He had seen tough times and had been in many brawls. He had faced thieves, bullies, and thugs, but he had never faced a trained fighter. This man looked like he knew his business.

It didn't matter. He'd beat him to a pulp like he had with the rest of them.

With a roar he rushed forward, ready to drive his fist into the man's face and knock him out with a single blow.

But that's not how it worked out. Instead of running, or raising his arms to block the blow, the Frenchman did something completely unexpected. He kicked Moustafa in the thigh, making him stumble, then dodged to the left and threw a punch to the side of Moustafa's head.

Moustafa shook it off and swung at the Frenchman again, but he'd already danced out of the way. Growling, Moustafa closed in on him, only to get kicked in the thigh again, spoiling his attack.

Before he could recover, the man spun and kicked him just below the ribs.

Moustafa grunted in pain, barely managing to get his hands up in time to block a third kick aimed straight for his head. Then came a pair of punches to his stomach that Moustafa took with a grimace, responding with a wild swing that managed to connect. The Frenchman got his guard up just in time, but the force of the blow knocked him back anyway.

"No technique, but plenty of spirit," the Frenchman said with a smile. He spoke in Arabic.

"I'll turn you into a spirit once I get my hands on you!" Moustafa thundered, rushing at him.

The Frenchman spun and tried to kick Moustafa in the head, but the Nubian anticipated this and came in low, driving his fist into the man's stomach.

At least that was his plan. Instead the nimble Frenchman ducked to the side and only took a glancing blow to the ribs. Moustafa got another one of those annoying kicks to the thigh that kept him from turning and punching again, then a punch to the kidney that almost knocked him down.

He backed up, trying to buy some breathing time, but the Frenchman didn't allow him any. He kicked at Moustafa's thigh again, then threw a punch Moustafa barely managed to block, and followed with a kick square in the breastbone.

That knocked the wind out of him, and he barely saw the kick that took him down. The Frenchman's foot whipped out and smacked him straight in the temple. The world spun, the ground rushed up to meet him, and for a moment all went black.

The instant awareness returned, Moustafa tried to leap up and get back in the fight, but only managed to get on his knees, one hand clutching his throbbing temple.

The Frenchman stood several feet away, casually putting his jacket back on.

"Now you know how Apaches fight," he said. "Consider this a warning. Don't interfere with our business or I'll kill you. That goes for both you and your boss."

"We didn't even know about your business until you involved us in it."

His opponent gave a little shrug. "That wasn't my decision. Either help or stay out of the way."

"Help? You're mad. You left a dead man in the house. My boss and I don't give up when we're on a case."

"Then you'll die," the Apache said as he strolled past him. When Moustafa moved into a crouch, he warned, "Don't get up. I have a pistol in my pocket I didn't use."

The man drew it out and flourished it. Moustafa paused.

"Why didn't you?" he asked.

"Because you are going to remember how you were bested in combat by a man half your size. You will tell people how well the Apaches fight, and our reputation will grow."

"You speak Arabic like an Algerian. Are you Edmond Depré?"

The Apache bowed. "You honor me. No, my name is Vincent. You assume I was in the penal colony with him because I speak your language? No, while he and other comrades languished in prison for no other crime than fighting for their rights, I was narrowing the disparity between the rich and poor in Algiers and plotting their escape. Now we have come seeking richer pastures. Good night."

Vincent strolled off. Moustafa struggled to his feet, leaning against the wall for support. He did not try to follow. Instead he went directly home. He did not want his boss to see him like this.

9

Faisal had just turned the corner onto Ibn al-Nafis Street when he saw the Englishman leading two other Europeans inside, one a man and the other a woman. The woman chatted merrily with the Englishman.

"Who are they?" he asked Bisam the water seller, who stood hawking his wares nearby.

"You don't recognize that man? It's Russell Pasha. I'd like to slap him across the face with my sandal."

"Is that woman his wife?"

"No, can't you see the family resemblance? That must be his sister."

Faisal bit his lip. More trouble! If a man was bringing his sister to another man's house, that meant only one thing—marriage!

The Englishman was getting married too? Why was everyone getting married all of a sudden?

Having a woman in the house would be even worse than

having jinn. Right now the Englishman had a cleaning woman who took his laundry away to wash it in another place, but a wife would do the laundry herself up on the roof. She'd probably fix the trellis and put plants in the pots too. She'd be up there all day. Faisal would be kicked out of his home!

Faisal stormed off. He had some work to do.

Khadija umm Mohammed sat where she usually did, in the courtyard between four ramshackle buildings crowded with the families of poor workers. She sat mending an old headscarf, trying to coax a few more years of life from the threadbare garment. She held her work as far away from her eyes as her arms would allow so that she could focus on it.

"Back again?" Khadija umm Mohammed said as she spotted Faisal.

"I need a different spell this time."

The old woman put her work down and rubbed her arthritic hands. "What is it now?"

"I need a marriage spell."

A smile spread across Khadija umm Mohammed's lips. "Who would marry a little street boy like you?"

Faisal frowned. "I come from a good family. My mother was a respectable woman who died giving birth to me."

"Of course she was," Khadija umm Mohammed replied patiently.

Faisal nodded. "It's not for me, and it's not really for marriage. I need a spell to stop a marriage. Actually I need to stop two marriages."

"Why would you want to interfere in someone else's love life?"

Faisal thought for a moment. How much of the truth should he tell? "The first is a spell to keep the Englishman over on Ibn al-

Nafis Street from marrying. If he gets married, I won't be able to work for him anymore."

"You work for an Englishman? I don't believe it."

"I do! I even got to ride in his motorcar. Well, actually his friend's motorcar."

Khadija umm Mohammed did not look convinced. Faisal went on.

"I also need to stop an Egyptian marriage. A friend of mine is going to be wed to an old man, and she's even younger than I am! If she gets married, I'll never see her again!"

"Mina at the *ful* stand," Khadija umm Mohammed sighed.

Faisal blinked. "How did you know about that?"

"When marriage is in the air, everyone's tongues start wagging. And I've seen you loitering around the *ful* stand. You want her for yourself one day."

"Nonsense! She's my friend. I'm just trying to save her."

Khadija umm Mohammed smiled again. "Your feelings will change. They might be changing already and you don't even know it."

"Can you help me or not?" Faisal asked, annoyed.

Khadija umm Mohammed did not answer at once. Her eyes unfocused, as if she was looking at something far away.

"Marriage is something a woman is never prepared for, but when the bride is a girl, it is ten times as hard. You move away from your sisters and your parents to a strange house filled with strangers. Oh, they try to make you happy. The wedding is like something out of a story and all the women of both families fuss over you, but it is like the old saying goes, 'Forty days of tea and honey followed by a lifetime of thankless toil.' And then you look back on the time when you were still a carefree little girl and wonder if it was all just a wonderful dream."

Khadija umm Mohammed looked directly at him. "My marriage curse usually costs fifty piastres. It is a powerful spell that is guaranteed to work. But for Mina, I will only charge you ten piastres. And I will give you the spell for the Englishman for the same price. Who knows? Perhaps you really will get a job with him and then when you are older you'll get what you don't realize you're looking for."

Faisal didn't quite understand all that, but if Khadija umm Mohammed was offering a discount, he'd take it.

"All right," he said.

"Do you have the money?"

"Yes."

Khadija umm Mohammed looked at him sharply. "Remember the rule of magic? You must pay for it with money earned honestly; otherwise the spell will not work."

Faisal bit his lip. Before coming over here he had gone up to his shed and gathered all the money he had been saving. That came out to only fourteen piastres. Lucky he had earned eleven of them posing for pictures for tourists in front of the Englishman's house. That was hard work because Moustafa usually chased him away and most of the tourists ignored him, but when they did take his picture they paid well. The other three piastres he had earned in the usual way—stealing.

"I have only eleven piastres. Can you give me both spells for that much?"

Khadija umm Mohammed shook her head. "The materials are expensive, and such strong magic tires an old woman like me. If you can only afford one, you have to choose one."

Faisal paused. What could he do? He couldn't let that old man marry Mina, but if he lost his home, where would he go?

Faisal thought of the cozy little shed he had on the roof, with its fine view over Cairo and the safety it offered from stray dogs and bullies. He thought of all the food he filched from the pantry, and his comfy spot on the loggia where he could lounge on the divan and eat the Englishman's dates. He'd never get a place like that again. People like him don't get much luck in life.

He stared at the money in his hand. At last he forced the words out.

"I'll pay for Mina's spell."

Khadija umm Mohammed smiled. "You are a good boy sometimes. Perhaps God will have mercy on you and forgive all your sins."

"This will work, right?"

"My magic never fails. Sit down here in the shade while I prepare it," Khadija umm Mohammed said.

Faisal did as he was told and watched, fascinated, as the wise old woman went inside and fetched some paper, a quill pen, and a bottle of ink. Faisal thought it strange to see such a poor person with items like that, but Khadija umm Mohammed was full of surprises. She also carried a few little paper packets.

With a grunt and a call to God she painfully sat back down.

"I wish there was a spell to make old knees young again," she groaned.

With deliberate care she laid out the packets in a neat row and then spread out a square piece of paper. Dipping the quill into the ink bottle, she began to write words on the paper, reciting verses from the Koran as she did so. Once she had filled the center of the paper with writing, she began to draw strange symbols all around the words. She continued her soft chant, but now she wasn't reciting anything Faisal recognized. It didn't even sound like a human language at all. The sentences, if they were sentences, were full of hoarse coughs, low growls, and high-pitched whines.

Faisal's skin prickled to hear it. This sounded like powerful magic indeed.

The old woman put the pen and writing materials aside and opened up the paper packets. Each had a differently colored powder inside. She took a pinch of yellow powder and sprinkled it on the page. Then she took a large portion of red powder and added it to the yellow. This was followed by a pinch of black, two pinches of orange, and a handful of blue. After that she folded up the paper to make a little packet. Then she made a second one.

Faisal handed over the ten piastres, feeling a little tug of regret to see so much money disappear into Khadija umm Mohammed's pocket. But it was for his friend, he reminded himself, so he needed to do it.

"So what do I do?" Faisal asked as she handed the packets over.

"You must stand on the threshold of the bride's house. Open one of the packets and blow on the powder, once to each of the four directions. Make sure all the powder is blown away by the time you are done. Then burn the paper. Then take the second packet and do the same at the threshold of the groom's house. The marriage contract will then be broken as if it had never existed."

Faisal stared in wonder at the little packets in his hands. With just ten piastres he would save Mina.

If only he had enough to save his home.

He grimaced. He'd been sleeping in alleys again soon.

Late that night, Faisal stood at the threshold of the little lean-to where his friend lay sleeping and did as Khadija umm Mohammed instructed. As the powder blew away in the wind and the piece of paper with its magical writing went up in flames, Faisal felt a wave of relief like he had never known. It wasn't the relief of getting away from a shopkeeper who was chasing you or the relief of finally getting some bread after two days of hunger. It was a different feeling, like the easing of future misery. Faisal had never worried about the future much; surviving the present took up all his thoughts and skill. But now he knew that he'd get to keep his friend, and that she wouldn't be stuck married to an old man and locked away in his house forever.

Faisal looked at the little lean-to of reed mats and took a deep breath. The air still carried the faint smell of the food that had been cooked here all day. He smiled. Next time he came to get some *ful*, Mina would be allowed to speak with him again. Maybe she'd even slip him and extra portion like she used to.

Now for Abbas Eldessouky's house. That afternoon he had asked around and found out the man was a successful cotton merchant and had learned where he lived. His house stood only twenty minutes' walk away along a busy street. The house was narrow but four stories tall, and the walls looked hard to climb. The front door was shut and all the windows covered with latticework, of course, so there was little to see.

At night there was even less to see. A single light shone through a crack in the shutter on the top floor. The street was more used than the one where Mina lived, and even at this late hour a steady trickle of people walked past. There were even streetlamps here, not the new gas lights, just old style oil lamps, but they gave enough light that Faisal would be visible as he stood on the threshold.

Faisal bit his lip. How could he finish the spell without being seen?

All this he saw as he passed by the house without slowing

down. Anyone seeing him would think he was walking somewhere just like the other people on the street.

A few doors down, he noticed the neighborhood watchman coming his way. He was a portly old man in a dirty turban with a large ring of keys in his hand that he jangled absentmindedly as he walked. The man gave him a suspicious look and Faisal quickened his pace like he was frightened. Ha! Like he'd be frightened of someone like that. He looked as stupid as Karim, and the way he jangled those keys, Faisal would know he was coming a mile off.

Still, it paid to be careful, so he walked some more before turning and retracing his steps. He could just make out the watchman far ahead, appearing in the pools of radiance cast by the distant streetlights and disappearing as he moved into the shadow. Faisal picked up the pace and drew closer to him. He could hear the jangle of those keys.

The watchman passed Abbas Eldessouky's house and shortly thereafter a bend in the road hid him from view. The soft jangle of his keys could still be heard, gradually getting softer.

Faisal slowed down as he got close to the house, awaiting his chance. A small group of men walked in his direction. He slowed even more to let them pass, then doubled back to get to Eldessouky's threshold. The men were walking away from him and the sound of the watchman's keys had faded into the distance. No one else faced him.

He gave a quick glance at an alley that opened up on the opposite side of the street and a little toward where the road bent. He didn't see anyone there either, and it might make a good bolt hole if someone saw him. Plus he could run either way down the main road. Good. You always needed at least two escape routes. Three was even better.

Faisal pulled the packet out of his pocket, opened it up, and as fast as he could he blew the powder out in all four directions. Once he was sure all the powder had been carried away by the breeze, he glanced around. The group of men still walked away, unaware. He could see no one else. Yanking a match out of his pocket, he struck it against the doorjamb and set the flame to the paper just as the match head flared up.

Faisal jumped as the flew open behind him.

"Tawfik, is that you?"

Abbas Eldessouky stood in the doorway, looking anxious. No light was on in the front hall behind him. Faisal got the impression that he had been standing on the other side of the door listening and flung it open the instant he heard a sound.

The pot-bellied man stared in confusion at Faisal.

"What are you doing here? What's that?"

Abbas looked at the last bit of paper get consumed by the fire. Faisal thought fast.

"I, um, was smoking. I found some tobacco and rolled it up in some paper."

Abbas took a swipe at him. Faisal ducked out of the way.

"Get out of here, you little wretch. Go smoke somewhere else!"

Faisal hurried off, but the man's strange behavior kept him from going far. Why had he been hiding in the dark in his own house? Why had he been so nervous about someone named Tawfik?

Faisal looped around back to the house. Having grown up on the street, he had a sixth sense for how Cairo's winding lanes and alleyways linked together, and in a few minutes managed to find the tiny alley that opened up almost opposite Abbas Eldessouky's house.

He made it just in time to see three men knock on the door. Abbas opened the door instantly, gave a nervous look around the street, and hustled them inside. Faisal wondered what the cotton merchant's family thought about all this, but he suspected his wives and children had been told to stay upstairs where that light shone.

A few minutes later the door reopened. Abbas peeked out, but just at that moment came the sound of the neighborhood watchman's keys jangling. The door closed. After a minute the watchman appeared, jangling his keys. Faisal grinned. What a fool! Didn't he realize that his little habit announced to the whole neighborhood where he was? On second thought, perhaps the cotton merchant had bribed him to do just that. He wouldn't be the first neighborhood watchman to be paid to look the other way.

As the sound of the keys faded into the distance, the door reopened, and the three men appeared, each burdened with a heavy bolt of cloth. They ran down the street as Abbas Eldessouky watched nervously from the doorway. After a minute they came back empty-handed and got more bolts of cloth from the house.

"Plenty more coming in a few days," Abbas told them. "I'm awaiting a shipment from Upper Egypt."

The men nodded and hurried off with their burdens.

Curious, Faisal took a back route to where it looked like they were going. It didn't take long to find a bullock cart standing in a darkened portion of the street with a man guarding it. The three fellows appeared, dumped more bolts of cloth in the back, and ran back to Abbas Eldessouky's house.

Faisal moved out of sight, and then reappeared on the street, walking casually. The man guarding the cart glanced at him but otherwise took no notice. No one ever took much notice of him. That came in handy.

Faisal went up to the man with his hand out.

"Can you give me half a piastre? I'm hungry."

"Get lost."

Faisal shrugged and walked off. He had seen what he wanted to see. The bolts of cloth didn't have a stamp on them. All cotton had to get a stamp from the English to prove the merchant had paid tax. That tax was pretty high. Abbas Eldessouky was dodging taxes.

It didn't matter, he thought as he walked away. Mina wouldn't be marrying him anyway. His friend was safe. He knew that eventually Mina would get married to someone, but that was a long way off.

Or was it? The sudden question jabbed at Faisal's calm. Mina's father wanted to marry her off because he couldn't support her anymore. That hadn't changed. Sooner or later, probably sooner, he'd find some other husband for his daughter.

Faisal gritted his teeth in frustration. Now what was he going to do? Cast a spell on Mina so that she never got married? No, that wouldn't be fair. Every girl needs to get married eventually. He had to figure out a way to get her father some work again so that he wouldn't have to marry off his daughter so early.

But who wants to hire a man with a bad back? What work could he do? Plenty of healthy people couldn't find work. Who would give him a chance?

With these impossible problems whirling around in his mind, he headed back to the Englishman's house.

As he came to Ibn al-Nafis Street, he saw Karim walking ahead of him, checking out each house to make sure it was secure. Faisal stuck out his tongue at him and waited for him to round the corner. That fellow was always looking for an excuse to beat him. Didn't Karim know that he guarded the Englishman's house better than he ever could?

And now Faisal would lose that job. Unless he could earn nine more piastres honestly—an almost impossible task—the Englishman would get married and he'd have to move back with the other boys to their shack in the alley.

Faisal wrinkled his nose in disgust. He hated that place. It got drafty on cold nights and stank of cats' piss. Plus the other boys always pestered him for food, which after he lost his job he wouldn't be able to provide.

Once Karim had safely disappeared around the corner, Faisal went around to the back of the building and climbed up to his little home on top. He looked at the snug little shack longingly for a time, wondering how much longer he would get to enjoy it.

The sweet voice of Mohammed el-Hajji lilted through the air from the neighborhood mosque, calling the people to prayer. Faisal looked out over the moonlit rooftops, his mind troubled. He hadn't really solved any of his problems and he knew they'd only get worse once he lost his home. But the sound of Mohammed's singing and the beauty of the moonlight soon eased Faisal's boyish mind and brought him back to the present. Having lived on the streets since he was eight, and having spent most of his time fending for himself even when his lout of a father had still been around, he had learned to enjoy the moment, never knowing when it would be his last. He decided to go down into the house and relax in his favorite place.

Squeezing through the window, he got down to the third floor, confident now that the darkness held no jinn ready to attack him. He took the stairs to the second floor and strolled out to the loggia, a covered porch overlooking the courtyard. The Englishman had furnished it with a comfortable divan, a low table, and a few chairs.

Faisal lay on the divan and took the lid off a covered dish of dates that the Englishman had kindly left on the table. The dish was always heaped with dates and the Englishman never missed one or two. Or three. Faisal started munching away, content as a Sultan, studying the intricate designs of the mashrabiya on the interior windows as they gleamed silver in the moonlight. The burble of the fountain lulled him into relaxation. He reminded himself to take care. Once he had fallen asleep here, to be awoken by the dawn call to prayer. Luckily the Englishman slept late, otherwise he would have been caught.

Ah, this was the life! Lazing on comfortable cushions and chomping on fresh dates.

A soft sound from above caught his attention. It sounded like the rattle of a window in its frame.

Faisal perked his ears and became immobile as a stone. Had one of the other boys discovered his secret? A moment later he heard a soft padding sound, as of an animal, on the stairs inside. His sharp hearing followed the sound as it descended to his floor and then continued down. A moment later, the same sound repeated, as if another creature followed the first.

His skin crawled. What was that?

Then he remembered the baboon prints on the glass. In all the excitement he had forgotten. The baboon jinn were back!

No, wait, the charm still worked, and the Englishman had said Europeans had brought the stone box and dead body into his house. That sound wasn't made by jinn, but by something else.

Plucking up his courage, Faisal crept inside to the staircase. He listened for a moment and heard nothing but the soft sound of the Englishman snoring.

Then, from a distant part of the house below, he heard a faint scrape.

Hurrying down the steps on bare feet, Faisal didn't make a

sound. He heard the scrape a few more times and could tell it came from the front room.

When he got to the doorway leading to the room with all the ancient things, he peeked around the corner, his heart thudding in his chest.

At first he saw nothing. Little moonlight filtered into this room and so it was almost pitch black, and he didn't dare light his candle.

Then that scraping sound came again, and Faisal immediately located it.

It came from the front door.

He stared at the dark rectangle of wood at the far end of the room, looking slightly to one side to improve his night vision. There seemed to be a darker mass in the middle of the door, a shadow on a shadow.

Scrape.

Faisal's eyes went wide. It was the bolt on the door! Something was opening it.

Scrape. Clack.

Faisal jerked as the bolt snapped open. The door opened with a creak, and the silhouettes of some men briefly appeared before the door shut again. Faisal moved back behind the doorway, leaving as little of his body exposed as he could while still being able to see.

A match flared in the darkness, making him blink. He saw three men—two European and one Egyptian. The Egyptian—a cunning-looking man with sharp, lean features—held the match. He lit a lantern he carried in his other hand. The two Europeans carried a large sack between them.

Then Faisal saw something that made his blood freeze.

A pair of baboons squatted on the floor nearby.

He almost ran off, thinking that the Egyptian with the lantern had summoned two baboon jinn, but then he remembered what the Englishman always said. He said that Faisal should use something called "logic". That meant he should think things through instead of latching onto the first story that came into his head.

The charm was still in place behind the crocodile-headed jinni, and Khadija umm Mohammed's spells always worked, so the logical explanation was that the magic still worked. That meant that the baboons would have turned to stone by now. So these weren't baboon jinn, but real baboons, trained to get into the house and open the door.

Faisal felt like bowing in respect. These were the best housebreakers he had ever heard of.

But respect gave way to fear and anger. These thieves were breaking into *his* house. Such dishonesty! Had they no respect for private property? People like that should be in jail.

Faisal's suspicions about the baboons were confirmed when the Egyptian motioned to the two animals and they obediently trotted over and squatted next to him. One of the Europeans turned on a flashlight. The light caught the gleam of a pistol in his hand. He turned and moved straight toward Faisal.

Faisal ducked back around the corner, but no shot came. Good, he hadn't been spotted. He guessed the man would go upstairs to check on the Englishman. As quietly as he could, Faisal rushed upstairs, hurried through the Englishman's room, and hid in the bathroom, peeking out through the crack of the open door.

Just as he suspected, the European peered in through the Englishman's doorway. Faisal looked around the bathroom, wondering what he could use for a weapon if the intruder decided to hurt his employer. But he didn't need to fight. The European stared for a moment at the Englishman's sleeping form, then turned and went back downstairs.

Faisal scratched his head. So they didn't want to rob him or hurt him, even though they had broken into his house. These people were strange even by European standards.

It took some nerve to go back downstairs, and by the time he did he saw the three men leaving the house, shutting the door behind them. The baboons stayed inside, and once the door closed, they leaped up on the bolt and started yanking it shut. While the animals were strong like all baboons, they were too small to stand and reach the bolt so they had an awkward time moving it.

Faisal retreated once more, this time into the hallway bathroom, shutting the door behind him. He waited in the pitch black.

Pressing his ear against the door, he soon heard them passing down the hallway, their claws lightly scraping the stone floor.

The sound stopped. Faisal strained his ears.

Then, right on the opposite side of the door, came a sniffing sound. Faisal bit his lip and trembled.

He heard the doorknob turn.

Faisal yanked the door shut, fumbled in the darkness for the latch, and snapped it closed.

The door rattled. Faisal backed up, pressing himself against the far wall, almost paralyzed with fear. Baboons could be vicious. These two could tear him apart as badly as any jinn.

The door shook again, followed by a loud bang that forced a cry from his lips.

Then there was silence. Faisal could not hear if they left over the sound of his own pounding heart.

It took him an hour to summon the courage to open the door a crack, and several more minutes to reassure himself the baboons had gone.

Once he did, he lit a candle and went into the front room. What had the thieves been doing in here? Everything looked in place …

… Except the lid on the stone box. It had been slid back to seal the box shut again.

10

"It's about time you fellows showed up again," Augustus said the next morning when he saw the lid on the sarcophagus had been moved.

He immediately drew his automatic pistol from his pocket, although he felt reasonably safe. They had come in again while he slept, probably looked in on him, and had done nothing. These people didn't want to hurt him; they wanted to play with him.

"Well, if it's a game you want, I'm happy to play along," he said.

Like the last time, he scoured the house from top to bottom looking for evidence of a forced entry or any other clue, and found nothing. As he passed the downstairs toilet on his way back to the showroom, he stopped short. The door to the toilet had a few scrapes on it about a third of the way up, as if some animal had scoured the wood. He felt pretty sure those had not been there before. Had the intruders brought a dog with them? And if so, why had it scraped at the toilet door?

The door was closed, and Augustus eased himself to one side of it, pointing the pistol at the doorway and putting his hand on the doorknob.

With a single fluid motion, he flung the door open and jammed his pistol through the open doorway.

Nothing. The toilet was empty.

"This just keeps getting better," he said with a chuckle.

He went back to the showroom and smoked a cigarette while he waited for Moustafa to show up, barely able to contain his curiosity.

As usual, his employee impressed Augustus with his sharp perception.

"Not again!" he cried as he came through the door, eyes fixed on the sarcophagus.

"Shall we fetch the crowbars?" Augustus asked.

"Very well," his employee said with a sigh.

Augustus laughed. "You seem less than enthusiastic about this, Moustafa."

"And you seem too enthusiastic," Moustafa grumbled as he left the room.

Poor Moustafa, Augustus thought. *He certainly gets more than he signed up for, but he's a good sport.*

When the Nubian came back, Augustus noticed he moved stiffly and the side of his face was swollen.

"What happened to you?"

"I followed the doorman to a low den of iniquity and got into a fight with one of the Apaches."

"Ah, good! Where is he? I presume you captured him."

"No, Mr. Wall," Moustafa replied, shaking his head and looking at the floor.

"But you said you fought him." Augustus had seen Moustafa fight, and knew he didn't lose.

"He used some strange fighting technique on me and … got away before I could knock him out."

Moustafa walked stiff-legged over to the sarcophagus with the crowbars.

"Did he kick you in the thighs then follow up with kicks to the chest and face?" Augustus asked.

"That he did, sir."

"Oh dear, I'm terribly sorry. It's a French fighting technique called savate. A mixture of classic boxing and a kicking style developed by sailors in Marseille. I should have realized the Apaches would fight that way. I've heard it is most effective."

"It is, Mr. Wall."

Augustus noted a trace of impatience in his employee's voice.

"Well," Augustus clapped him on the shoulder, "you and I will get them in the end. Let's see what they left for us this time, eh?"

Moustafa told him all about what had occurred the night before, ending by saying, "They warned me that they'd kill us if we kept after them."

Augustus sized him up. "But you want to keep going, don't you?"

A spark lit in Moustafa's eyes. "More than ever."

Augustus smiled. "That's what I thought."

Together they fitted the crowbars on the sarcophagus lid and heaved the stone aside.

A loud bang and flare of light made them jump back.

Augustus blinked from the light, his vision wavering. Day turned into night, and the Germans were sending star shells to burst over No Man's Land. The roar of the big guns in the distance filled his ears.

"An assault is coming!" he shouted to his unit.

Someone shook him. He blinked again, and the room came back into focus. A big African stood by him. Who was this?

Oh, right.

"Mr. Wall, are you here?" Moustafa said, still gripping his shoulder.

Augustus shrugged him off. "I'm fine."

Unfortunately, Moustafa had learned about his little slips of the mind and worried over him like a mother hen. Most humiliating. He'd have given Moustafa the sack if he hadn't been so damned useful.

Moustafa stared at him doubtfully. Augustus ignored him and approached the sarcophagus, shaking a little from the vision.

"Mr. Wall …"

"I said I'm fine!" he barked, and peeked inside. "But this poor bugger most certainly is not."

A head lay within. Moustafa moved to his side and gasped.

"That's Claude Paget! They must have killed him for talking to me."

Moustafa turned away, hands over his face. Augustus hesitated a moment, then put a hand on his shoulder.

"It's not your fault. This only goes to show that we have to stop these barbarians."

Moustafa squared his shoulders. "We do. Claude was a drunken lowlife, but he didn't deserve this."

Augustus looked in the sarcophagus again. Attached to the lid was a small pressure device similar to the mines they had all used in the war. White smoke issued out of a small metal tube next to it. The flare must have been inside.

Claude Paget's head sat in the center of the sarcophagus, wearing a look of surprise. Not much blood surrounded the severed neck. The murder had obviously taken place elsewhere and the head taken for some distance.

His vision wavered again as he remembered other severed heads. It wasn't such a strange sight on the front, when shells ripped men apart. Heads took some time to bleed out. He supposed it was all those veins and capillaries of the brain slowly draining. Whoever had done this hadn't wanted a mess on his hands and had waited for a time. That meant that the bastard knew that grisly little detail like he did. Also, that booby trap with the pressure plate and flare had been cleverly done. He'd had someone in his regiment who had been equally expert until a German trench mortar had blasted their foxhole and torn the poor man apart.

That explosion had torn Augustus apart too …

"Mr. Wall?"

Augustus shook his head. "Just, um, examining the evidence." He forced himself to look at the head again and for the first time noticed a small slip of paper had been rolled up and inserted in the ear. The shock of the flare and the sight of poor Claude's head had kept him from noticing it at first.

He reached for it.

"Good morning!" a cheery voice called behind them.

They whirled around to see Cordelia and Aunt Pearl standing at the doorway. Augustus almost jumped in the air with fright.

"One moment!" he called, "Just cleaning the place up. Haven't really opened yet. My, what a state it's in. No, don't come in."

Augustus and Moustafa heaved on the lid to move it shut.

"Is something the matter?" Cordelia asked, stepping into the showroom despite his injunction not to.

"The matter? What would be the matter?"

"It's smoky in here," Aunt Pearl said, waving her handkerchief.

Augustus' mind raced. "Ah, yes! Bad habit. I really should give up. Moustafa is always telling me I smoke too much. Isn't that right, Moustafa?"

"Terrible habit, sir," Moustafa said, nodding.

"Why does it smell of explosive?" Cordelia asked, looking around curiously.

"Explosive? It doesn't smell of explosive. Do you smell explosive, Moustafa?"

"No, sir."

Cordelia cocked an eyebrow. "I worked for two years as a nurse in France. I know cordite when I smell it."

"You do? Um, I mean, yes of course you do! Yes, cordite, works wonders on cleaning old stone. Burnishes it right up like new. Silly of me to forget. We were using cordite to clean the statues."

"Yes," Moustafa hastened to agree. "Cordite is most efficacious, but smelly. So terribly smelly."

"Whatever are you two babbling about?" Aunt Pearl said. "Oh, this is nice!"

She was examining a set of alabaster canopic jars. The lids were of painted wood and carved to represent heads. Only one was human, the others being a baboon, a jackal, and a falcon.

"Those are canopic jars from the New Kingdom," Augustus said, glad to change the topic. "The figures are of the four sons of Horus. They contained the mummy's liver, stomach, lungs, and entrails."

Aunt Pearl chuckled. "Well, I hope they're empty now."

She lifted the jackal head off one of the jars, screamed, and let the head fall to the floor with a crash.

"Is this your idea of a joke!" she demanded.

"What?" Augustus rushed over.

"There's a real stomach in there!" Aunt Pearl looked ready to swoon. Augustus caught her just as she started to tip over.

"Moustafa, get a chair and the smelling salts!"

Cordelia hurried over to her aunt, waving her handkerchief in front of her face. Moustafa returned in a minute with a chair and they sat her down. As Augustus opened the bottle of smelling salts and put it under her nose, waking her up with a start, Cordelia stepped away.

"What's all this about a real stomach?"

She peeked in the canopic jar, frowned, and turned to Augustus, hands on her hips.

"There really is a stomach in there, and a fresh one at that! Just what is going on here?"

Augustus peeked in the jar and saw she was correct.

"Um …"

It wasn't the wittiest answer he had ever given to a tough question, but it was the best he could come up with under the circumstances.

She pulled the lids of the canopic jars one by one. "And a pair of lungs, and entrails, and a liver. A liver with cirrhosis at that. The man had obviously been a heavy drinker."

"Too much red wine, I suspect," Moustafa mumbled.

"Moustafa, go get another chair for the lady," Augustus said. His assistant ran off, looking only too happy to leave the room.

"I'm not going to faint," Cordelia said. "I've seen as much blood and gore as you have."

Augustus gave a little bow. "Not to diminish your service to the empire in any way, madam, but I must beg to differ."

Aunt Pearl bellowed from her seat. "Why do you have real human organs in your canopic jars?"

"Oh, um, that. Yes. Well, you see, it's a …"

"A wealthy and eccentric collector," Moustafa said, rushing back in with a second chair. "He wanted the canopic jars to be as realistic as possible but we didn't have any with mummified remains inside, so we got an unclaimed body from the medical school."

"Yes!" Augustus said. "Yes we did! You're quite right, Moustafa. Terribly sorry to give you a fright."

"That's perverse," Cordelia said with a frown.

"All in the name of science," Augustus replied, hoping he had finally quelled her annoying interest in him.

"I need my morning constitutional," Aunt Pearl groaned.

"I think we all do," Augustus said. "Let's move into the drawing room, shall we?"

The ladies agreed, and as Augustus ushered them out, he looked around the room uncertainly. Had the Apaches left any other little surprises?

He sat them down in the drawing room and went to the liquor cabinet.

"Will whiskey do? I'm afraid I don't have any gin," Augustus said.

"As long as it isn't made by Presbyterians," Aunt Pearl sniffed.

Augustus cocked his head and studied the bottle. "I don't think it is."

"One of our ancestors was killed by Convenanters at the Battle of Bothwell Bridge," Cordelia explained.

"My great-great-great grandfather, Jack Russell. Saved the battle for the monarchy and Episcopalianism at the cost of his life," Aunt Pearl said.

Augustus poured her a double, thought the better of it, and made it a triple.

"None for me, thank you," Cordelia sniffed when he turned to her.

He poured himself one and raised his glass.

"To the great Jack Russell, terrier of the north."

Aunt Pearl gave him a level stare. "Young man, I've heard that joke so many times I barely even notice it anymore. If I didn't know better, I would think you were trying to alienate us."

"I'll have to try harder next time," Augustus mumbled into his glass.

"I beg your pardon?" Cordelia asked.

"Nothing," Augustus replied in an innocent voice. He turned to Moustafa for help, only to discover he had already beaten a hasty retreat. "So, um, how can I be of service you ladies?"

"The tour," Aunt Pearl said. She looked much recovered now that her drink had disappeared as quickly as Moustafa.

"Tour?"

"You promised us a tour of Old Cairo," Cordelia said. "Most kind of you. I'm anxious to see the native quarter, and my brother says you know it well."

"I prefer it."

Cordelia stood up and gave him a warm smile. "Shall we go?"

Augustus cast about for an excuse, but the mention of her brother the police commandant dampened his creativity.

"Well, I'd be happy to, it's just that it's so terribly hard to find a carriage in this neighborhood and—"

"My nephew already provided one," Aunt Pearl said, lifting herself out of the chair with a noticeable wobble.

"I see."

The two ladies walked out to the showroom. Augustus reluctantly followed.

They found Moustafa poking around all the artifacts.

"Find anything?" Augustus asked in Arabic.

"Nothing, boss."

"The head has a note tucked in its ear. Examine it once I've left. Unfortunately, I'm forced to play tour guide to these two. I'll shake them as quick as I can."

"Really, Augustus!" Cordelia said, putting a hand on his arm. "Your servant speaks English. Don't cut us out of the conversation. You'll make me feel lonely."

Augustus detached himself. "Just a few technical terms better expressed in his native tongue."

"Speaking English tires me after a while, madam," Moustafa said. "Languages are most difficult for me."

Suddenly Augustus had an idea. "Oh, wait. You wanted to go to the old native quarter? They've been quite restive since the protests. It might not be safe."

"My nephew provided us an off-duty policeman as a driver," Aunt Pearl said, her words coming out somewhat slurred. "And he said the protestors have been quiet as church mice since they were taught their lesson."

"Oh."

Aunt Pearl turned to Moustafa. "I hope you aren't caught up in all this independence nonsense."

Moustafa gave her a broad grin and bowed. "Of course not, madam. The English are a blessing to this country."

"Well, I'm glad to see some of the natives see sense," she declared, heading out the front door.

"Kill me now," Augustus told his assistant in Arabic. Cordelia had her hand on his arm again.

"Enjoy yourself, boss. You get to play the tourist while I chase a pack of bloodthirsty murderers."

"As I said, kill me now."

Cordelia nudged him. She was getting much too familiar. "English, Augustus. Speak English. My brother warned me you had gone native."

"Did your brother warn you that I'm an ill-tempered recluse who regularly gets into gunfights with the lowest elements of society?"

Cordelia laughed. "Did my brother warn you that I'm unstoppable?"

Good Lord, what does it take to shake her? Dump the contents of those canopic jars on her head?

They went to the street, where a carriage was waiting, driven by a burly Egyptian with a pistol-shaped bulge in the pocket of his jellaba. Augustus shook his head in wonder. Sir Thomas obviously wanted to protect his relations, so why on Earth did he not let them fester in the hotel instead of foisting them on him? Was he really so desperate to solve the case by himself?

They got into the carriage, ignoring the stares of loungers in the café across the street. As the driver cracked the whip and the carriage pulled away, Faisal appeared out of nowhere.

"Wait!" he shouted, leaping onto the carriage.

"Thief!" Aunt Pearl cried, bringing her parasol down on the boy's head.

"Ow!"

Augustus grabbed the parasol. "Stop, Aunt Pearl. This is a local lad. He's harmless."

"He'll give us all the plague. Just look at him!"

The driver turned around. "I'll get rid of him for you, sir."

"No, wait." Augustus turned to Faisal. "I don't have time to watch street entertainers at the moment."

"It's not that," Faisal said, rubbing his head. "I saw who broke into your house last night."

"Really? Tell me everything you saw."

Cordelia cut in. "What a pitiful looking beggar child. Is he asking for alms? Here."

Cordelia gave him half a piastre. To Augustus' surprise, instead of the usual gratitude, followed immediately by a plea for more money, Faisal shot her a look of open hostility.

"Behave," Augustus warned. "Now tell me what's going on, but get out of the carriage first, you're making the ladies nervous. One of them has already fainted once this morning."

Faisal hopped down.

"I saw all of them, and I know how they broke into your house."

"Go on."

"Are you going to lunch?"

"Not with you."

"I need ten piastres."

"Ten piastres! Not on your life."

"I need it," Faisal whined.

"Whatever for?"

Faisal gave Cordelia a hostile look and then looked at his feet.

"Nothing," he mumbled.

"I'm busy, Faisal. I'll give you two piastres and you'll be happy with it."

"I'm trying to help you!"

"By robbing me blind? Come now. You know you don't need that much. Tell me what you know and I'll give you two piastres, plus lunch some other day."

"All right," the boy moped. He then explained how he was lounging across the street that night, curious if anything more would happen to the house, when he saw a pair of Europeans and an Egyptian appear out of a darkened alley after Karim had passed by. They had obviously been waiting for him to pass, not wanting to be seen like the first time. The Egyptian had a pair of trained baboons that scaled the wall and must have gone through an open window. A short time later the baboons slid back the bolt to the door.

"Are you trying to tell me baboons broke into my house? Ridiculous!" Augustus scoffed.

"It is possible, sir," the driver said. "We have had cases like this in the past. Baboons are clever animals. They can be trained to snatch jewelry off women and money right out of your hands. They could probably be trained to enter a house and unbolt a door."

"See? Even the policeman agrees with me."

The driver frowned. "How did you know I was a policeman?"

"You wear boots instead of sandals and you have a pistol in your pocket. Plus you're driving the police commandant's sister."

Augustus laughed. "You're quite the little detective!"

"Which is why I deserve ten piastres."

"Two and lunch. Consider it beginner's pay. You're not a full detective yet. Can you describe these men?"

Faisal gave a general description that matched the one Karim had provided after the first break-in. He also mentioned they carried a sack, not that Augustus needed to ask what was in it.

"Anything stolen, sir?" the driver asked.

"No, they're just left a warning note," Augustus replied. He'd tell them about the body once he'd solved the case.

"What did it say?" the driver and Faisal asked at the same time. They glanced at one another.

"They told me not to pursue the case, but I wasn't going to anyway. I'm leaving it up to the authorities."

The driver nodded. Faisal got a sly look on his face, and winked at Augustus, who smiled back at him.

"Thank you for your help," Augustus said, "Go tell all this to Moustafa."

"He'll beat me!"

"Just tell him I sent you. And don't be a pest. Tell him what you know and get lost."

Faisal stared at the carriage. "Where are you going?"

"For a tour around the city."

His eyes narrowed. "With them?"

"No, with the Ottoman Sultan."

Faisal's jaw dropped. "He's in Cairo?"

"No he's not. Good-bye, Faisal." Augustus threw him some coins. "Driver, carry on."

"I wish more of the natives learned English so we could be part of the conversation," Aunt Pearl declared. "All this Arabic is liable to give me a headache."

Nothing another constitutional wouldn't fix, I'll wager, Augustus thought. Out loud he said, "Never fear, it's all English from here on in, Aunt Pearl. Later we'll stop for tea at the Windsor."

Aunt Pearl nodded, but her frown remained. "Who was that beastly little monster you were jabbering with, and why did you give him money when Cordelia already wasted some of her own?"

"A local beggar boy. He's a good source of information on, um, local events. Plus a show of generosity helps smooth over affairs with the natives."

Cordelia's face lit up. "Oh, you've taken that poor child under your wing. How splendid! Aunt Pearl, isn't that splendid?"

Aunt Pearl clucked. "Charity of that sort is best done through institutions. The child is liable to pick your pocket or give you fleas. Did you see how he glared at you, Cordelia, when you gave him a coin? Such ingratitude!"

"He's just naturally skittish," Cordelia objected. "Think what a hard life he must have on the streets."

"Faisal can take care of himself," Augustus said.

"Oh, is that his name? So nice of you to take care of him," Cordelia said.

"I am not taking care of him."

To change the subject, Augustus instructed the driver to head for the mosque of Ibn Tulun.

"Quite an interesting mosque," he told the ladies. "Completed in 884 and modeled after the mosque in Samarra, where Ibn Tulun studied. Its minaret has the stairs on the outside. Don't worry, there's a railing, but I don't suggest a climb if you have vertigo."

"There's so much to see here I've felt dizzy ever since I arrived," Cordelia said.

Augustus bit his tongue.

They passed down a narrow lane crowded with people, the way made narrower by stalls selling mounds of colorful fruit and spices. The smells tickled their nostrils. A few passersby gave them dark looks. This was the native quarter and foreigners were a rare and not particularly welcome sight, especially after the independence demonstrations had been crushed a few months before.

Augustus fiddled with his cane, ready to defend himself and the ladies if anything untoward should happen. He also had a small automatic in his pocket. Damn Sir Thomas for making him play tour guide at such a time! Was he really so desperate to keep him off the case?

Someone called out in Arabic from behind the carriage, his shrill voice rising above the general hubbub.

"A lovely lady you have there, Sir Augustus. Or should I call you by your real name? Take care that she remains lovely. The Apaches are loyal to their comrades and cruel to their enemies, and we will run this city before long."

Augustus felt a chill go through him as he looked around for the caller, but whoever it had been had melded into the crowd. The driver looked around too, then caught his eye.

There was a question on his face. He had obviously heard the part about Augustus' real name.

How could they know that? Only Sir Thomas knew, and he had sworn he wouldn't tell anyone. The people back home didn't know his new identity. His transition between his old life and his new one had been complete.

How could the Apaches have discovered his real name? He didn't even have any French friends in his old life, unless you counted those he had met whilst in the army.

The army ...

"What's the matter?" Cordelia asked.

"Nothing, just a bit of native nonsense," Augustus mumbled. "Driver, keep going."

The driver did as he was told, but the looks he kept giving Augustus over his shoulder made the rest of the day pass in a tense haze.

II

Moustafa studied the piece of paper that had been stuffed in the ear of the decapitated head of Claude Paget.

On it was a crude drawing in pencil of a man tied to a post being shot by a firing squad. Beneath was scrawled in French:

"The ruling class turn us into murderers

We should murder them!

Too low. Too high. Perfect. Under the bridge. 100 cm.

The Apaches ruled Paris, and they will rule Cairo!

Will you be RULER or ruled?"

He stared at the slip of paper for a time and could not make head or tail of it. Perhaps Mr. Wall would be able to shed some light on the message. The second and final lines sounded like an invitation, and the third line like a clue.

"These savages warn us off but lead us on," Moustafa muttered. "Are they insane or do they have some secret purpose?"

Leaving the sarcophagus lid ajar, he went over to the canopic jars.

With a grimace, Moustafa checked each one, and found they were all filled with Claude's interior organs, each in their correct place. The Apaches obviously had someone with them who knew a bit about Egyptology. Well, perhaps not too much. Such information could be found in even the more basic texts, but it showed they had thought this crime through. These weren't the usual class of street thugs.

He carefully replaced the tops on each of the four jars, feeling a surge of guilt. Poor Claude. He'd be still alive if Moustafa hadn't gone to that wretched belly dancing bar and questioned him.

Moustafa secured the lock on the front door. This mess meant they couldn't open today. The Apaches were beginning to hurt their business.

Even worse, he'd have to call the authorities and report the body. Mr. Wall would certainly want to avoid any further entanglements with Russell Pasha, but that made no difference. The law was the law, and what remained of poor Claude deserved a decent burial.

That didn't mean he'd tell the police about the paper, though. Mr. Wall had been right about that. The Apaches had made this personal by breaking into the house not once but twice. And it would be good to show up Russell Pasha again. Let the police commandant conduct his own investigation. Mr. Wall could find out what he was up to and perhaps the vile oppressor would give them a useful lead or two.

A knock came at the door. Moustafa groaned. This was the first time he had ever worked in a shop, and he had discovered that the worst part of working in a shop was the customers.

He slid back the cover on the view slit, ready to make his polite excuses in whatever language the customer required.

He saw no one.

Immediately he ducked back, fearing a bullet. None came.

"Hello?" a small voice called in Arabic from the other side.

"Who goes there?" Moustafa demanded.

"It's me, Faisal."

"Go away, Little Infidel!"

"The Englishman has a message for you."

"Well, give it and go away."

"It's a secret, I shouldn't give it on the street where everyone can hear."

Moustafa growled. What a pain in the backside this boy was!

He opened the door, hauled the brat inside, and slammed the door shut behind him.

"What?" Moustafa demanded.

"I saw how the Apaches broke into the house, and I saw how they did it. The Englishman told me to tell you."

"Fine. Out with it," Moustafa said, trying to hide his interest. Showing the brat he could occasionally be useful only encouraged him.

Faisal cocked his head and smiled. "He said that you should give me ten piastres and lunch."

"Nonsense! Tell me what you know or I'll wring your neck so hard your head will pop like a balloon."

"OK. I only need seven piastres. Oh wait, actually only six and a half."

"You'll get half a piastre and lunch. If you're not satisfied with that, I'll beat the information out of you." Why did he have to be plagued with such vermin?

"But I need six and a half," Faisal whined. A growl from Moustafa made him get to the point. "It was a pair of Europeans and an Egyptian. They had trained baboons with them that went through one of the windows and opened the bolt on the front door after one of the Europeans picked the lock."

"Baboons? Nonsense!" Moustafa scoffed. Then he remembered an entertainer he had seen in Khartoum. That fellow had a baboon who could perform backflips, smoke a pipe, and ride a camel all at the same time. Perhaps it wasn't so far-fetched as it sounded.

Faisal went on to describe the men. Moustafa's heart beat faster as one of the people he mentioned sounded like the man he had fought in the alley.

So the boy was telling the truth and not just looking for money as usual …

Moustafa fished out a half paistre coin from his pocket and tossed it to him.

"And lunch?"

"I'll get you some bread and fruit from the pantry."

"You'll give me more if I find the Apaches, right?"

"Fine," Moustafa said, heading for the pantry.

"Get me one of those apples. They're good."

Moustafa hesitated. "How do you know there are apples in the pantry?"

"Um, the Englishman told me."

"You better find those Apaches for all the trouble you're putting us through."

"I'll find him," Faisal said.

"You'll find him, God willing," Moustafa said.

"What?"

"God willing. Why do you never say 'God willing'?"

"Why does everyone always say that? Either you do it or you don't."

"Bah! This is what happens when children are raised without

religion. Not only do you defy God's commands, but you deny his power. Everything happens by God's will."

"The stone box ended up in the Englishman's house by the Apaches' will."

"Of course they were bad for doing it, but God decided it should happen."

"But they killed a European! Why would God let that happen?"

"Why knows? Maybe he was an evil man and deserved it. Or maybe he was a good man and is now enjoying Paradise."

Faisal blinked. "Europeans go to Paradise? I thought that was only for Muslims."

"They'll get there quicker than little street thieves," Moustafa snapped. "Who knows? God is mysterious. Perhaps some good Christians go to Paradise. They are People of the Book, after all. What I'm trying to say is, that everything happens according to God's will."

Faisal frowned. Moustafa was taken aback. He'd never seen such an angry face on the boy before.

"So it's God's will that I have no parents and I live up ... I live on the street?"

"God assigned everyone their portion," he replied in a calming voice. "Maybe you'll take the right path and be successful one day."

"But only if God is willing. Why can't I do it myself?"

Moustafa hesitated. For someone of such low station, this boy had remarkable pride. Then a story his father had told him back in his village in the Soudan came back to him.

"Look, do you know the story of Creation?"

"Sure! That's when everything was created." Faisal looked at him. "Right?"

Moustafa resisted the urge to throw him out the window. "Look. When God created the world, he created each animal one at a time. He created the monkeys, then the mice, then the scarab beetles—"

"Why did he create the monkeys before the mice?"

"I don't know if He did. It's just an example."

"That why did you say it? Why not the mice first?"

"Shut up and listen! Anyway, as each animal was created, it said 'God willing, I will fly.' The monkeys said this, but it did not happen and they accepted their fate. The mice said it and they didn't get to fly either. Then crows said it and they did get to fly and praised—"

"But the scarab beetles came after the mice."

"Pay attention! The point is that each animal put their faith in God and left it in His hands. But when it came the ostrich's turn, it said 'I will fly.' It didn't say 'God willing'. Thus it became the only bird that cannot fly. It even has wings but they don't do any good. Have you ever seen an ostrich? We have some in the south of my country. They flap their wings and flap their wings but they will never fly. At Creation they were too proud to put their faith in their Creator. God knew this because He knows all, and the ostriches were denied the flight the Creator had planned for them."

Faisal rubbed his chin, deep in thought.

"So God knows all?" he asked.

Moustafa beamed at the boy and put a hand on his shoulder. "That's correct."

"And everything is according to God's will."

"Exactly! There's hope for you yet."

"Then God knew that the ostrich was going to say that, and so He never planned on letting them fly in the first place."

"What? No, that's—"

Faisal looked at him eagerly. "So if I say 'God willing' it doesn't really matter, because God already knows whether I'm going to say it or not."

"That's crazy! What I mean is—"

Faisal jumped up and down. "I get it! So I can say whatever I want because God already decided what I'm going to say. And if I rob someone, that's God's will too!"

"You impertinent little—" Moustafa swung his arm out to knock him on the side of the head, but Faisal was too quick and ducked back.

"Thanks! It's all clear to me. It's God's will that I'm poor and it's God's will that I'm a great thief. So it would be against religion for me to stop stealing."

"Damn you, Little Infidel, I'll tear you apart!"

Moustafa rushed after him, but Faisal darted out of reach. After chasing him around the showroom for a minute, Moustafa gave up.

Shaking his head, Moustafa went to the pantry, Faisal's giggles taunting him. When he returned with the little brat's lunch, he found Faisal crouched in a ball at the foot of the sarcophagus, pale and shivering.

"T-there's a head in there!" the boy wailed.

"That should teach you not to peek around where you're not welcome," Moustafa said. It didn't come out as cross as he intended. The boy looked beside himself. "Come on, get up. Here's your lunch. Try to put it out of your mind."

"They had a sack with them," the boy whispered. "The head must have been inside."

"I suppose so."

At the door, Faisal turned to him, his face long with fear and worry. "These Apaches are as bad as the Egyptian gangs. Will the Englishman stop them?"

"Yes, with plenty of help from me, not that he'll appreciate that enough."

"Me too! I helped."

Moustafa thought for a moment. "And you can help even more. You make a good spy. No one sees you. Search around and see what you can find out about these people. They seem to be establishing themselves here. All those thieves and lowlifes you waste your time with must be talking about them. Find out what you can."

Faisal glanced at the sarcophagus and rubbed his neck. "It's dangerous."

"If you find out anything, we'll pay you."

Faisal looked at him as if he hadn't thought of the possibility. Moustafa realized the boy really was scared. "Oh, um, all right."

"Be careful, and report back as soon as you find out something useful," Moustafa said as he let him out the door.

The boy wandered down the street, looking sick and not even wolfing down his food as he usually did.

As Moustafa watched him go, he felt a growing unease. He had already gotten Claude killed. He hoped he hadn't put Faisal in danger too.

He sat down and studied the slip of paper, trying to puzzle out its meaning. After nearly an hour of staring, pacing, and staring again, he gave up. He got the feeling that the message was not intended for him anyway, but Mr. Wall. Perhaps he could shed some light on it once he got back from the grand distraction Russell Pasha had put in their path.

Moustafa went around the neighborhood again, asking if anyone had seen anything. He did not mention that the house had been broken into a second time, merely that he wanted to know if anyone had been seen lurking about. A sleepy-eyed Karim irritably told him that he had kept a sharp watch on the house and no one had even come close to it all night. Leaving the man without giving him the slap he so deserved, Moustafa checked on the neighbors and street idlers, but no one had seen a thing. The Apaches had been more careful this time.

Feeling at loose ends, he returned to the house and worked some more on his scientific paper. No one, not even the Apaches, would distract him from it. This would be the first step in a lifetime of scholarly work.

His tension eased as his mind was transported back to that wonderful time when Egypt and the Soudan were first among nations. The books Herr Schäfer had lent him were a gold mine. Just look at this frieze from a little-known tomb near Aswan. The style of the figures was Nubian through and through, and this in the XIV Dynasty, the late New Kingdom! And then there was this temple pylon just south of Thebes with exactly the same features. Of course this was XXII Dynasty and much later, but considerably further north. The Nubian incursion in the XXV Dynasty was only the political culmination of a cultural diffusion that had begun centuries before.

And he could prove it—with drawings in excavation reports, artifacts in the National Museum, and a stack of photographs.

Moustafa worked intently, the hours slipping by, but not unnoticed. He knew time was short. At any moment Mr. Wall would show up and whisk him off on that damned manhunt again.

Marcus Simaika's offer whispered in his ears. Good pay. Artifact hunting trips. Learning a new language. He even would get to work with a fellow Egyptian, although a Christian one. A chance to be in the new order. And most of all, no murder investigations to waste his time and risk his life. He still hurt all over from Vincent's kicks. Working for an Egyptian, he wouldn't have to suffer any kicks.

He picked up the note the Apaches had left. One line in particular needled him.

"Too low. Too high. Perfect. Under the bridge. 100 cm."

While the rest of the short note was just revolutionary babble, this line seemed to have substance.

But what?

A hundred centimeters was a meter. So something was a meter under a bridge? And why would that be the perfect level? The bridge over the Nile was higher than that.

Wait, no. While for most of its span it was higher than a meter above water, on each side the riverbank gradually rose to meet it, so at some point the bridge was a meter above the surface.

He set the note aside and tried to get back to work, but the idea pestered him and wouldn't allow him to concentrate. A meter under the bridge. There was a meter stick among Mr. Wall's things. A "ruler" as some called it. The note had even had that word in all capital letters. He could go and check the bridge. There were only two spots to check, one on either side of the river.

Moustafa shook his head and tried to get back to work on his paper. Why couldn't Mr. Wall check? It was that man's ego insisting on doing work that should be better left to the police. He started to write.

A minute later he threw down his pencil with a growl. How maddening! He couldn't do a thing until he had checked that bridge, and he didn't even know what he was looking for! Stomping to the storeroom, he grabbed the meter stick and headed out the door. If this fool's errand ended up with getting someone killed or himself beat up again, he would quit for sure. A week from now he could be exploring medieval monasteries and learning Coptic.

He got a tram to the bridge, standing in the second class carriage as it trundled along the tracks, leaving the native quarter behind and entering a richer neighborhood of Greek grocery shops, Jewish tailors, and Italian wine merchants. The independence movement still had a boycott against the tram, but that had mostly faded as the city eased back into a semblance of normal daily life. The car looked only a little less crowded than usual, and no one shouted at them from the street to get off like in the heady days of mass marches.

Had that been just a couple of months ago? It seemed like forever. The whole city had been in an uproar, with tens of thousands of people taking to the streets—Muslims, Copts, rich, poor. Even women.

He found his heart beating faster at the thought of it. The British had crushed the demonstrations, of course, but they had been put on the back foot. You could see it in their eyes. A lot fewer tourists ventured out of the international quarter. The police had a wary look to them. And while those here for a month or a season acted just as imperious as ever, longtime residents spoke to Egyptians with a bit more courtesy.

But what next? Sa'ad Zaglul and the rest of the independence leaders had been deported. Many of the students and shopkeepers who had organized the street protests were locked up in the Citadel. Besides posters plastered up in the dead of night and the occasional strike or two, not much was happening. Yet the tension beneath the surface was palpable. All the cafés buzzed with talk about the movement. Even the European press was covering it.

He got off at the foot of the bridge. A European hotel stood not far off, three stories of balconies looking out over the Nile and the pyramids in the distant desert haze. At the ground floor was a terrace, carefully enclosed with an elaborate ironwork fence with spiked tops. The terrace was raised so this protection from the natives didn't obscure the view of the whiskey and gin drinkers. Moustafa walked by on the street outside. None of those drinkers looked at him.

But he looked back at them. Many of his countrymen looked at Europeans with awe, thinking they were almost magic. Even those who made fun of Europeans behind their backs, or swore to kick them all out of the country, always did so with a trace of inferiority in their attitude.

Moustafa did not feel inferior. He had spent enough time around Europeans to see their virtues and their flaws. Yes, they were more clever than Africans in many ways. They were masters of engineering and far more organized than any of the other races, but at the same time they were as impulsive and spoiled as rich children. Look at the last war. Owning the world wasn't enough for them and so they decided to fight over Europe too. The Russians, the Germans, and the Austro-Hungarians all lost their governments. The Austro-Hungarians had even lost their empire. The Ottomans had too. God had punished them for being foolish enough to join in a European war.

The British had dragged Egypt into that war too, diverting much of the grain and cotton to war use and "hiring" men for the Labor Force to serve in France. Recruitment had been left to village headmen who took bribes to overlook some men and grabbed the poorest to send to Europe. Many had never returned, and those who did found the price of food twice what it had been when they had left. Those poor men had become the core of the independence movement and now the English called them troublemakers.

Moustafa snorted as he left the road and followed the gentle curve of the riverbank down to the water. Typical European arrogance. They thought they could use hundreds of thousands of Egyptians to do their bidding without it affecting the situation back in Egypt. Oh, yes sir, we will be happy to dig trenches for you as the Germans shell our position with a thousand cannons. We will be happy to take your meager pay and then be sent back home without so much as a thank you. He had talked to the veterans of the Labor Corps. He had heard their stories. He knew their opinions. Every one of them supported independence.

As he reached the water, looking out over its glittering surface at the feluccas sailing along like quill pens, the palm trees waving in the breeze on the far shore, he heard the call to prayer lilt through the air. Noon already?

He looked around. The only minarets he saw were a fair way off. He'd have to retrace his steps.

"Brother!" someone called. "Come join us."

Moustafa turned and saw a group of boatmen a little way down the shore laying down prayer rugs on the sand near where their feluccas were beached.

"We have spare rugs!" the boatman said.

Moustafa smiled and strolled over. The boatmen were all Egyptian, and while some Egyptians acted all high and mighty with dark-skinned Soudanese, these men were obviously true Muslims and knew that all believers were equal in the eyes of God.

Together they took off their sandals, hitched up their jellabas, and did their ablutions in the shallows. Once done, they took their places on the row of prayer rugs and prostrated themselves in the direction of Mecca. As Moustafa came up from his first prostration, muttering the familiar words of prayer he had learned as a child far to the south, he saw a European woman on the terrace of the hotel taking pictures. A trace of irritation passed through him but he dismissed it and focused on his prayers.

As he continued to pray, he kept glancing at the woman, who continued to snap photos. A couple of men joined her, drinks in hand. Now that the muezzin had finished his call to prayer he could hear the happy conversation from the terrace, jolted by the occasional sudden laugh.

Were the Europeans laughing at them? Was the sight of a scholar and some simple boatmen prostrating themselves, all equal before the Almighty, a source of amusement to them? He imagined himself and the boatman in that woman's photo album, brought out at cocktail parties to impress and entertain all the drunks back home. Anger boiled in his veins.

"You have to control that anger," Nur always said. "It does you no good, no matter how justified it might be. God had made the world according to his plan. There is no sense in shaking your fist at it."

How many times had she said those words to him? Their children were growing up with those words. Nur was a village girl, just as humble and far less worldly than these boatmen he was praying with, and yet she saw some things clearly.

He finished his prayers and stood up. Just as he turned away and reached for his sandals, he turned around and went back to the prayer rug.

"Praying again, brother?" one of the boatmen asked, putting on his own sandals.

"My mind wasn't on it," Moustafa said with some embarrassment.

This time it was. He didn't look at the hotel terrace even though he faced it, but rather imagined the holy city of Mecca far beyond. He ignored the woman with her camera and the men with their drinks and laughter, and focused on his submission to God.

When he finished, he felt that familiar clear-headed calm that prayer usually gave him. He put on his sandals and rolled up the prayer mat with a smile.

By then the boatmen had made tea and invited him to sit. They had a pleasant chat for a time about nothing in particular. Moustafa, remembering his purpose for being here, asked if they had seen any Europeans beneath the bridge recently.

"Ha! All the time," the man who had invited him to pray said. He looked at where the bridge met the land. The level span of metal and macadam joined the gentle curve of the riverbank, leaving a portion of it in deep shadow.

"Really?" Moustafa asked.

"Oh yes. That's where the easy girls gather."

Some of the men chuckled. One of them, a bit sterner than the others, said, "Must we talk about this right after prayer?"

"Easy girls?" Moustafa asked.

"A whole group of them. You see the Europeans every evening, strolling along and eying the merchandise."

"I thought they went to belly dancing bars for that sort of thing," Moustafa said.

"You seem to be quite the expert," the stern one said.

"I work for a European," Moustafa hastened to explain. "Not that sort. A good man. But one of his … associates might have been loitering around here and he wants to find out why."

"He wasn't the man who got robbed, was he?" one of the boatmen asked.

"Robbed?"

"I'm surprised it doesn't happen to all of them, walking back and forth in the dark like that," he said.

"That's because Aziz the Pimp keeps most of the thieves away. Bad for business," another said.

"Who was robbed?" Moustafa asked.

"Some European the night before last. English, I think. A man came up from behind and put a garrote around his neck. Then two more rushed in and stole his wallet, his watch, his ring, everything."

"Did they kill him?"

"Oh no. Once they had everything they choked him until he was unconscious and left him there. The strange thing is, the easy girl who was with him swore the thieves were European."

Moustafa leaned in with interest. "So she got away?"

"Here's the strange part. They didn't do anything to her. They kept her from shouting or running away, of course, but didn't hurt her at all. They even gave her some of the European's money!"

"That's odd."

"Aziz was furious, of course, but now he's gone missing. None of his girls have seen him."

The boatmen knew nothing else, so Moustafa changed the topic to trivial matters for a time before finally excusing himself.

He headed for the bridge, cringing at what those kind boatmen would think of him for inspecting such a place. As he approached the bridge, he studied the shaded area beneath. No one was there the moment, and besides some fish heads and some bits of broken crockery, typical trash along the Nile, he didn't see anything.

The shade of the bridge felt cool after the noonday heat. He studied the metal struts and the flat span of the road that stretched like a roof above him. The vibration caused by the lorries and carts passing overhead made the metal bridge hum. He studied the sand under his feet too, but saw no disturbance. It didn't look like anything had been buried here or dug up.

Holding the meter stick vertically, he moved toward where the bridge met the riverbank, hunching as he did so. When he got to the point where the bridge was a meter above the ground he looked around again. Nothing.

The other end of the bridge was equally lacking in interest.

What was he missing?

Shaking his head, he caught a tram back in the direction of Mr. Wall's neighborhood. He was no closer to deciphering the note than he was before, but he had figured out one thing.

The Apaches were taking territory from local criminals. That pimp named Aziz wouldn't come back, or if he did he would come back as a body floating in the Nile.

12

Faisal walked down the street, trying to steady his breath. He'd seen a lot of ugly sights in his life, but that head without a body had been the worst. These European Apaches weren't like the ones in the Wild West at all. Chief Mohammad had honor. He'd never cut off an innocent person's head like that. He wouldn't threaten the Englishman, either, because the Englishman had honor too.

He didn't like having to tell the Englishman how baboons could slip through the window because that was his only way into the house. Now the Englishman would keep the window closed. Luckily Faisal had foreseen this trouble and fashioned a thin bit of metal that could slip between the window and the frame and open the latch. Still, it was inconvenient, and he didn't like having to break into his own house.

But how long would it remain his house? Faisal's shoulders slumped. Not only had that woman come to visit the Englishman with her brother, now he was taking her for a carriage ride with her mother. Or maybe that old woman with the deadly parasol was the matchmaker. The woman's family had obviously made a deal with the Englishman and now they were spending a bit of time getting to know one another and planning the wedding.

When would she move in? A month from now? A week? Then Faisal would be back on the street. If only he could earn enough money to buy another spell!

He needed to earn six piastres honestly somehow. Perhaps they'd give him more money if he found out something about the Apaches, but how was he supposed to do that? Moustafa assumed that just because he lived on the street he knew all about the local gangs. He knew enough to avoid them, that was for sure. There had been rumors that some of the gang leaders were being roughed up, that a new gang was pushing for territory, but that sort of talk only made him avoid the gangs even more.

But now he had to find out about them. He needed time to think about how to do that without ending up a head inside a stone box.

A plaintive voice broke him out of his thoughts.

"Do you have any food, Faisal?"

It was Abdul, one of the smaller ones. He got beat up a lot and didn't know how to beg right. He was a head shorter than Faisal and even dirtier. Despite his grubby face, Faisal could make out a partially healed black eye.

"Here," Faisal said, giving him some bread and one of the apples he'd gotten from Moustafa.

"Thanks," Abdul said around a mouthful of food. "It sure must be nice working for the Englishman."

Faisal smiled. A lot of the street children looked up to him now.

"You doing all right?" Faisal asked.

Abdul shrugged. "Sure."

"I've heard there's a lot of trouble with the gangs."

Adbul nodded eagerly. "Yeah. Mohammed the Club got stabbed the day before yesterday and is in bed not knowing if he'll live or die. And Amir disappeared. No one has seen him."

Faisal thought for a moment. Those were two gang leaders that had territory near the Citadel.

"Anyone know who did it?"

"No. That's all I heard. I stay away from those guys, just like you told me."

"Good."

"I have to go," he said.

"Are you doing something for the Englishman now?" Abdul asked.

"Yes."

"Can I help?"

"No, this job is for men. Stay safe, boy."

Faisal hurried off in a random direction. He didn't want Abdul dogging his footsteps all day. The smaller ones did that sometimes, knowing he had food and that they'd be safer with him around. They weren't independent like he was.

Once he shook Abdul, he slowed his steps. What to do? He had no idea how to hunt down the Apaches.

Then it struck him. Baboons were used by entertainers! He needed to ask another entertainer.

He hurried to the square where Tariq ibn Nagy usually set up his show and to his relief found him there, busily entertaining a trio of children while their father looked indulgently on.

"... and the Great Chief Mohammad flew into a rage. He vowed that the vile Snaketongue would never have Princess Fatima as his bride. He took up his trusty tomahawk ..."

Faisal closed his eyes and imagined the show he had seen so

many times. This was the best part, when Chief Mohammad and Snaketongue had their duel. He could imagine every swing of their tomahawks, every dodge and feint, and the cries from the three children told him they were happening right on time.

What a hero he was! If only Chief Mohammed were here. Too bad America was so far away, further north than Europe even. Chief Mohammed probably didn't even know that bad Apaches were in Cairo dishonoring the name of the good Apaches.

With a final "oooh" from the children, the duel came to an end, Snaketongue's head flying off his shoulders and Chief Mohammed striding away with the Princess Fatima. The children clapped.

After the father led the children away, Faisal went up to Tariq ibn Nagy. The entertainer turned and smiled at him.

"Ah! Back so soon? And where is your Englishman friend?"

"Oh, he's busy. He sent me to do a job for him."

Tariq ibn Nagy bowed. "I must admit I doubted you when you said you worked for an Englishman. Now I see you are a young man full of potential."

Faisal nodded eagerly. "I need your help to find a baboon trainer."

"A baboon trainer? What does your Englishman want with a baboon trainer?"

"It's, um, for a party. He wants to see the best trained baboon in all of Cairo. Two baboons, actually. Do you know someone who does a show with two baboons?"

Tariq ibn Nagy scratched his little pointy beard for a moment, deep in thought.

"No, I don't know anyone like that. The animal trainers all tend to live together. They don't make the best neighbors, as you might guess, so they have their own neighborhood well away from everyone else."

"Where?"

"In the City of the Dead."

Faisal gulped. The City of the Dead was a vast cemetery not far from the Citadel. Only the poorest of the poor lived there, turning the old family mausoleums into houses. He had never ventured there, had never wanted to. There was nothing worth stealing in that neighborhood and the gangs there were tougher than anywhere else in Cairo.

Tariq ibn Nagy seemed to read his thoughts, because he said, "It would be better to spend some time in the big markets waiting to see one of the baboon shows. Then you could ask them without having to go."

The storyteller's words tempted him, but he sighed and shook his head. "No, this needs to be done quickly. I guess I'll have to go."

"The Englishman's party is so important?"

"Um, it's more than that, but I can't say what. If you hear anything about a trainer with two baboons, tell me, won't you? He's thin, and about your age, with a short beard. But don't tell anyone I'm looking for him."

Tariq ibn Nagy raised an eyebrow. "What trouble have you gotten yourself into this time, Faisal?"

"Not me, the Englishman."

"Well, if you're going to the City of the Dead for him, he better give you more than a ride to Giza in his motorcar."

Faisal grinned and waved as he ran off. "He already has!"

The City of the Dead was a long walk from Ibn al-Nafis street in the heat of the day. Faisal had to stop at a crumbling old public fountain to get a drink of water. As he refreshed himself, he looked around uncertainly. Dust choked the broad avenue, and all the people and buildings looked unfamiliar. In the distance, he could make out the thick ramparts of the Citadel through the haze. Up there were hundreds of English soldiers, and enough cannons to blow Cairo apart. To the south, past an old aqueduct, was a miserable bazaar to which only the poorest went, and beyond that, he knew, lay the City of the Dead.

He had never been further than the bazaar, and there only once. He had found little worth stealing, and the hungry eyes of the people who worked the stands made him to afraid to try.

But he had been hungry that day and decided to chance it. He had waited for the right opportunity, sidling up to a date seller while the man talked with a customer. He had slipped a handful of dates into his pocket and casually walked away.

He had made it three steps before they grabbed him.

He didn't remember much of what happened next. They had beaten him, slapping his head with their sandals until he fell down and then a whole circle of them kicked him. He thought he would die that day, but the date seller and his friends had tired of the game and carried him out of the market and threw him onto a pile of trash. He lay there for more than an hour, trying to recover, while local children jeered and tossed offal at him.

Faisal shuddered at the memory. His stomach growled.

"Oh no," he told it. "You can't start complaining now."

Faisal stared at the broad avenue and the aqueduct and the bazaar beyond. He turned away. Why had he given half his breakfast to Abdul? Now he had to steal some food.

At least it delayed him having to cross that street.

He found a bread seller a block away, an old woman hawking little round loaves. Faisal loitered in the area, pretending to watch a group of men loading bags of millet onto the back of a donkey, while really keeping half an eye on the bread seller.

The old woman was sharp, though, and glared at Faisal once or twice to tell him she was onto his game.

Faisal bit his lip. Perhaps he should try some other place. Another growl from his stomach convinced him to be patient. Something would distract the old woman. Cairo was a city full of distractions.

It came in a few minutes. A young man strutted down the street with a scowl, looking like he wanted to smash the whole world. Those angry eyes fixed on something just beyond Faisal.

Faisal turned and saw another local tough, a bit older, standing on the street just past the bread seller, chatting with a couple of the stall owners. The man looked up, scanned the crowd, and his eyes fixed on the tough young man walking toward him.

"Hey! I thought I told you never to come down this street!"

"I'll walk where I like, you son of a whore!"

"I'll rip your arms off, you piece of trash!"

Both men rushed at each other, fast enough to look impressive and slow enough for people to intervene. As the pair's insults got drowned out by the general hubbub and all eyes turned to the drama in the street, Faisal strolled past the bread seller, whisked a loaf off the stack and with nimble fingers folded it in half with one hand and stuffed it in the pocket of his jellaba. He stuffed his other hand in the other pocket, making a fist so both pockets bulged equally.

Then he walked away, not bothering to watch the fight because there wouldn't be any fight. You could tell a real fight from a fake one by how much noise the two people made beforehand. A lot of shouting and insults and there would be no fight. A silent rush at each other and watch out.

The moment he turned the corner he gobbled down the bread.

Faisal got back to the broad avenue with the old aqueduct on the other side, its pointed arches sheltering the ragged marketplace where he had once nearly been killed. He made it halfway across the dusty avenue, picking his way around ox carts and dog droppings, before he hesitated once more.

He looked back the direction he had come. Why was he risking his neck like this? Sure, the Englishman would give him some money, but there were safer ways to get what he needed. And the Englishman probably wouldn't pay him enough to buy the spell to end the Englishman's marriage. He'd end up on the street just the same.

Faisal helped out the Englishman all the time and didn't get enough credit, or enough pay. Half the time the Englishman didn't even know he was doing it. And did Moustafa appreciate him? Ha! So why did he keep running around helping those two, just so he could have a secret little shed on a rooftop?

No, Faisal realized. He didn't do it for the free food or the occasional tip or even that little shed. He did it for something else. When he was helping the Englishman and Moustafa solve their murders he got to be something more than just a dirty little street boy. He got to be somebody special, like Chief Mohammed. It didn't even matter so much that they didn't know, because he knew.

So he would go through that market and into the City of the Dead, and he would track down that man with the vicious baboons, because if he didn't then he was just what everyone thought of him—a nobody. He didn't want to be a nobody. Even if he lost his house and ended up back on the street he'd keep helping the Englishman, because every now and then the Englishman looked at him through that scary mask and saw Faisal as somebody more than a street urchin, and that was the best feeling ever.

Puffing out his chest and squaring his narrow shoulders, Faisal continued across the avenue and plunged into the marketplace.

After the brilliant light of the street, the marketplace was dark. Ragged, filthy awnings stretched over the narrow lanes and stalls. Faisal glanced this way and that, checking for danger. Would they remember him? That had been a couple of years ago so hopefully not. But there were bullies here, like that sharp-eyed teenager leaning against one of the pillars of the aqueduct, sizing everyone up. The stall owners looked tough too as they brayed out exaggerated praises for their used clothing and half-rotted fruit.

Half a dozen street urchins shot out of a space between two stalls, laughing and swearing. They spotted him and descended on him.

"You don't live here," the leader said. He was a bit smaller than Faisal, they all were. But six against one was always bad odds.

"I'm delivering a message," Faisal replied, not slowing down. Sometimes urchins got hired to deliver messages for a bit of food or a few millemes. It was a reasonable explanation for why he would come here.

"To who?"

"None of your business."

"We can show you the way."

"I already know the way."

"Well if you're so smart you should know that you can't pass through here without paying a tax. We run these streets."

"Yeah, right. Go away." Faisal tried to keep his voice sounding tough and confident.

The leader and one other cut him off. Faisal stopped.

"Pay the tax or get out of our neighborhood."

The others surrounded him.

Faisal did the only smart thing to do in that situation—he turned on the smallest in the group, slugged him, and ran past as the boy fell down.

He just managed to break out of the circle, but the boys came right at his heels like a pack of dogs, braying and screeching.

Faisal vaulted over a stand selling slippers, sending a heap of the cheap wares falling all over the place. His pursuers followed, ducking under the stand or running around it. The slipper seller yelled out in fury and grabbed one of the boys by the hair.

Faisal didn't see what the man did to him, because five on one was still bad odds and he kept on running. He zigzagged through the crowd, dodging as hands tried to stop him, then ducked past a soup stand and upended the big brass pot. The soup splashed out in a big steamy wave, catching the gang leader in its spray and causing him to yelp and jump back. His friends behind him stopped. A plume of steam obscured them from view, and Faisal hurried around one of the big pillars holding up the aqueduct and kept on running.

After a few minutes he had caught his breath and assured himself he had lost he gang. He hated going out of his territory. Something like this always happened. Back in his own neighborhood he was known. Rejected, but known. He had a low place but he still had a place. Here he was a stranger, and fair game for anyone who wanted something from him. He had to take care.

By now he had moved past the sprawling market and into the City of the Dead. It was an old cemetery for rich families dating from the days of the Sultans. Each family had a plot of land about ten paces wide and twenty paces long surrounded by a high wall. The tombstones—simple stone slabs—stood inside. A single gate allowed entry. In the old days the family tombs would have been locked and guarded, but these family names had all died out or moved on and nobody cared about the dead who lay here any more. Thus the poorest of the poor moved in, breaking open the gates and installing new doors, creating roofs with canvas awnings or reed mats, and clearing away the tombstones.

They had turned the family tombs into homes. Faisal shuddered. Think of the ghosts and jinn that must lurk around here at night!

But the people he saw here didn't look like they feared anything. They had the dull, resigned look of the abject poor, or the cunning, animal look of those who preyed on them. They were either too hopeless or too brutal to fear any spirit from the unseen world.

The tombs stood in tidy rows, each the same as the other, so that the lanes in between made a grid like the mesh in a strainer. Faisal found it baffling to have all the streets look the same. It was much easier to find your way when streets twisted and turned like normal. At least he could use the aqueduct as a landmark to find his way back, and he'd make sure to find his way back before sundown. If he ended up stuck here after dark, the ghosts and jinn would get him if the human predators didn't get him first.

Plucking up his courage, he asked an old woman weaving in front of one of the tombs where he could find the neighborhood of the animal trainers. She fixed him with suspicious eyes, grunted out a terse response, and told him to be gone.

Faisal hurried off. He could feel eyes on him. Luckily no more gangs, child or adult, tried to stop him.

He had to ask for directions twice more before he found the right area, deep within the City of the Dead in an old section where the tomb walls had crumbled and had been shored up with rubble from a vast stretch of wasteland on the other side of the cemetery. Faisal could see it in the distance, a field of sandy hillocks through which poked portions of old wall. Half-wild dogs picked through trash as vultures wheeled overhead. He had heard that an old city had been there once that had since disappeared, its decay helped along by people stealing its stones to make newer places to live.

His ears told him he had made it to the neighborhood of the animal trainers before his eyes confirmed it. A cacophony of barks, growls, roars, squeaks, and hisses brought him right to the spot.

Faisal turned a corner and his breath caught. Before him stretched a lane crowded with cages and pens. Jackals, hyenas, monkeys, and countless other animals paced behind the bars, calling out in a deafening cacophony.

Beyond the street stretched an open area where men and even some women put the animals through their paces. A woman in a scandalously tight costume stood on the back of a horse as it trotted in tight circles. A man nearby urged a small army of monkeys to jump through hoops and then form a line. He made a gesture and uttered a short cry, and several of the monkeys climbed onto the shoulders of the others, then more monkeys climbed on them, up and up until there was a pyramid of monkeys all screeching and chattering. The man tossed them bits of banana which they caught with their nimble, humanlike hands. One banana fell short, and the whole pyramid collapsed as the monkeys dove for it.

"Damn you, get back into position!" The man shouted, cracking a whip. The monkeys screeched and scattered. This made the man angrier and he laid about with his whip as the other trainers laughed at his expense. Faisal made a wide circle around him and continued to look for a baboon trainer.

After an hour he found him. The distinctive cry of a baboon led him to the open door of one of the tombs. It was bright inside, because the owner had cut a window in each of the three walls not pierced by the door. The shutters were all open, as was the door, so that light streamed in.

Faisal tensed as he recognized the thin Egyptian with angular features who had broken into the Englishman's house. He sat on a dirty old carpet in the center of the room. Nearby stood a table made from a tombstone with broken bits of other tombstones as legs. There was little other furniture except for an old wooden chest, a lamp, and a few bundles of raw cotton piled in one corner. In front of the Egyptian thief squatted the two baboons, their beady eyes fixed on him.

The man gestured with his hand and muttered a strange sound. One of the baboons sprang out of the window and in an instant got on the roof. Faisal could hear the scrape of its claws on the palm trunks that made up the roof as the baboon hurried across to the other side of the tomb and then swung down through the opposite window. It returned to its place before its master.

He made the same gesture and sound, followed by a second gesture, and this time the baboon went to a corner, grabbed a key lying on the floor, jumped out the same window as before, ran across the roof, came in through the opposite window, and returned to its place. It no longer had the key.

The trainer turned to the other baboon, flicked his fingers out like he was spraying water from his hand, and made a low hiss through clenched teeth. The second baboon leaped out of the window and scrambled onto the roof. Faisal stepped back so he could see it. The baboon turned around a couple of times, then its eyes widened and it bolted for a spot out of sight. In another moment it came through the back window with the key in hand

and dropped it in its master's lap before taking its place once again.

Faisal realized he should leave. He had found out where the baboon trainer lived. All he had to do was tell the Englishman and collect his reward. But he was fascinated by these animals and the power the trainer had over him. He'd stay just a little longer and then get out. There were still a few hours before dark.

The trainer reached into his pocket and pulled out two bits of mango. He balanced a piece on each baboon's nose. The animals sat still, eyes focused on the treat. For a moment they sat there, silent, and Faisal waited for the trainer to give the signal to eat. He'd seen this trick before. It wasn't as complicated as the key trick, but getting baboons to hold off on their appetites was still impressive.

But the man did not give the signal. Instead he got up and went to one of the bundles, which he opened, pulling out a pipe and a little pouch of tobacco. Without any haste he filled the pipe, the two baboons obediently awaiting the signal, squatting like a pair of statues on the dirt floor.

"Instead of gawping there by the door, why don't you come in?" the trainer said without looking up from his pipe.

"I-I didn't want to disturb you," Faisal said.

The man smiled. "You're not disturbing me. I always like an audience. Are you impressed by my baboons?"

"They sure are well trained," Faisal said. He felt himself growing cold. He suddenly had the urge to pee.

"That they are," the trainer said, waving his hand without taking his eyes off Faisal. The two baboons jerked their heads back and brought their powerful mouths down on the pieces of mango with a snap. Faisal flinched.

"Allow me to introduce myself. My name is Hakim, like the great Sultan of old. And what might your name be?"

"F-Faisal."

"You're a quiet one, Faisal. I think you have been standing at the doorway for some time before I noticed you. You live on the street, isn't that right?"

"Yes," Faisal lied.

Hakim shook his head sadly. "I thought so. You have the look of a street boy. Such a shame. You don't deserve to live on the street. You deserve to have a place to sleep and money in your pocket. Would you like that, Faisal?"

"Sure." Faisal didn't like the way this conversation was headed.

"Come inside."

"I, um, need to be going."

"No need to be suspicious, Faisal. I'm not going to hurt you. I'm just curious about you."

Faisal thought about running, but he knew those baboons would be on him before he made it past the next tomb.

Hakim held up a half piastre coin. "Come in and I'll give you this."

Faisal shook his head. The rest of him shook too.

Hakim glared at him. "Come in."

The baboon trainer's expression was like an iron grip around his neck. Faisal found himself moving forward. Once he got a few steps inside, he stopped just out of reach of Hakim, who gave him a satisfied smile.

"Much better. Now we can talk as friends. But first we need a bit of privacy."

He darted a glance at his baboons and hissed out a command. The animals sprang up. One bolted past Faisal, who ducked out of the way with a cry, and the baboon slammed the door shut. The other went and closed all three windows, plunging the room into darkness.

After the bright light of the noonday sun, Faisal was blind inside the suddenly darkened chamber. He stood stock still, ears perked for any sound of the baboons.

"Are you frightened, Faisal?"

"Y-yes."

"There is no shame in that. The mark of bravery is not the lack of fear, but the mastery of one's fear. Someone who has been through the great war in Europe told me that."

A match flared, making Faisal blink. Hakim's thin face appeared like a bloody crescent moon.

"Now Faisal, we're going to play a little game. I'm going to tell my baboons to chase you, and you are going to run away. When this match burns out, the baboons will stop, and you will be safe. Ready?"

"Wait, I—"

Hakim shouted a command, and the baboons let out a screech that tore at Faisal's eardrums. He ducked to the right, and the baboon behind him flew past, missing him by an inch. The other one bounded across the room and threw itself at him. Faisal tucked into a roll that ended up right next to Hakim. Glancing over his shoulder, Faisal saw the baboons making for him again.

"Run, Faisal!" Hakim shouted through his laughter.

Faisal did not run, instead he blew out the match.

For a second there was silence. The baboons had stopped.

"Well," Hakim said, the surprise evident in his voice. "That was quite the solution. Your mind is as quick as your reflexes. But the test isn't over."

Another match flared to life. Hakim cupped a hand around it to protect it as the baboons lunged for Faisal.

He ducked behind Hakim, who still sat placidly in the center of the room. The baboons circled around their master, reaching for Faisal.

The boy leapfrogged over Hakim, who laughed, and sprinted for the door. Instinct made him veer off a second later and a baboon flew past, its fur brushing his face, and banged against the door. Faisal kept running, then jumped in the air as the second baboon swiped at his legs.

Faisal grabbed a big bundle of cotton from the corner and threw it at the pursuing animals. The weight of it knocked them back and they screeched in rage. Faisal picked up another and brought it up as a shield just in time to stop one of the animals from tearing his face off. Instead its thick claws raked at the cloth wrapping, almost yanking the bundle out of his hands and sending bits of cotton everywhere.

Faisal pushed with all his might. The baboon was stronger than he was, but lighter and shorter, and he managed to knock it off its feet.

Then he had to jerk to the side again to dodge the second animal, losing grip on his improvised shield as he did so.

He ran. The match burned out. Faisal stumbled and stopped.

A low chuckle emanated from the darkness. "Well done. Very well done."

The animal trainer made a couple of short cries. Faisal backed away as he heard the baboons' claws skitter across the dirt floor. After a moment there was silence.

Hakim lit a third match. One baboon stood sentinel by the door. The other squatted beside its master. Neither moved. Hakim lit an oil lamp and held up the coin.

"I think you have earned this."

He flicked it through the air. Faisal caught it and stuffed it in his pocket. Hakim nodded with satisfaction.

"Look at that. Panting and trembling as you are, you still snatched that coin out of the air like a pleasant thought. I think I might have work for you. Yes, I bet you're quite the little pickpocket and housebreaker, aren't you?"

"I'm not good at any of that."

"Oh, don't be modest, Faisal. One has to make a living in this cruel world. I have need of an assistant. My baboons are quite useful, quite clever, but they are still animals. They have their limitations, but a clever little boy like you could be just the thing I need. Whatever you do not know I will train you to do. And you will be rewarded, Faisal. You can have a roof over your head and money in your pocket."

"Thank you, but I really—"

Hakim raised a silencing hand. "Oh, but Faisal, I insist. God has placed us in each other's path. You need someone to take care of you and give you shelter. I need a little thief. It is ordained."

"But I already—"

"Accept your fate, Faisal. You're mine now."

13

As soon as Moustafa showed Augustus the note the Apaches had left, reality shattered.

The crude drawing of the firing squad became a real one. The Frenchman stood lashed to a post, a defiant look on his face. When he had refused a blindfold, the French officer had put one on him anyway, but while it could hide the contemptuous gleam in his eyes, it could not hide the fanatical pride graven on his features.

"Do you have any final words?" the officer asked. It was Captain Fortier, who had held the line next to his own detached unit of Oxfordshire and Buckinghamshire Light Infantry.

"I forgive the working men who do this deed, and condemn the tools of the ruling class who make them do it!" the man shouted.

"What did he say?" Mark asked beside him. He was the only other Tommy on the firing squad, the rest being French poilus like the man they had to execute.

"Nothing," he muttered.

Captain Fortier stood aside, raised his saber.

"Ready, aim, fire!"

The saber came down.

They fired. He had decided to deliberately miss, but at the last instant shifted his aim and put a bullet dead between the man's eyes.

The other shots ripped apart the prisoner's chest, all save one, which lodged in the post several inches above the man's head.

The man slowly crumpled, seeming to deflate, the ropes going slack. Blood poured down his face and chest.

Captain Fortier strode up to the executed man and tapped at the bullet hole in the post with the tip of his sword. He gave the two Tommies a suspicious look but when he asked the question he asked it in French.

"Who missed on purpose?"

The only answer was silence.

Captain Fortier walked slowly down the line. Mark stood on the far right and the officer passed him first. He stared at Mark for a moment, who held his gaze, and the officer continued to where he stood. He couldn't bring himself to look at his French counterpart. He could only look at his hands, hands that had never trembled before but now could barely keep a hold of the rifle. Sweat poured down his face. He felt like he was going to be sick. That brought more fear, the fear of heaving up his half-digested bully beef and spattering it all over Captain Fortier's shiny boots.

He felt a hand on his shoulder.

"You didn't miss, did you?" The words came out almost kindly.

All he could do was shake his head.

"Executions are never easy," Captain Fortier said as if from a father to his son. "But they are vital to maintain the fighting spirit of the army. You saw what this man did. You saw how he tried to turn my regiment into some rabblerousing workers' collective.

Why, if he spoke English he would have tried to do the same with your regiment."

The gorge rose in his throat, and he just managed to turn enough away that his breakfast ended up on the grass and not on the captain.

"Easy there, easy," Captain Fortier said, his fine, upper class Parisian French sounding oddly beautiful in this ugly scene. "Mustn't let the men see you waver. You set a good example by volunteering to be on the firing squad instead of ordering one of your men. Don't ruin it now."

Captain Fortier continued his slow walk down the row, his saber waving slightly over the grass as if he would suddenly bring it up high and swing it down on the guilty party. The captain stared at each man in turn, forcing them to look him in the eye.

His own gaze slipped past Captain Fortier to a man further down the line. When they had all raised their guns in unison, he had glanced to his left to avoid looking at the prisoner, and saw one rifle raised slightly above level. The way the man held it, he got the sense that he would raise it a little further before he fired.

The man had a calm look on his face, too calm. The others all looked sick or angry, but not this fellow. That made it even more likely that he was the culprit.

Then the fellow returned his gaze. Suspicion, anger, fear, and collusion all flickered through his features like the windows of a passing train.

Then his face became a mask again, and remained so as Captain Fortier stood before him.

"So it appears that miss was accidental," Captain Fortier declared when he got to the end of the line. "With shooting like that, no wonder we still haven't defeated the Bosche. All you men will have gunnery practice for an hour each morning until further notice, and fatigue duty for the rest of the day."

Captain Fortier turned to him.

"Captain ----," Fortier said, addressing him by a name long buried. "I suggest you do the same with your man."

"My man did not miss," he replied, then added, "Nor do I think any of yours did, at least not deliberately."

Captain Fortier's expression was unreadable. "So you say." He nodded to the bloody mess tied to the post. "At least there's one less of his kind. Men, return to your duties!"

The line broke up. He staggered away with Mark at his side, feeling dizzy. Mark walked faster, eager to get away, and once Mark had gone ahead of him a few steps, he sensed another figure come to his side.

It was the poilu who had deliberately missed.

"Thank you for not turning me in," the man whispered. "I am Yves Savatier. Remember that name, comrade."

"Don't call me comrade. And as for remembering your name, I doubt I'll forget anything of this day, although I will certainly do my very best to."

Yves Savatier glanced at his captain with a sneer. "Fortier is a fool. He thinks there is one less for killing Gascon. No, he created a hundred replacements."

Augustus came back to reality on the floor of his own showroom, one hand pressed against the floor and holding up his upper body, the other arm extended, the hand spread out as if to ward off a blow.

Or to warn off his assistant.

Moustafa stood a few feet away, a grim look on his dark face.

"You went away again, boss."

"Thank you for informing me," Augustus said as he stood up. The drawing lay on the floor. He picked it up without looking at it.

"All you all right, boss?"

"Don't be a pest, Moustafa."

"What does that note mean? Do you know the man who sent it?"

Augustus nodded. "An old partner in crime."

"Crime? You?"

"Murder. But all quite legal. Quite neat and tidy."

For a moment neither said anything. Moustafa broke the silence.

"I need to know everything if I am to be of help, sir."

Augustus didn't look at him as he replied.

"You've probably heard of the Great Mutiny, when the French poilus as a mass refused to go on any more of those pointless, bloody attacks. They also demanded better living conditions and leave. Some of those poor fellows hadn't had leave in a year, and spent their days in damp, lice-ridden funk holes ten times worse than what we had, wondering when their lives would be thrown away by their idiotic commanders. Well, the mutiny didn't happen all of a sudden. There was a great deal of discontent in the ranks in the months leading up to it. In March of 1917, after another mess of a battle, a portion of my regiment had become detached from the main body and ended up fighting side by side with the French. A certain Captain Fortier ordered a counterattack to even up the line. The Germans had taken a hill from where they could fire down on our position and he wanted to retake it. Perfectly sound reasoning from a military point of view, but hundreds would die for this perfectly sound reasoning, just like millions had already died for the sake of other perfectly sound decisions."

"I cannot even imagine what it must have been like, boss."

"No you can't, and for that I am glad. So this one private named Gascon stirred up some trouble among the poilus. He said that their regiment had already taken fifty percent losses in the past two days, and why should they take more? When zero hour came and Captain Fortier ordered the assault, my men went over the top but virtually none of the French did. We got hit hard, and scampered back to our starting positions as quickly as we could. The good captain was beside himself with rage, smacking at his men with the flat of his sword. Gascon punched him, and urged the men to kill him then and there. Luckily his comrades balked at that, but just barely, and I and a few of my men managed to pull Fortier out of the tussle before Gascon could rile them enough to do it.

"We got out of there and back to the support trench, where Captain Fortier gathered some officers and men made of sterner stuff and went up to arrest the lot. A good thing the Germans didn't choose that moment to make another attack, or the whole sector might have collapsed."

"Did you have to fight the mutineers?" Moustafa asked. They had moved to the side of the room where they kept a couple of chairs for customers. Augustus sat down hard in one of them, rubbing his temple. Moustafa remained standing.

"No, they gave up, thankfully. Captain Fortier did the right thing. As we came up, he declared that only Gascon would be brought up on charges of mutiny. The others would only have to face charges of gross insubordination."

"What is the difference?"

"One carries the death penalty and the other merely fatigue duties or some time in military prison. If he had charged them all with mutiny, we would have had a firefight on our hands."

"Divide and conquer."

"Indeed. We held a military tribunal that same evening in regimental headquarters. Gascon was found guilty and sentenced to be shot. The others got sent to rear areas to build roads on suspended pay. Since my regiment had been imperiled as much as Captain Fortier's, he asked that two of my men be on the firing squad. While that was highly irregular, those were irregular times. I didn't want to do it, but Fortier got his commission five months before me and thus was the most senior officer present. To spare one of my men I volunteered to be on the firing squad. We drew lots for the second."

"So how does this connect with the Apaches?" Moustafa asked.

Augustus shook his head and looked at the sarcophagus that had contained two of the gang's victims. "Gascon was an Apache, one of the more political ones. He had never been arrested and so when he got drafted he wasn't sent to a convict brigade but rather the regular army. Once there, he started to foment insurrection much like the Bolsheviks in the Czarist army. It turned out one of the poilus forced to be on the firing squad was an Apache sympathizer. Yves Savatier. That act pushed him over the edge and I suppose he joined the Apaches. It could only have been him who could have done this little sketch. The question is, how did they learn my assumed name and learn that I live in Cairo?"

"It also doesn't answer why they have chosen to focus on you."

Augustus sighed. "War is a strange thing, Moustafa. It creates ties between the most unlikely of men. I will always be tied to the men who made up that firing squad, even a low-bred slouch with revolutionary pretensions like Savatier. He might be chasing me for his own reasons, just like I cut myself off from all my fellow veterans for mine."

Augustus stopped talking. He hadn't meant to reveal so much to his assistant, but it had all come tumbling out.

So was that what all this was about? Savatier wanting to put the war behind him somehow? He had picked a funny way to do it. Unless Savatier thought he could convert him to the cause …

Augustus glanced at the message again.

Fools. If they think that, they're barking up the wrong tree.

"So what else have you learned?" Augustus asked in order to get his mind off the past.

Moustafa told him about his experiment with the meter stick and what he had learned from the boatmen.

"Hmm," he said, scratching one side of his chin. "I agree that particular line is a clue of some sort, but we're obviously missing the mark. No, I must admit it eludes me as it does you. But that detail about the attack on the waterfront and the disappearance of the procurer Aziz might just be the lead we need."

"How so?"

Augustus looked at him and grinned. Moustafa got a guarded look on his face. Why did the poor fellow always turn sour just as everything was getting fun?

"We wanted to meet the Apaches, and the Apaches are down by the waterfront attacking foreign men looking for ladies of the evening. Well," Augustus straitened his tie, "I'm a foreign man, and I just so happen to feel a mite lonely tonight."

The waterfront was quiet, the only sounds the not-too-distant chatter of the hotel terrace and the occasional *clop clop* of a horse or mule on the road. The streetlights did not give much illumination as far as where the sand met the water, and Augustus realized that from the relative brightness of the road or hotel terrace, people walking along the riverbank would be impossible to see. The dear departed Aziz had chosen a good spot to set up his nocturnal business.

Augustus strolled casually along the roadside until he found a spot where one of the street lamps had guttered out. Hoping this patch of darker road would be enough to hide his disappearance, he quickly made his way down the slope leading to the river.

He had dressed up for the occasion, favoring a winter suit because it was darker than his light summer suits and thus hid him better at night, and had added a formal shirt with a high collar. On his head he wore a broad slouch hat pulled down over the masked half of his face. He hoped this would hide his features enough that the Apaches wouldn't recognize him. Completing the ensemble was his walking stick, which he swung jauntily in time with his steps. His automatic rested in his pocket and his assistant, also armed, tailed him about two hundred yards behind.

Augustus looked out over the Nile. The water rippled under the faint yellow gleam of the distant streetlamps. All remained quiet but for the palm trees rustling in the breeze and the slap of oars from an unseen boat far out on the river.

He took a deep breath and smiled. It felt peaceful here. No people. He would have come here more regularly if not for its bad reputation. Augustus had, of course, heard that this was a spot for assignations. When social or business duty forced him to spend time with other Europeans, he'd heard many a drunken boast about the commercial transactions along this stretch of the river. Such encounters interested him not at all.

Far more interesting would be the encounter he presently encouraged.

He stopped his descent a few steps from the water and turned to the bridge, visible as a string of lights spanning the river. Eyes and ears alert, he made his way slowly toward it.

About halfway there, he spotted the form of a woman standing by the river ahead, staring out over the water. She wore a loose caftan over her plump body. A headscarf hid her features. After Augustus had taken a couple of more steps the figure turned and he could just make out a careworn but still pretty face.

"Hello, mister," she said in broken English, her voice coming out soft.

"Good evening," he replied in English. Best not to give the game away by speaking in her own language.

"Is the good mister looking for something?"

"Yes. Yes I am."

"Come."

She walked away toward the bridge. Augustus followed a few paces behind. He glanced around but saw no one. She was obviously a professional, completely at ease with the situation. Briefly he wondered if this wasn't a trap, and what he would do if he found himself alone under the bridge with her. How does one make excuses to a woman of this sort?

They passed a few boats beached on the sand. Augustus gave them a wide berth.

The woman turned, as if to make sure he still followed. Then she stopped and looked him full in the face. In the dim light he could see her expression of open invitation.

Yes, a professional. She didn't even change expression when they jumped him.

14

The Apaches came out of nowhere. One moment Moustafa was following his boss at a safe distance, the fallen woman almost invisible in the darkness further along the riverbank, and the next moment there was an explosion of motion.

A man seemed to appear out of the very earth just behind and to the left of Mr. Wall. Silent as the shadow he resembled, he ducked behind Mr. Wall and reached around his neck.

It must have been a garrote, because the attacker jammed a knee against Mr. Wall's lower back and pulled against his neck, making Mr. Wall arch backwards, his feet nearly coming off the ground. From behind the beached boats, two more figures sprinted over to him, angling in from either side.

Moustafa drew the heavy English Webley revolver his boss had lent him from the house arsenal and rushed forward.

He hadn't made it three steps before his boss made his move. Gripping his cane by the knob and by the shaft, Mr. Wall separated the two to reveal a sword hidden inside. Splaying his arms, he swiped at the man on his left with the sword and the man to his right with the metal shaft.

The man on the left jerked to the side. In his haste to avoid being slashed he lost his balance and stumbled to his knees in the sand.

The man on the right wasn't so lucky. He took the metal shaft right in the head, the impact making a loud thwack that Moustafa heard over the sound of his running footsteps. The Apache spun and fell.

That left the man strangling his boss. He put extra effort into the garrote, grinding his knee into Mr. Wall's back and lifting him further off his feet with an impressive display of strength.

Mr. Wall, however, appeared rather unimpressed. Turning the tip of his sword cane downwards, he jabbed it into the man's foot.

The strangler howled and let go of his prey. Mr. Wall tumbled forward and the man with the garrote fell backwards, to land on the one who had dodged the first swing of the blade.

All three Apaches were down, but not for long. The man who had cut in from the left remained unhurt and jumped up, landing a fist in Mr. Wall's stomach. He doubled over, letting out a great gust of air, and the Apache gave him a vicious bow to the head that sprawled him flat.

"Stop right there!" Moustafa shouted in French. "I have a gun."

He was still several paces away but had a clear shot, so he didn't expect the man to face him and for fire to erupt from his fist.

The bullet whizzed by like an angry hornet, barely missing. Moustafa stopped and dropped to one knee. The next shot nicked his shoulder. He still couldn't see the man's gun.

Moustafa ignored both the wound and the mystery, leveled his revolver, and took the man out with a single shot.

As the man fell, one of the other two lobbed something at

Moustafa. It looked small and round. Other than that he could not tell what it was, except that he should get as far away from it as possible.

Moustafa sprang to one side.

Too late. A blinding flare and an earsplitting bang ripped the night.

Blinded, Moustafa fired twice more, aiming high and not hoping to hit anything but just to drive them off.

A garish afterimage shrouded his eyes. Moustafa squinted, trying to see. He heard the sound of running steps moving away.

"Moustafa," he heard Mr. Wall cry out.

"You all right, boss?"

"Not particularly, no."

Moustafa blinked, his vision slowly returning. He could make out a dark figure staggering to his feet.

"Is that you, boss?"

"What's left of me, at any rate. They've scarpered. No point giving chase or firing after them in this dark. They're too far. Despite having stabbed one in the foot he seems to have legged it with some alacrity."

Mr. Wall stumbled over to a dark figure lying on the sand.

"We have this one, though. Good work, Moustafa."

Moustafa came up and saw the man he had shot. A neat hole had pierced the Apache right through the heart. The man's gun was missing. Moustafa assumed the other two had taken it.

He peered around. He couldn't even see the Apaches any more.

"What happened to that woman?" he asked.

"Long gone." Mr. Wall bent over the body and pulled a pair of brass knuckles off the man's hand. "This hurt quite a bit."

"I'm surprised he didn't knock you out with that blow to the head."

"Oh, that." Mr. Wall said with a grin. He pulled his hat off. "Feel inside."

Moustafa did as he was bidden and felt a thin metal cap lining the inside of the hat. A slight divot told him where the brass knuckles had struck.

Mr. Wall pulled down his collar to reveal more metal protection.

"I'd read that the Apaches' favorite attack was to garrote you from behind or kosh you. Forewarned is forearmed."

He knelt back down and rummaged through the Apache's pockets. All he found was a bit of money.

"Well, that's that I suppose." Mr. Wall said, standing up. He sounded disappointed. Then he bent down again and pried the brass knuckles off the man's hand.

"These look unusual but it's difficult to see in the dark."

Moustafa glanced around. Waiters urged everyone off the hotel terrace. "I think it best that we move, boss."

"Hmm, right." He sounded disappointed.

They hurried down the riverside. Glancing over his shoulder, Moustafa saw two figures running along the bridge toward their side of the river. As they came into the light cast by one of the streetlamps, he saw they were policemen. He was tempted to stop his boss and call over to them, but of course Mr. Wall wouldn't want that. No, he'd get into a fight with a criminal gang and not tell the police about it at all. He'd rather solve everything himself.

Why? Was it the war? His injury? Was Mr. Wall trying to prove to himself that he was still useful?

Perhaps. But what was Moustafa trying to prove to himself by going along with all this nonsense? Because he couldn't deny the thrill that went through his veins any time his boss got him into a mess like this. It made him feel alive.

But more importantly, it made him feel superior to those bumbling colonial policemen.

They got away from the scene without too much trouble and went back to the house. Once there, Moustafa bandaged the nick on his shoulder and made some tea and sandwiches for them both. When he came to the little sitting room where his boss took most of his meals, he found Mr. Wall examining the brass knuckles he had taken from the Apache.

"This is a curious device," he said, turning the weapon over in his hands.

Now that Moustafa could see it clearly, he noticed it was far more than a set of brass knuckles.

It was actually a small pocket pistol with brass knuckles for a grip. The cylinder had six chambers for small bullets such as the old Derringers fired. There was no barrel, the bullets firing straight out of the chamber.

Moustafa pointed at it. "I'm surprised he was able to hit me with that little thing."

"I suspect it's not terribly accurate, but in close quarters it would be deadly enough. And look here."

His boss reached under the cylinder where a small spike was tucked beneath. He turned it and it snapped into place, creating a miniature bayonet protruding from below the cylinder.

"This is a nasty bit of work," Mr. Wall said. He fitted his fingers through the brass knuckles. "A bit awkward to use for punching, though."

Moustafa pointed at a button. "I think the gun collapses if you press this, sir."

Mr. Wall tried it and found his assistant was correct. The cylinder tucked behind the brass knuckles perfectly and with the spike extended below his fist it made for a weapon that could be used for punching or stabbing.

"This is one for the arsenal, Moustafa," Mr. Wall said with a grin.

Moustafa suppressed a shudder. In a locked room upstairs, his boss kept a rack of rifles, a couple of machine guns, a collection of pistols and bladed weapons, and even a German trench mortar from the war. No further evidence of his madness was needed.

Moustafa hesitated, knowing his question would be unwelcome, but also necessary.

"Um, boss ..."

"Yes?" Mr. Wall asked, still fiddling with the Apache pistol like a child with a new toy.

"Did you have ... any trouble during the fight?"

Mr. Wall looked up at him sharply. The flash in his eyes was so fierce that Moustafa almost took a step back. Then his gaze softened.

"No. I suppose I didn't have time. Before I knew what was happening I was in the thick of it. It's gunshots that usually set me off, and by the time you and that other chap were blasting away at each other I'd already been given a good rap on the head. Hurt like the Dickens even with that metal lining."

"I see," Moustafa said. "Now what do we do?"

"We try to figure out that note and await their next move. I doubt they'll be so charitable in their little game of cat and mouse now that we have killed one of their own. I think it best if you stay here tonight."

Moustafa sighed. He had suspected as much. Nur had gotten accustomed to his absences, and although she never complained he knew they bothered her and the children.

Still, he didn't see any way out of it. And at least in the morning he could take care of something he needed to do. Something for his own future, rather than for this strange madman whose fate God seemed to have tied up with his.

The next morning, Moustafa walked into the offices of *The Journal of Egyptian Archaeology* with his head held high, his paper on the impact of Nubian art proudly tucked under his arm. The journal's office was in a fine colonial building just off Tahrir Square near the Egyptian Museum. After the grandiose exterior, the office itself came as a bit of a disappointment. A desk stood to one side, at which an Englishman sat, busily typing. The desk and the shelf behind were stacked with papers and correspondence. Several large filing cabinets lined the opposite wall. Above them hung a photograph of King George. A door on the far wall had the word "director" stenciled on it. In short, this office looked much like any other colonial office. But what did that matter, Moustafa asked himself with a smile. This was the home of one of the most prestigious archaeological journals in the world. He asked the man in the front office to see the director.

"What's your business?" the Englishman asked, barely looking up from his typing.

"I've come to submit this paper for consideration to be published in *The Journal of Egyptian Archaeology*." Just saying the words swelled up Moustafa with pride.

The secretary stopped typing and looked at him. "For whom are you submitting it?"

"I beg your pardon?"

"Who is your dig director?"

"Oh, you misunderstand, sir. I am submitting it for myself."

Moustafa extended the paper. The secretary did not take it.

"You wrote it?" the man asked with a notable tone of disbelief.

"I did. I have several years of experience with excavations both here and in the Soudan. I have worked under Professor Somers Clarke and—"

"I really don't think the journal would be interested. Run along now."

"You haven't even read it yet," Moustafa said, waving the paper in front of his face. What was wrong with this man?

With an indifferent air, the man took the paper and leafed through it. His eyes did not follow the lines of text.

"It's a study of how the XXV Dynasty was only the culmination of the Nubian influence on Egyptian monumental art," Moustafa explained, "and that in fact the influence started much earlier, and runs much deeper, than previously thought. For example, if you look at the pylons of the temple at—"

"Thank you for your time, but I don't think we will be needing this," the secretary said, handing it back to him.

"Why not?" Moustafa asked, dumbfounded.

"We have a high standard of quality at this journal. Now if you please, I have much to do." The man started typing again.

"This paper is a high standard of quality," Moustafa said, his anger rising.

"Then your dig director must have written it and it should have his name on it," the man replied, continuing to type.

"What's that supposed to mean? This is my own work!" Moustafa bellowed.

The man didn't seem phased by Moustafa's outburst. He glanced up from his typewriter and said in a cool voice, "Very well, it is your own work. As I said, we keep very high standards here at the journal."

"You didn't even read it!"

A door behind the secretary opened partway and a pasty-faced, older Englishman poked his head out.

"Any problem here, Winston?"

"No sir, I was just showing the boy out."

Moustafa recognized Dr. Lansing, the editor of the journal.

"Ah, Dr. Lansing!" he said, bringing his voice to a polite level again. "Most honored to meet you. I attended your lecture on Middle Kingdom anthropoid sarcophagi last month. Allow me to introduce myself. I am Moustafa Ghani El Souwaim. I have extensive experience on excavations in Egypt and the Soudan and wish to submit a paper to your esteemed journal."

"All papers must go through Winston," Dr. Lansing said, and shut the door.

Winston smirked at him. "Well that's that, my boy. No work for you here. It's been a dusty day, though. Perhaps I can find you some shoes to shine."

Moustafa slammed his fist on the desk, making the typewriter leap into the air and crash back down.

"Once we have independence you people will learn some respect!"

Dr. Lansing called from the other room. "Winston, shall I call the police?"

"I think that might be a good idea, sir." Winston had backed into a corner.

"They'll be thrown out too!" Moustafa shouted and kicked the desk. He was happy to see he left a crack in the wood. "Apologize this instant!"

Winston rallied.

"When pigs fly, as the Yanks say," he said with a sneer.

Moustafa almost lost control of himself. He almost took the

three steps separating him from Winston and gave him the thrashing he so thoroughly deserved.

But he did not. He'd be arrested, thrown in jail, and Mr. Wall would be stuck trying to solve the murder alone. Plus who would take care of Nur and the children?

Good God, did he just think of his employer before his own family? These English were like mosquitoes—when one is in the room you can pay attention to nothing else! They nag you and nag you until you go mad!

He glared at Winston, who made a bold attempt to glare back but remained pressed against the corner. The only sound in the room was their heavy breathing and the low voice of Dr. Lansing in the next room, no doubt speaking with the local police station.

Oh, how he'd like to beat them both to a pulp! If they were Egyptian they'd be lying on the floor already for showing him such disrespect.

If they were Egyptian.

But they're not Egyptian, Moustafa thought.

"What's my name?" he asked Winston.

"W-what?"

"I said my name just now, do you remember it?"

Winston managed to curl his lip, although his voice was less than steady. "Why should I?"

"You people never do, do you?"

Moustafa picked up Winston's typewriter and hurled it against Dr. Lansing's door. It crashed right through the paneling, leaving a beautiful typewriter-shaped hole in the wood. Dr. Lansing face appeared behind it, looking even pastier than before.

"I bet you don't remember my name either!" Moustafa said and laughed.

"I sure do, Mohammed el-Gawani, and I've told the police too!"

"Fools!" Moustafa snatched his paper and stormed out of the office. He shoved past a few curious Europeans who had gathered in the hallway, confident that none of them would be able to adequately describe him, and left the building. He swore to God he would return. He'd show them all.

15

Faisal couldn't believe he lived to see the dawn. Hakim hadn't laid a finger on him all that long afternoon and the even longer night that followed it. Instead he had asked endless prying questions about his life and how he made his way in the world. Faisal had tried to lie, but Hakim was quick to find even the slightest inconsistency in his story and chase it down like a hunting dog that has caught the scent. Hakim learned all about how he had ended up on the street and that he was a good housebreaker and pickpocket. Faisal had managed to hide the facts that he worked for the Englishman and lived on his roof.

Faisal had done this by playing a trick with his own mind. He blanked out everything that had happened since the Englishman had come into the neighborhood, instead talking about how he slept in the entrance of the Mosque of Sultan Hassan, something he had done before the Englishman appeared. He talked about how he and his friends had a shack in an alley he sometimes used as well, and how he begged with an old blind beggar who had died.

Hakim learned nothing about the Englishman. Faisal didn't even let himself think about the Englishman or all the good things that had happened since that man had moved to Ibn al-Nafis street. It was like he was eleven again, still alone and hopeless and prey to neighborhood bullies like Hassan and his cousins, who the Englishman had first beaten up and then gotten arrested. It was like he had no protector in the world, just like before. That's how talking with Hakim felt.

During all this the baboons had squatted nearby, watching him.

Then Hakim had put him through a series of tests. He had made Faisal grab objects out of the air. He had made him climb halfway up the wall of the tomb in which he lived and then traverse all the way around it to end up at the spot where he had started. He had taken him out to the market and made him pick a pocket, the baboons coming along in case he made a run for it. To Faisal's surprise, Hakim let him keep what he had stolen.

"You see?" Hakim said when they returned. "Working for me can be quite profitable. I will feed you and give you some of the take and I will not hurt you unless you defy me. And if you defy me, I will hurt you very, very badly."

That night they had dined on bread and *ful*. Despite his fear, or perhaps because of it, Faisal ate ravenously. As he ate he kept thinking of Mina.

Hakim didn't have any spare blankets so Faisal had to sleep on the dirt floor with only an old jute sack as a carpet. Hakim laid himself down on one side of the tomb and Faisal laid down as far away from him as possible. The baboons slept in the center of the room.

"Do not try to unlatch the door or any of the windows," Hakim had warned. "Baboons have very good hearing and I might not wake up in time to stop them from ripping your face off."

Faisal shuddered. He would end up looking like the Englishman. He wished the Englishman were here. He'd defeat Hakim and his filthy beasts in less time than it took to pick a pocket. Faisal thought he would never fall asleep that night but exhaustion finally overtook him.

That morning he woke to a hand touching his face.

He screamed and scrambled back, pressing himself against the wall. A baboon squatted next to him. Hakim sat on the other side of the room, contentedly smoking.

"Pleasant dreams?" he asked.

"Can I go now?" Faisal pleaded.

Hakim chuckled. "Just as things are getting interesting? Oh no. I'm taking you to see some friends of mine. I think they'll like you very much."

Faisal gulped. He must be talking about the Apaches. He hoped they wouldn't scalp him or cut his head off and put it in a big stone box.

After a breakfast of bread and dates, Hakim led him through the City of the Dead, the two baboons trotting behind like faithful dogs. At the edge of the old cemetery they met with a burly Egyptian in a filthy jellaba who took one look at Faisal, snorted, and joined them without a word.

"His name is Abasi," Hakim said. "He rarely talks."

They left the City of the Dead and moved through a better neighborhood, ending up close to the river in a warren of streets lined with a mixture of old houses and new. The people were mixed too, and included some better-off Egyptians and various Europeans. While most Europeans still all looked the same to Faisal, he had come to realize that not all were rich. Some had humble jobs, working in the shops of richer Europeans. These were the kind of Europeans who lived in this neighborhood.

They came to a grimy building with an open entryway leading to a flight of steps. A European lounged at the entrance. Faisal could tell he was a thief and a bully. Europeans thieves and bullies looked just like Egyptian thieves and bullies. They had the same hardness to their eyes, the same way of standing that showed they were just as likely to lash out at you as to light a cigarette. Hakim led Faisal to a closed door right next to the open entryway and knocked three times, then twice. The European pointed to Faisal and said something in his language, followed by a cruel laugh. Faisal trembled.

To Faisal's amazement, Hakim replied back in the same European language. It didn't sound like English, which he had heard a lot of by listening at the Englishman's window.

Hakim noticed him staring and smiled down at him. "Are you surprised I speak French? I was stationed in France with the Egyptian Labour Corps. I was forced to go, like so many others, but I learned so much. Just like you will learn, Faisal, even though you don't want to be here."

The door opened, and a suspicious-looking European man standing inside said something to Hakim, then glanced up and down the street. He pointed at Faisal and grunted something. After a quick conversation, the European nodded and they went inside.

They entered a low-ceiling room crowded with old, worn tables and chairs. At the back wall ran a counter and behind it several shelves filled with bottles. Faisal wrinkled his nose at the stench of alcohol that hung in the air.

At a large round table in the center of the room sat half a dozen Europeans. Each had a glass in front of him and several half-empty bottles stood on the table.

Despite his fear, Faisal looked at them with disgust. He hated drinkers, especially morning drinkers. His father would open a bottle before breakfast, and by the time he had finished the morning meal would be in his usual angry, slappy mood.

These Europeans looked like they'd be a lot worse.

One of them leaned forward and studied Faisal. He had the brown skin Europeans got once they had lived in the desert for a while. As he reached for the bottle, Faisal saw his hand and forearm were covered with thin scars. Faisal had seen those before. People got them by fighting duels with razors.

"So what do we have here?" the man asked in Arabic.

Hakim smiled. "My new assistant. He's quite the little housebreaker and climber. It solves our problem."

"Do you trust him?" the European asked.

"I trust his fear."

"Fear isn't enough."

They switched to French for a minute before the man with the razor scars turned to Faisal and continued in Arabic. "My name is Edmond Depré. I speak your language because I was in a French prison in Algeria for many years, crammed in a tiny cell with inmates of your race. I learned a great deal from them, enough that once I escaped, I knew the ways of your kind. Enough to stake out territory here."

"You're the ones who have been taking over the gangs," Faisal said.

Edmond nodded and smiled. There was no mirth or friendliness in that smile. "You're well informed, I see. Does it bother you that a group of Europeans are taking over the streets?"

"No," Faisal said, hoping that was what he wanted to hear.

"Good. Because we are like you. We are oppressed, just like you. It is the rich Europeans who you should hate. People like the English generals who run the army of occupation here. People like the police commandant."

Faisal repeated the words Bisam the water seller had said to him. “He’s a bad man. I’d like to slap him in the face with my sandal.”

Edmond grinned.

“I bet you would, but you don’t have sandals. That’s how poor they want to keep the Egyptians. Would you like some sandals, Faisal?”

“Um, sure.”

“And a new jellaba?”

“OK.”

“And some money in your pocket and food in your belly, eh? You can have all that. You deserve all that. Hakim tells me you’re the quickest, most agile little boy he’s ever seen. You were even able to get away from his baboons for a time. We can use you. We need you to do a little job, not much different than the little jobs you do every day to keep yourself alive, and you will get to strike back against the rich Europeans who have hurt you and your people. I know you hate them. All Egyptians hate them. I hate them too for the war they started and we suffered in.”

“Rich Europeans suffered in the war too,” Faisal blurted out. He stopped before he went on. He had almost revealed that he knew the Englishman.

To his surprise, Edmond Depré did not get angry at being contradicted. Instead he took a swig from the bottle, set it down, and said in a quiet voice, “That’s true. Yves here knows such a man. He was in the army. The stories he tells show me that I was lucky to be in prison the whole time. He tells me of a man, a rich man, who suffered worse than he did. You know what happened to him?”

“What?”

Edmond Depré ran a hand slowly down one side of his face. "A German shell took half his face off."

Faisal's eyes went wide and he started to tremble more than before. They were talking about the Englishman!

Edmond chuckled. "Terrible, isn't it? Terrible enough for me to feel sorry for a rich man. There are more than a few like him. They will be valuable in the revolution to come, because they have connections, they have knowledge. They hate the European elite just as much as the working man, perhaps more. They got betrayed by their own kind."

"You think he will join you?" Faisal didn't mean for it to come out as a challenge, but the idea that the Englishman would ever team up with these fake Apaches made him angry.

"He will," Edmond nodded. "We have watched him and know that he has come to hate Europe. He is always showing up the police commandant because of his hatred. He will join us when the time comes. But never mind that. The question is, will you?"

Faisal blinked. Was he really being asked? He glanced at Hakim and the baboons. Edmond smiled.

"Don't be scared. I won't let Hakim hurt you. I'm not one of those street thugs boys like you have to watch out for. The only people who have to fear me are the rich and powerful."

Faisal had his doubts about that.

Edmond got a distant look in his eye. "I had a little boy once. My, he'd be a young man now. Seventeen years old. Eighteen next month. But he died of fever when he was eight. I was in prison at the time, but that cold, dank cell they put me in was no worse than the filthy tenement where he and his mother lived. Rats, fleas, mold, it's a wonder any child can grow up in such places. He caught a fever and I had no money to send for medicine. The bastards wouldn't let me out to see him, not even to attend his funeral."

Edmond slammed a fist down on the table and looked at Faisal with such fierceness that the boy almost ran for the door. It might be better to take his chances with the baboons than stay here.

"He was a clever boy too, just like you. Yes, he was a lot like you. He already knew how to filch candies from the sweet shop to feed all his friends. I was teaching him how to pick pockets too, just like you can. Oh, I would have taught him so much."

"Sorry you lost your son," Faisal said.

Edmond looked at him. "I bet you mean that. You've lost family too, so you know what it's like. But the Apaches are like a family, protecting each other from the cruel, greedy world. You can be part of that. You can have new clothes and three meals a day and a safe place to sleep. You can have money to buy the things you can't steal. And all you have to do is deliver a message."

"What will that do?"

"Help us kidnap Sir Thomas Russell Pasha."

Faisal's jaw dropped. "He's the police commandant!"

"Exactly," said another Frenchman in Arabic. He, too, had a deep tan. "If we take him, think what a blow it will be to the empire! All of Cairo will rise up, and we will be at the forefront of the revolution."

"I thought you were thieves," Faisal said, confused.

Edmond reached over and put a hand on Faisal's shoulder. Faisal pulled away.

"Silly boy. Don't you know that theft is a revolutionary act? The rich steal from us every day, so it is only right to steal back from them. And as my comrade Vincent said, stealing the police commandant will be the most revolutionary act we've ever done."

Faisal stared at them. These people were crazy. Stealing was all right if you needed to, but they were talking like it was some big noble thing, like what Chief Mohammed did. But wait, Chief Mohammed killed and robbed from the Americans to protect his own people. Weren't these fake Apaches trying to protect their own people too?

No, that couldn't be right. These people were bullies, bad people. Weren't they?

He decided to test them.

"The, um, the European who lost his face. If he doesn't join you, will you kill him?"

"Only if he continues to fight against us. Why do you care?"

"What if I don't join you?"

Hakim cut in. "Haven't I treated you well? I could have hurt you when I had you in my house but I didn't. And didn't I give you money and food? What have the Europeans ever given you?"

"You'll pay me if I help you?"

"Of course," Edmond said.

"But what if I don't help you?"

Vincent smiled. "Then we'll stick you in a cage with the baboons and sell tickets so people can see what they will do to you."

Edmond, who seemed to be the leader, did not contradict him.

Faisal nodded. Yes, that's what he thought they would say.

"Then I'll work for you."

Edmond nodded. Vincent poured some wine into a glass and pushed it over to him.

"Here you go. Now you're one of us. Are you hungry? We'll get you some lunch."

Edmond snapped his fingers and an Egyptian came in from another room with some bread and olives. He set them before Faisal and without a word left the room. After he went through the door, Faisal heard him say something to someone in the other room. Both laughed.

Edmond gestured to the food with a grandiose wave of his hand.

"Eat!"

Faisal ate as the Frenchmen drank and spoke in their own language. Hakim and Abasi drank too.

"Why aren't you drinking?" Abasi asked, speaking for the first time.

"I don't like wine. It smells gross," Faisal said.

"Drink it," he said. The man sounded drunk already. He sounded like Faisal's father.

Faisal kept on eating, hoping that if he kept quiet and didn't look at him the Egyptian would lose interest. That had worked with his father. Sometimes.

Abasi grabbed him by his hair and yanked his head back. With his other hand he brought the wine glass up to Faisal's lips.

"Drink!"

Edmond leaped up and smashed a fist into the man's face, sending him to the floor.

Within an hour they were crossing the Nile in a felucca, headed for al-Rawdah Island in the middle of the river. Faisal had never been there and didn't know anyone who had. Besides a little village of fishermen, he had never heard of there being anything else on the island.

"You know why we're going here?" Edmond Depré asked.

"It's your hideout," Faisal said.

The Apache leader nodded and smiled. "Clever boy. But living on the streets would make you clever, wouldn't it? You'll make a good Apache some day."

When Faisal didn't respond, Edmond went on.

"Of course you're still scared of us. Perfectly reasonable considering Hakim kidnapped you. But think of it this way. You've slept under a roof and you've had three big meals in a day. When's the last time you had that?"

"A long time ago," Faisal lied.

"Exactly," Edmond said and patted him on the shoulder, making Faisal flinch. "We are good to our friends. We've been on al-Rawdah Island for a couple of months now and the fishermen who live there have been enriched by our presence. Smugglers, the lot of them, and now they're *our* smugglers. Oh, their village headman didn't want to cut a deal with us, but now he's the village headless man. The rest fell in line quickly enough, and they're making more money than they ever imagined."

They reached the island and Hakim dragged him out of the boat, his fingers digging into his arm. Hakim always kept a close eye on him. The Apaches moved out ahead, scanning the shoreline for trouble. But they looked confident, only searching out of habit. This had obviously become their island.

An Egyptian carrying a rifle emerged out of the shade of a grove of palm trees, nodded, and without a word disappeared back into the gloom.

"I know you want to run," Hakim said. "Try that and I'll set the baboons on you,"

He let go of Faisal's arm and whistled. The baboons loped up like a pair of dogs and flanked him. Faisal shuddered and bowed his head.

They moved through the grove's cool shade, at times having to push their way through thick underbrush, and came to a clearing.

Faisal saw a strange mosque standing at the far side. It had no building, only a short minaret with no window for the muezzin to call from.

"You've taken over a mosque?" Faisal said with disbelief. If these Apaches had even taken over the religious teachers, they had more power than he suspected.

Edmond Depré laughed. "In time, my little anarchist, in time."

Faisal had heard him use that term before. "What's an anarchist?"

"It's a man who is free."

Like I was before you captured me, Faisal thought gloomily.

An Egyptian man opened a small door in the minaret and Hakim pushed him toward it.

"Relax, my friend," the Apache leader told Hakim. He put an arm around Faisal's shoulder.

They passed through the doorway and entered the strangest mosque Faisal had ever seen. Just inside the door they stopped on a landing. A spiral staircase went down the inside of the wall. The space in between was open like a giant well. In the lamplight Faisal could see a circle water rippling far below. A thin pillar with writing and lines on it ran from the ceiling to the water. High above, a domed ceiling was painted with calligraphy, the windows surrounding it letting in light.

"This isn't a mosque," Faisal said.

"No it isn't," Edmond said, squeezing his shoulder. "This is the Nilometer."

"The what?"

"See these markings?"

"I can't read."

Edmond grimaced. "Of course not. Reading would allow you to get ahead in the world, and the wealthy who run your country don't give a damn if you progress or not. In fact, they want to keep you in your place. These markings show the level of the Nile. A clever boy like you knows that the level of the Nile's annual flooding is vital for the peasants working the land. Too little of a flood and the crops don't grow. Too much and the fields flood. This is an old place, from a time when your people were ruled by Egyptians and not British. The Egyptian rulers would check the level to know how much they could tax the peasants. It's not used anymore because the British will tax the peasants whether they've had a good crop or not."

"The British are bad," Faisal said, repeating what he had heard so many adults say. "They should be kicked out of Egypt."

"That's right, and you're going to help make that happen."

"How?"

"With that message you're going to deliver."

"Deliver where?"

Instead of answering, Edmond moved over to a large chest standing by one wall and opened it.

"We have a new suit of clothes for you," he said, holding up a clean white shirt and pantaloons, plus a green vest with red embroidery. "I even have a little fez to go with it."

"That looks like a servant's uniform."

Edmond nodded. "This is the uniform the tea boys wear at the Citadel. I have connections there and can get you in without you having to show your papers. Once inside, you can pass without notice."

Faisal's heart pounded. "You want me to break into prison? Who does such a thing?"

Edmond laughed. "No, not the prison part of the Citadel, although we will break out those prisoners in good time. I want you to go into the offices."

Faisal blinked. That did not sound like an improvement. Then a realization struck him.

"Sir Thomas Russell Pasha! You want me to get at him."

"Look at this clever boy," Edmond said with a smile, and Faisal could not help but feel good at the compliment. Hardly anyone ever said nice things to him. "Yes, you will meet with my contact. He's an Egyptian policeman we have in our pay. He will get you inside and then you can pass unnoticed among the buildings."

"Won't they notice I'm a new face and stop me?"

Edmond cocked his head. "Will they?"

Faisal thought for a moment. "No. No they won't. They never recognize us."

Except for the Englishman.

"Exactly. And when you get into his office, you will put a letter on his desk. That's all you have to do."

"What does the letter say?"

At that, Edmond only smiled.

16

"Damn it, Moustafa, why did you have to call them!"

"Because there's a dead man in our showroom, boss. The canopic jars are beginning to smell funny."

Augustus grunted and went back to the front door, where Sir Thomas was still patiently knocking.

"Just as I thought," the police commandant said as Augustus let him in, "taking police work into your own hands."

"Why do you say that?" Augustus asked, trying to put an innocent tone in his voice. A colonial policeman followed Sir Thomas in. Augustus looked past them and did not see Cordelia or Aunt Pearl.

Thank God for small favors, he thought.

"Because you hid a body and interfered with a crime scene," Sir Thomas said. "Those are criminal offenses, my good man. Now where is it?"

Augustus glared at Moustafa, who gave him a defiant look in return, and led Sir Thomas and the policeman to the sarcophagus and canopic jars. He lifted the lid of one and Sir Thomas peered inside, wrinkling his nose.

"All four are full with Claude Paget's internal organs. His head is in the sarcophagus," Augustus told him. "Paget was a doorman who acted as a messenger for the Apaches."

"So you actually slept last night knowing these body parts were in the house?" Sir Thomas sounded more angry than shocked.

"I spent three years in France sleeping with body parts. One gets used to it."

"That was France, this is Cairo. The war is over and it is about time you accepted that."

"The Apaches haven't accepted it, so why should I?"

Sir Thomas frowned. "What do you mean?"

Augustus paused. How much should he tell him?

He glanced at the sarcophagus. Two men were dead and he was still far from finding the culprits. As much as he wanted to solve this himself, at this point the police needed to know everything.

"Let's step away from the others, shall we?" he said in a low voice.

Augustus took him to the other side of the room and showed him the note left by the Apaches. Sir Thomas paled as he stared at it, and his hand began to tremble.

"Whatever is the matter?" Augustus asked.

"Nothing. Go on," the commandant said, handing the note back to him.

Augustus related what had happened in the belly dancing bar, although replacing Moustafa with himself. He had no doubt that if he told Sir Thomas the truth, Moustafa would get in trouble. He did not mention the fight by the river. The fight would land him in even more trouble.

Sir Thomas seemed to listen with only half an ear. He looked at the floor, still pale, nodding occasionally.

"Do you have any idea what this note means?" Sir Thomas asked softly.

"I've been puzzling over it for some time now."

"And the ... firing squad?"

Augustus' breath caught. "No."

The police commandant gave him a sharp look. Augustus didn't say a word. His wartime crimes were his business, and taking on the Apaches was his fight.

After a moment, Sir Thomas shook his head and chuckled. The laughter sounded false. "My good man, leave police work to the professionals. If you wanted to tail this Claude Paget fellow, you should have sent your man instead of yourself. You would be easily recognized, while he could have blended in with the crowd. He could have also questioned the native doormen on Paget's street to find out more information."

"I must admit I didn't think of that. Yes, I suppose I should leave it to the professionals."

Sir Thomas patted him on the shoulder.

"You got lucky with the khedive's jewels. Don't let it go to your head. Now I'm willing to overlook the crime of hiding a body, and I'm willing to overlook the fact that you engaged in police work without permission, but here's my price. You will stay out of it from now on. I have enough on my hands without having to keep an eye on you. The whole city is going mad."

"I haven't heard of any more protests."

"No, not that. We've taken the wind out of their sails. It's the underworld. Several major crime figures have turned up dead. An illegal casino owner was found with his throat slit, a couple of gang leaders found strangled, and a pimp was found floating in the Nile. There's probably more we haven't found yet."

"The Apaches are gaining a foothold."

Sir Thomas scoffed. "You read too many illustrated papers. They aren't criminal masterminds, just a few political fanatics here on a vendetta. No, I suspect it's some native group."

"Natives led by the Apaches."

Sir Thomas shook his head.

"No, my good man. Now where will you be today? I want to know so I can keep an eye on you."

Augustus almost came out with a lie until he realized he would be in too public of a place not to be seen.

"I am having lunch at the Continental. After that I'll be here in my shop."

"Very good. My man is cleaning up that mess in your showroom. I'm afraid we'll have to take those jars as evidence. Stay out of trouble."

Within a few minutes Sir Thomas, the colonial policeman, the canopic jars, and Claude Paget's head were all gone.

"I got you off the hook for the belly dancing bar by saying I went," Augustus told his assistant. "Although I was tempted to let you hang. You've severely interfered with our ability to solve this case."

"Monsieur Paget deserves a decent burial. It is humiliating to be chopped up like this."

"It might happen to the two of us if we're not careful. You want out?"

Moustafa thought for a moment, then shook his head. "The Apaches need to be stopped."

Augustus smiled. "And we're the ones to do it, not that windbag who just left."

Moustafa smiled back. "Now what do we do, boss?"

"I have a lunch date with Zehra," he said, his heart lifting. "Perhaps she can throw some more light on this. After that I suspect there will be more night work."

The dining hall at the Continental more closely resembled a post-Reformation cathedral than a restaurant. Lofty ceilings held up by soaring arches, painted white and devoid of decoration and all but the simplest of architectural embellishment, dwarfed the guests seated at the tables. The atmosphere seemed to encourage a respectful hush. Even those already well into their third drink—and there were many of those of both sexes—managed to keep their voices to a respectful level. This was encouraged by the waiters, all Nubian, who asked what the "good gentlemen" and "good madam" would like in voices barely above a whisper.

If Augustus had to go through the ordeal of dining outside his home, he preferred coming here. The lack of inane babble, or at least his inability to hear very much of it, made it an attractive option.

Today it seemed like the most beautiful place in the world, because Zehra Hanzade was in it. She looked radiant as usual in one of her unlimited number of gorgeous Ottoman caftans, this one a brilliant turquoise with silver embroidery. As usual, she let her luxuriant black curls fall around her shoulders.

She was the only Turk in the dining room, and the sharp looks she got from the English ladies filled Augustus's heart with joy. He was equally happy to see that her husband had not come. Not that he had anything against Suleiman. He was a good man, a trustworthy business partner, and an expert in forging antiquities, it's just that Augustus wished he didn't exist.

"It is so good to see you again," Zehra said as they sat down. "We really must see more of one another."

A waiter, obviously charmed, hurried up to take their order.

"Mango juice and the Greek salad. It's always nice to have something from the former colonies," she told him.

"Those Greek statues you have in your house make quite the collection," Augustus said. He and Moustafa ordered. His assistant looked ill at ease but Augustus barely noticed.

"Ah, but the Greeks sculptors were masters at creating beautiful bodies," Zehra said. "Do you remember my gladiator? The one in the drawing room? Such a perfect example of the manly form."

Augustus gulped. Zehra extended a hand. On her wrist was a slim gold Rolex studded with emeralds.

"I just bought this downtown. Do you like it?"

"It's exquisite, but didn't you already have a Rolex?"

Zehra laughed, a clear resonant sound like church bells.

Oh, church bells, Augustus thought. *Ringing for me and her.*

"Really Augustus, a lady can never have too many Rolexes. Or gladiators."

Zehra took off the watch and laid it on Augustus's wrist. Her touch nearly gave him a coronary.

"Hmmm, not suitable for a man. You need something more robust."

"I most certainly do."

"Speaking of robust warriors," Zehra said, fixing him with a delicious look that he knew he'd carry with him for days to come, "we have a new stock of friezes showing battle scenes. Pharaohs smiting enemies and shooting from the backs of chariots. Would you be interested in some for your shop?"

"Oh, I'm sure they'll sell well. Send them over. We'll arrange the price later."

Zehra smiled. "You have such excellent taste, Augustus." Her gaze lingered on him. "I'd like to think I have excellent taste too. In fact, I know I do."

Oh, Zehra. You do have a way with words.

They chatted amiably through the appetizer and the main course, and it was only after some persistent nudging from Moustafa that he remembered the supposed reason for this meeting. The nudging also reminded him that Moustafa was still at the table.

"Ah, yes," Augustus cleared his throat. "The case."

Augustus outlined what they had learned and experienced since last they met. Zehra listened with interest, and Augustus swelled with pride at the admiring look she gave him when he recounted the fight on the river. Once he finished, she thought for a moment and shook her head.

"I haven't learned any more about the Apaches. They haven't approached any other antiquities dealer. I suspect as experienced as they are, they wouldn't try the same trick twice. They know you're after them."

"Hmm, then we're stumped."

Zehra brightened. "Ah, perhaps not! I did hear that one of the families in our neighborhood suffered a break-in. The thieves took a number of diamonds from the safe."

"From the safe? Had it been blown open?"

"No, the robbery happened while the family was at home asleep. Someone snuck in somehow, opened the safe with the combination, and then left. There was no sign of a break in."

"Where is the safe?"

"In the study."

"Was the front door bolted like mine?"

"Yes."

"Sounds like our men. One of the Apaches must be a professional safe cracker."

"Or the master slipped up and opened the safe in front of a servant, who then sold the information to the Apaches. None of the staff who live in the servant's quarters did it. They were thoroughly questioned and their rooms searched."

"Who does that leave?" Moustafa asked.

"The chef and the second footman," Zehra said. "They both live in their own homes."

Augustus smiled. "Been doing a bit of sleuthing, have you?"

She fixed him with those warm brown eyes. "Anything for you, Augustus."

If only that were true, madam.

Moustafa began to speak. It took Augustus a force of will to put aside his fantasies.

"I'm sorry, what did you say?" Augustus asked.

"I said that the chef is an unlikely suspect because he would be in the kitchen most of the time and would rarely come upstairs, and when he did would more than likely take instructions from the lady of the house, who would generally be in the drawing room. The second footman serves drinks and takes mail, so is much more likely to enter the gentleman's study."

Zehra nodded. "That's good reasoning."

"So we must find out where this second footman lives," Augustus said.

Zehra handed him a slip of paper. "His name is Idris Wakil. Here's his address. I had one of my servants go to the house where he works to deliver a letter and check on him. He's working today and will be off at sunset. Shall we go pay him a visit?"

"Best if you don't go. The last time we ran into these chaps we had a bit of shooting."

Zehra tut-tutted. "Why do men have all the fun?"

"There's nothing fun about getting shot at," Augustus said. Moustafa nodded, rubbing his shoulder where the Apache's bullet had grazed him.

"Then why do you keep finding opportunities for that to happen?" Zehra asked.

"They seem to find me," Augustus grumbled, then saw trouble. "Oh good Lord."

Sir Thomas and Cordelia had made an appearance. They spotted him from across the room and approached their table. Augustus and Moustafa stood.

"Augustus! What a coincidence!" Cordelia said.

"Yes. Coincidence," Augustus grumbled.

She barely glanced at Moustafa and then her eyes settled on Zehra. A trace of a frown, quickly suppressed, passed over her features.

"And who is this?" Zehra said.

"Cordelia Russell, may I introduce Zehra Hanzade, a fellow antiquities dealer and close friend." Augustus decided to emphasize "close" and leave out the "Mrs."

"Charmed, I'm sure," Cordelia said in a flat voice.

"And this is Sir Thomas Russell Pasha, commandant of the Cairo police."

"Ah, you poor man!" Zehra said. "You have inherited all the troubles we Ottomans used to have with this country."

"The Egyptians are a spot of trouble, madam, but we have them well in hand," Sir Thomas said, bowing slightly but not taking his eyes off her. He turned to a waiter standing nearby.

"Bring the menu, will you? And get the lady whatever she wants."

"A lemonade, please," Cordelia said.

"And a scotch and soda for me," Sir Thomas said.

They all sat. Cordelia beamed at Augustus. To his eternal gratitude, Zehra shifted her seat ever so slightly closer to him. Just a little. Just enough. The look on Cordelia's face was priceless.

"Hard at work on the case?" Augustus asked the police commandant, lacing his question with an ironic tone.

Sir Thomas lit a cigarette.

"A fellow deserves some rest once in a while. After all, it's just the underclass killing one another. I have several good men on it."

"Only the underclass? I heard a European was attacked by the river," Augustus said, then realized he had slipped.

Sir Thomas gave him a sharp look. "That wasn't in the papers."

Luckily Zehra came to his rescue. "I heard about it through the rumor mill. One hears such things when one deals with the public."

"He was a rather low character, despite his station," Sir Thomas said.

"Oh I don't think that would stop Ms. Hanzade from knowing him," Cordelia said, then as a cover quickly added. "All sorts buy antiquities, just think of that odd gentleman who wanted canopic jars full of actual organs."

Sir Thomas nearly dropped his cigarette. Augustus turned away. He didn't want to know the expression on his face. In any case, the front was flaring up in a different sector.

"Yes, you do get the occasional low person coming to look at my stock. Mostly those here for the season," Zehra said, giving Cordelia a withering look.

"Oh, I bet you get all sorts of men looking at your stock," Cordelia replied.

"Perhaps that's because my stock is more attractive to them than what others have to offer."

"Cheap price, too."

Augustus cleared his throat. "Ah look, drinks!" He grabbed a glass of whiskey off the tray.

"Sir, that is for a different table," the waiter said.

"Then it's on me," Augustus said, downing it.

The drinks did not douse the fireworks.

"You have quite the unusual name," Cordelia said. "What is it, gypsy?"

Zehra's eyes sparked, showing Cordelia had landed a hit. To Zehra's credit, Cordelia lived through the next several seconds.

"No, it is Ottoman. You'll find it to the east of Greece."

"Oh, my relations found it easily enough during the war."

Sir Thomas tried to cut in but his words got drowned out by Zehra's riposte.

"Pity your relations didn't find it four thousand years ago when we had a great civilization and you were painting yourselves blue and dancing around stone circles."

Augustus made a quick decision. He needed to get out of here not only for his own sanity but to shake Cordelia once and for all.

17

Moustafa watched with a mixture of wonder and horror as the two ladies—the woman Mr. Wall didn't want and the woman he couldn't have—dueled it out with words sharper than razors. While he didn't understand the motivations of either woman, he realized it had stopped being about his boss after the second or third insult.

But what was far more interesting was how Russell Pasha, whom all native Cairenes feared and hated in equal measure, seemed incapable of controlling his younger sister. Yes, the Europeans were definitely weak when it came to women.

Just when Moustafa was looking forward to one of the women throwing her drink in the other's face, Mr. Wall stood.

"If you'll excuse me, we must make that telephone call, Zehra," he said. "You have the number, yes?"

Zehra didn't skip a beat. "Why yes. Do excuse us, important business."

The last two words were directed at Cordelia, and seemed to

imply that a silly little English girl like her would never have important business, and that whatever business she ever did have, would most certainly not have anything to do with Mr. Wall. She rose and put a hand on Mr. Wall's wrist.

"Don't run off again," Cordelia said with a weak smile. The words came out halfway between a plea and an order. Mr. Wall's face turned into a mask on both sides. With long strides he crossed the room and was gone. Zehra could barely keep up with him. Cordelia and her brother turned to each other and began to chat about trivial matters. Moustafa found himself cut out of the conversation, not that he had ever been a part of it in the first place.

Moustafa didn't say anything. He had spent enough time with Europeans to know that every African had a secret magical power —the power to turn invisible. All he had to do was sit still and remain quiet and they would start ignoring him. After a time, they would forget he understood their language. Eventually they would forget he was even there. Then he would hear their true thoughts.

After a few minutes listening to their small talk, he did.

"I don't like that Turkish woman," Cordelia said with a frown.

"I don't have to be a policeman to notice that. She was perfectly pleasant until you started in on her. I thought you liked the exotic."

"I think she's far too forward. I know she's just a Turk, but one of her station should have learned some of the social graces."

Russell Pasha took a sip from his drink. "I daresay she's not lacking in graces."

Cordelia scoffed. "Men!"

Russell Pasha changed the subject.

"I've arranged dinner with the Ambersons. They have a son in the Royal Engineers. A couple of his friends will come too."

"Oh Thomas, why do you volunteer me for these dreary social events?" Cordelia asked. "I'm here to have fun."

"You're here to plan for your future. You don't want to end up like Aunt Pearl."

"Better a spinster than the wife of some dull colonial officer."

"There's some wheat among the chaff; you just have to keep looking. You'll find an interesting man."

A slow smile spread across Cordelia's lips. "I think I may have already found one."

Russell Pasha looked surprised, glanced in the direction that Mr. Wall had gone, and looked back at her.

"You don't mean …"

Cordelia blushed.

"Cordelia, you can't mean it! He's a good sort, but he's an ill-humored recluse and he's, well he's …"

Moustafa was astounded. Her interest had been perfectly obvious to him. Was Russell Pasha really that dim-witted?

"He's ill-humored because he doesn't have someone to share his life with," Cordelia said. "As for the other matter, a decent woman can overlook these things. Didn't Alicia have a child after Charles came back from the war missing both legs?"

"They were already married."

"What difference does that make? Unless you know something you're not telling me." At this point Cordelia's blush deepened. "He's not injured in … any other way, is he?"

"Good Lord! How should I know?"

There was a pause. Cordelia hid herself behind her glass of lemonade, and Russell Pasha kept glancing in the direction Mr. Wall had gone, as if checking for, or hoping for, his return. Russell Pasha broke the silence first.

"You're being impulsive. You hardly know the man."

"I'm not saying he's the one. I'm only saying I'm interested in spending more time with him. Do you know he's taken a little street urchin under his tutelage? He has a good heart. More than I can say for some of those officers you've introduced me to."

Russell Pasha shook his head. "This is my fault. I should have foreseen it. You were always taking on charity cases. Every bird with a broken wing ended up in our conservatory. Your pocket money always ended up in the grubby hands of local beggar children. At least you put your soft heart to good use during the war with your nursing, but this isn't the war and Augustus doesn't need any nursing, nor does he want it."

"I think a woman can sense these things better than a man," Cordelia objected.

Russell Pasha leaned over and put his hand on hers. "I just don't want you to get hurt."

"How could I get hurt?"

"By giving your heart to a man who doesn't want it."

"Who's to say he doesn't want it? I don't think he knows what he wants."

Russell Pasha laughed. "That man knows exactly what he wants. And it's far, far different than what you want."

"Oh, what would you know? He's—"

Mr. Wall appeared without Zehra, and Cordelia changed the subject.

"Zehra was called away on urgent business," Mr. Wall said. "She says she hopes you have a fine time here in Cairo. Now if you'll excuse me, I must be off."

Cordelia looked crestfallen. "So soon?" Suspicion flickered across her features and she glanced at the door, as if expecting to spot Zehra waiting for him.

"Yes, urgent business myself, you see. The antiquities trade has been rather, um, dramatic of late. Moustafa, let's go."

Moustafa gladly rose.

Russell Pasha gave Mr. Wall a piercing look. "I hope things go well in your shop. I'll pop by later and see how you're doing."

Moustafa wondered what the policeman's reaction would be when he didn't find them there. It didn't matter. It was Mr. Wall who would have to deal with the ensuing trouble. Meanwhile, Moustafa felt his pulse quicken. From his boss's eager attitude, he knew they would soon be on the hunt.

And then he knew why he followed this strange, selfish man into danger. He knew why he endured Nur's constant complaints. He had to tell her everything, of course. He couldn't hide the bruises or the bullet wounds and no lie he could think of would be more palatable than the truth. And the truth was he, like Mr. Wall, had become addicted to the thrill of the chase and the satisfaction of showing up the grand Sir Thomas Russell Pasha, friend of nobility and appointed personally by King George himself.

He also knew that if he didn't follow Mr. Wall, that maniac would get himself killed.

They were already heading out the door, out into the busy afternoon traffic of Cairo.

"Did you get the footman's physical description, boss?"

"Yes, Zehra was most obliging," Mr. Wall said with smug smile.

Not as obliging as you'd like her to be, Moustafa thought. *How much did you spend on her fake antiquities today? And all for a flirt and a smile?*

Moustafa made a mental shrug. That was none of his business. The fake antiques sold just as well as the real ones.

"First thing's first, my man," Mr. Wall said, clapping his hands together and rubbing them with glee. "To the arsenal. We must get kitted out for the night's fun. And then to interview a few diamond merchants. By then it will be time for the good Idris Wakil to get off work. That's when we'll pounce."

"But how do you know the Apaches are involved?"

"I don't. Just a feeling. There hasn't been a heist like this in Cairo in years. The Apaches are settling in and beginning to make a name for themselves. You hear what Sir Thomas said? It's not just Aziz the Pimp who has turned up dead or missing, but several criminal leaders all across town."

"They certainly work fast," Moustafa said as they got into a hansom cab waiting in front of the restaurant. Mr. Wall told the driver to take them to Ibn al-Nafis Street.

"Perhaps not so fast as all that. They may have been working this game for quite some time before they came to our notice."

"But why come to your notice at all?"

He saw Mr. Wall stiffen. "To revisit the past, and put it in the past."

"But surely that could have been done without endangering their operation. Yves Savatier could have contacted you privately, and not made his association with the Apaches known. Why would they challenge you to stop them? Why run the risk?"

Mr. Wall turned his face to look out the window, and all Moustafa could see was the half with the mask.

"They don't want me to stop them, Moustafa."

"Then why reveal themselves?"

"Because they want me to join them."

"That's ridiculous! Why would you help them?"

After a long pause, Mr. Wall murmured, "I have before."

Their meetings with the diamond merchants turned up nothing. All had heard of the robbery, because no one gossips more than those who serve the rich, but no amount of verbal entrapment or browbeating wrung a confession of involvement out of any of them. Moustafa suspected they were actually innocent. The Apaches were too clever to fence goods through known merchants. More than likely the stones would be shipped abroad and sold safely in some other city.

Now they waited in the shadow of a palm tree, hidden from view of the mansion where Idris Wakil worked. The night was well advanced before the servant strolled out from the service entrance and headed down the street. They waited until he was almost out of sight before following. Moustafa crossed the street to walk a little behind Mr. Wall. Idris Wakil turned a corner and they hurried to catch up before they lost him.

They followed him for a good twenty minutes before he turned down an alley between two closed shops. At the entrance Moustafa caught the rich smell of hashish.

"He's gone for an evening smoke," Moustafa said. "Wait at that café across the street, boss. You would stand out too much in such a place."

After a pause, Mr. Wall nodded and headed across the street. Moustafa checked the revolver in his pocket and entered the alley.

It was as he suspected. The narrow lane had been filled with chairs and tables, one of Cairo's countless cafés that appeared nightly and disappeared like stars with the dawn. Men sat alone or in small groups sucking on hookahs. None smelled of the flavored tobacco that Moustafa liked. Apple and pomegranate were his favorite. But these men weren't after the relaxing buzz of a good dose of tobacco. These men were all smoking hashish.

Moustafa tried to hide his distaste. Some Muslims claimed that since the holy Koran didn't specifically forbid hashish that it wasn't haram. What nonsense. The Koran said only wine was forbidden, but every Muslim agreed that beer and spirits were also haram, and therefore it stood to reason that all intoxicants were forbidden to the practicing Muslim as substances that took one further from God. Tobacco wasn't an intoxicant. All it did was lift one's spirits and momentarily take the weight of the world off one's shoulders. Tobacco was a blessing from God.

He spotted Idris Wakil easily enough. He had taken an empty table near the far end of the lane. The waiter had already brought him a hookah and was coming from the oven with the ladle full of coals, spinning them around to keep them bright red. Moustafa let out a contented sigh. That sight always cheered him. It meant that relief was on its way.

The waiter used a pair of tongs to place some coals on the top of the hookah. Idris Wakil puffed on it a couple of times and nodded to show that the draw was clean, and the waiter turned to Moustafa, who was just sitting down at the only other spare table, the one right next to the footman's.

"A tea," Moustafa ordered, and when he saw the waiter expected more added, "and some apple-flavored tobacco."

"We have some good Lebanese in just this week," the waiter said.

"I don't smoke the good stuff until after I've had a few draws of tobacco."

The waiter shrugged and went to fetch the hookah.

Soon tea and the hookah came and Moustafa settled in. He kept an eye on the footman, waiting to see what he would do. He doubted the fellow planned to meet any Apaches here. The robbery had probably been his only involvement with the gang.

But it was best to wait and spring the trap at the opportune moment.

Moustafa imagined Mr. Wall sitting at the other café seething with impatience. Europeans were always impatient, obsessed with the clock. They never understood that some things took time.

Getting a man thoroughly off his head on hashish took time, for example, especially a regular smoker like Idris Wakil obviously was.

Moustafa nursed his tea and tobacco pipe, ignoring the occasional look from the waiter. After Idris had taken a third brazier for his hookah, the waiter gave Moustafa a frank scowl of impatience.

"Another apple tobacco, please," Moustafa said.

"There are plenty of places to smoke tobacco. You're holding up a place for the regulars."

Moustafa glared at him and puffed out his chest. "Get me a new brazier before I pull your entrails out and let my daughters skip rope with them."

That got some good service. Luckily, Idris at the next table hadn't noticed the disturbance. It didn't look like he was noticing much at all. The footman gazed up at the thin strip of stars visible between the two buildings that formed the alley, a stupid look of awe on his face.

At last Idris set aside the hookah, wavered a little as he stood, and paid. He turned and went further down the alley. Moustafa called the waiter over, paid for his drink and smoke, and followed.

The alley connected with another street, this one quieter and darker. Idris hadn't gotten far. He was barely fifty paces in front of him, shuffling along and humming contentedly to himself.

Moustafa caught up with him.

"Diamonds," he said.

Idris stopped. Turned. His face had regained some sobriety.

"What did you say, brother?"

"I said diamonds. Who told you to steal the diamonds?"

"I don't know what—"

His protestation of innocence got cut short by Moustafa grabbing him by the neck and shaking him.

"None of that. Tell me!"

The man got a look of terror on his face and began to shake like a palm frond in the desert wind. A stuttering babble came from his mouth as he shook his head over and over again. Moustafa realized his roughness had made the paranoia set in. He gave Idris a slap to clear his head.

It worked to a point. The man still trembled, but at least now he could form a coherent sentence.

"Some Europeans. They call themselves Apaches. They gave me a hundred piastres and a promise of more once they sold the diamonds."

"How did they know about them? You must have told them."

"No, I swear! They came to me. The lady of the house recently bought a new necklace. Her picture was in the society page when she wore it to a ball. That must have been how they found out. They said I could either help them and get paid or they'd cut me up."

"How did you get the diamonds out of the house? The witnesses said you didn't leave before it was noticed they were gone."

"I didn't leave. A boy climbed up the wall and took the bag."

"A boy? A European boy?"

"He—"

There was a sickening thump and Idris jerked, his back arching. A knife had embedded itself into his spine.

Moustafa ducked to one side as another knife whistled out of the shadows.

Drawing his pistol, he rushed toward the entrance to a courtyard. He couldn't see the attacker, but he had come from there.

Moustafa pressed himself against the wall, then popped around the corner, his gun at the ready.

Not ready enough. A figure rose from the darkness and struck his hand with a blow that felt like an iron bar. The pistol clattered to the ground.

Moustafa backed off. The figure emerged from the shadow and into the faint moonlight.

Vincent.

Moustafa struck at that smug, sneering face, only to have the man duck back while at the same time delivering a painful blow to his shin.

That put Moustafa off-balance. Trying to ignore the pain, he went after him, swinging a heavy fist at the center of Vincent's chest, figuring that he would have a harder time dodging that than a blow to the head.

But he didn't even try to dodge. He landed another kick on Moustafa's shin that knocked him onto the ground as if he'd been poleaxed. His punch fell short, only hitting air.

A rush of air and an explosion in his head was all he knew of Vincent's final kick.

He lay on the ground, barely able to see. Vincent laughed.

"You have spirit, Nubian, I'll give you that. It's a pity you serve a foreign master. Your people could use someone like you. Cross my path again and you'll regret it."

Vincent walked off into the night.

After a minute, Moustafa picked himself up and limped

through the alley, ignoring the stares of the smokers at the hashish café, and made his way to where Mr. Wall sat in a more respectable venue across the street.

"What happened?" Mr. Wall said, standing up and putting his hand in the pocket where he kept his pistol. "Are you badly hurt?"

"Not badly sir, no. It was Vincent again. He killed Idris before I got a chance to get anything useful out of him."

"Blast! We're no closer than before."

"Hopefully Faisal will have found out something," Moustafa said.

Hopefully he has had better luck than me and didn't run into Vincent.

"He's looking around, is he? When did he last check in?"

Moustafa shook his head. "Too long. I'm worried something might have happened to him."

18

Faisal's fear had not left him, but it had subsided to a low tension that did not stop him from clearly seeing his situation. He now knew that he would not be hurt if he did as he was told. Hakim still threatened him with the baboons, but the Frenchmen fed him and told him how rich he could be if he stayed with the gang.

He pretended to be eager. While Faisal knew the Apaches were too clever to trust him yet, and Hakim would probably never trust him, at least they had begun to relax their guard.

Their attitude had improved after last night, when he had been instructed to climb into the upper window of a mansion to meet with one of the servants. Faisal had entered a darkened room and crouched by the window as instructed. After a wait of several minutes, the servant, an Egyptian, had walked in and handed him a small bag.

Without a word the servant had left, but Faisal had gotten a good enough look at him in the moonlight that he could recognize him again.

He had gotten a good look at the contents of the bag too. Before he had climbed back out the window, he had opened it. His breath caught as a heap of diamonds sparkled in the moonlight.

All the way down the outside wall, he dreamed of what he could do with such a stash, but of course Hakim, one of the Apaches, and both baboons waited for him at the bottom, silent as shadows.

The baboons could have easily performed that task, but that wasn't the point. It was a test and he had passed.

And now it was the next day. They woke with the muezzin call from the nearby mosque.

"Back to the city again, boy. We have a busy day today," Edmond said over breakfast. The gang had set up beds and a table in one of the lower floors of the Nilometer, and a loyal villager brought them their meals. Faisal was really beginning to appreciate all the food he was getting. It was far more convenient than sneaking into the Englishman's pantry.

"You're taking over all the gangs in the city, right?" Faisal asked. He had suddenly come up with an idea.

"We're making good progress. It's a big city, though."

"I know a good business you can get in on."

Edmond handed him a boiled egg. "And what is that?"

"There's a merchant named Abbas Eldessouky who trades in illegal cloth. He's buying and selling lots of it without paying tax."

Edmond nodded in approval. "Cheating the imperialists out of their unjust taxes. Sounds like man I should get to know."

"He's got a big shipment coming in from Upper Egypt in a few days. I'm not sure when. You better hurry."

"And how did you come across this information?"

Faisal shrugged. "Nobody notices me. I hear all sorts of things. Some things are useful, some aren't. This wasn't useful to me until I met you."

"And where does this merchant live?"

Faisal extended a hand. He knew the kind of man he was dealing with.

Edmond laughed and gave him a two-piastre coin.

"Good enough?" the Apache leader asked.

Faisal nodded, wondering whether it counted as honest earnings. He still needed to save money for the spell to stop the Englishman's marriage.

"He lives on Sebil al-Nimir street."

Edmond studied him. "You sold him out pretty quickly. You've been reluctant to help us and now this? Why?"

Faisal looked down at his food. "I needed the money."

Plus when the Englishman catches the lot of you, he'll put that greasy-haired son of a dog in jail.

"You'll make plenty of money with us. Do you need it for anything specific?"

"A spell to help a friend."

Edmond snorted. "Your rulers keep you in superstitious ignorance."

"Khadija umm Mohammed's magic works every time! She's the best."

The Apache leader shook his head and looked him over. "You'll need a new jellaba. You can't go into the Citadel wearing that old thing. They'd beat you within an inch of your life and throw you out on your ear, if they're feeling merciful. Come."

Faisal followed the gang leader, not having any other choice. Edmond brought him to the village tailor who gave them both a long look and then with a shake of his head took Faisal's measurements and got to work. Within an hour he was wearing a clean, brand new jellaba of light blue. Edmond hadn't even skimped on the material, buying him one better than the cheapest, something a shop owner's son would wear.

"I'd buy you the best," Edmond said. "But that would raise suspicion. Perhaps on another job you'll need to pretend to be someone rich, in which case I'll buy you the best material available."

Faisal looked in amazement at his new clothes. He hadn't had a new jellaba in two years, and the one he had been wearing was so patched and mended there was almost none of the original material left.

"You'll need sandals too."

They went and got him a new pair of sandals. Faisal had never owned a pair. Not even his father had ever bought him a pair. That would have been a waste of precious drinking money.

They went back to the hideout and Edmond had him clean up in the water at the bottom of the Nilometer, even providing a bar of soap. Faisal never washed except when he went swimming in the Nile. The soap made him smell funny.

"There," Edmond said, looking at him with satisfaction. "Now you're ready. Take a look."

The Apache leader pulled down a cracked mirror from the wall and held it at his level so he could get a good look at himself. Faisal blinked. He looked like a different person, like he had a home and a family and everything. He stared and stared. Edmond held the mirror patiently.

"You like it?" Edmond asked.

Faisal nodded.

"You like nice things, don't you? All those things they never let you have."

Faisal nodded again.

"If you cooperate you can have those things. But first you have a job to do."

Edmond handed him a parcel containing his uniform.

"The servant's uniform you don't put on until you get to the Citadel. That's their custom. They don't trust the boys to keep them clean otherwise. A guard named Selim is posted at the gate. He's with us. He'll get you past the other guards and inside. Once inside, no one will notice you. The Europeans won't spare you a glance and the Egyptians will assume you're someone new. The commandant's office is in the large stone building next to the prison. Second floor, the large office on the far end. You bring the tea in there."

Faisal climbed the long road up to the Citadel gate. The hot wind howled and the lane was shrouded with dust. He kept looking at his light blue jellaba, and the smile never left his lips. He noticed his new clothes made him stand a little straighter, and his walk was a bit more confident.

Be careful, he reminded himself. *This is the most dangerous thing you've done in a while.*

Faisal felt the letter in his pocket. It was inside a sealed, plain envelope with something written on the outside. He wished he could read. Why deliver a message to Russell Pasha like this? Was it to signal that the Apaches could get at him? They had told him that Russell Pasha and his secretary would be called away from the office just before Faisal entered. He was to put the note on the police commandant's chair, leave the tea like he was doing his job, and get out as fast as possible.

So they didn't want Russell Pasha to see him deliver the note. Why not? To keep him from getting captured and talking? That made sense, but what did the note say?

The gate loomed ahead. Several Nubian and Egyptian guards stood in front of it with their rifles at the ready. Behind him, he knew, one of the Apaches waited on the road below casually smoking a cigarette, while really keeping an eye on him in case he tried to bolt.

Faisal considered his chances if he told the police why he had been sent. They would keep him for questioning, and he had seen what happened to people questioned by the police. Plus he didn't know how many people the Apaches had inside the Citadel. If he told the wrong person, he'd end up with is throat slit.

He approached the guards, his heart beating fast. One of the Nubians stepped forward.

"You're late, boy. Get in here."

"Sorry," he mumbled. This must be Selim.

The guard gave him a shove and he hurried past the other soldiers, who barely glanced at him.

Beyond the first gate they came to a portion of the road flanked by a high wall on one side and the sheer cliff of the hillside on the other. Atop the wall stood more guards, their rifles resting on the parapet. A second gate stood further up. Faisal remembered hearing about this place. Tariq ibn Nagy did a show about it once. Way back a hundred years ago, the great Muhammad Ali Pasha wanted to get rid of the Mamluk soldiers who vied with him for power over Egypt. They pretended to be his loyal troops but really did whatever they wanted and ground the people down under their heels. The great Muhammad Ali Pasha heard his people's cries for justice, and decided to get rid of the Mamluk beys once and for all. He invited their leaders to a big party in the Citadel.

After serving them coffee and entertaining them with dancing girls, the great Muhammad Ali Pasha bade them good afternoon and they took their leave. As they marched in procession out of the upper gate, moving down this narrow lane toward the second, outer gate, both portals slammed shut, trapping them inside. Then the great Muhammad Ali Pasha ordered his troops to fire, and from the towers atop both gates and from the wall hemming in the road, the soldiers rained bullets, arrows, and spears on the treacherous Mamluks. From atop the cliff, more soldiers rolled great stones down on the Mamluks. Four hundred and sixty-nine were killed on the very spot where Faisal was walking now. Only one escaped. He rode a magnificent Arabian charger of the purest white. The Mamluk spurred his horse into an incredible leap that took him to the top of the wall. From there he leaped down to the street far below. The horse died from the fall but the Mamluk bey survived. He grabbed another horse and galloped off, not stopping until he reached Syria.

The Mamluks had been crushed, and the great Muhammad Ali Pasha sent their heads to the Sultan in Constantinople to tell him that Egypt was now free.

Faisal looked around and shuddered, imagining the carnage. Tariq ibn Nagy had shown him how it had been with his puppets. Horses falling over screaming with arrows stuck in their sides, Mamluks pitching out of their saddles as they got struck by bullets, or crushed by the great stones rolled off the cliff top. With so many killed in one place, this lane must surely be haunted by jinn. He felt thankful that he was walking here in the daytime.

"Keep up," Selim the Nubian guard said.

They passed through the second gate and into a wide courtyard. A large mosque rose to the right, its thin minarets touching the sky. Ahead of them stood a long, low building that

Faisal guessed was a barracks. A group of British soldiers stood in formation, then wheeled right at a barked order from their officer before marching off.

Selim led him to a smaller building to the left of the barracks, from which wafted the smell of cooking. Faisla's stomach grumbled.

"You can change in the kitchen," Selim said, leading him in.

"Can I get something to eat?"

"You have work to do."

They entered a busy kitchen where several Egyptian cooks stirred huge pots filled with chicken stew for the soldiers. Through a large arched doorway Faisal saw a pair of bakers hard at work at an oven. Selim gestured to a small alcove where a line of pegs held the cook's street clothes.

"Hurry up," Selim ordered.

Faisal changed as quickly as he could, reluctantly hanging up his new jellaba on one of the pegs. What if someone stole it? Then he reminded himself that this wasn't a shack in some dirty alley like he used to live in. Everyone here had a job and money. No one would be interested in stealing his jellaba. This was a different world.

"The cook is in our pay. Take a tray of tea from him. Russell Pasha normally takes his tea at this hour," the guard whispered.

Faisal did as he was told. The cook didn't even look at him as he handed him a tray with a teapot, cup, and bowl of sugar.

Faisal looked at it dubiously. "Did you poison this?"

"Keep your voice down," the cook said in an angry whisper, looking around him. "Now do as you're told."

Faisal noticed that Selim the guard had disappeared.

"Go on," the cook urged.

Faisal hesitated. Everyone said that Russell Pasha was bad, but his sister was going to marry the Englishman and the Englishman would never marry into an evil family.

"I'm not going to poison anyone," Faisal whispered.

The cook sighed and rolled his eyes. He poured a little of the tea into a spare cup, blew on it to cool it, and drank it.

"Satisfied?" the cook asked.

"What are you going to do to him?"

"Nothing compared to what I'll do to you if you don't do your job. Now get to the administration building. Just out the door and on the right. If you don't deliver the tea, I'll boil you in the soup and serve you to the soldiers."

The cook sounded like he meant it. Faisal hurried off.

Sweat trickled down Faisal's back as he approached the administration building. He struggled to contain his fear. This was no worse than breaking into a house, he told himself. If you break into a house and someone spots you, that's it. You better run away or they'll beat you to death. He'd been in a couple of close scrapes before. This was no different.

But it sure felt different. Here he was walking in plain view of dozens of soldiers and policemen.

But they think you're a tea boy, he told himself. *It's like when you're lounging around the market. You're invisible. Hey, you've even more invisible here because you have nice clothes. In the market everyone mistrusts you because you're wearing bad clothes.*

Faisal smiled at the thought of that new jellaba hanging on a peg in the kitchen. It was the nicest he'd ever owned, and this uniform wasn't too bad either. The vest and fez made him look like a servant, but he could keep the pants and shirt at least. That meant he had two sets of clothes. Two sets! Incredible. What would Edmond buy him after this job?

Immediately after that thought he felt sorry. The Englishman was after these people so they must be bad. He'd seen himself how bad they could be. Were a few nice clothes going to make him change his mind?

But still …

His mind in a turmoil, he strode up to the front door of the administration building, the tea tray in his hands. An English policeman stood there, a pistol in a holster on his belt.

The Englishman shouted at something and Faisal jerked in fear, almost sending the tea tray crashing to the ground.

The policeman shouted something again. Faisal realized he was trying to speak Arabic. It sounded something like, "Where are you going?"

"Russell Pasha," Faisal squeaked. Faisal couldn't have hidden his fear even if he had tried, and it was best not to try. Policemen liked to see you afraid.

The policeman grunted and motioned for him to go inside.

Faisal could barely keep the the tray steady as he passed through a large front hallway abuzz with conversation. Englishmen, many in uniform, stood in serious groups talking and smoking. He had never seen so many Englishmen all in one place before. He stared around him with awe. All that power. All those nice clothes. Not a single one of them even glanced at him. He was beneath their notice.

Fine by him. He'd love to turn invisible like the jinn's son in the *Thousand and One Nights* and sneak out of here. This was the next best thing, but he didn't get to sneak out. No, he had to see this thing through or the Apaches would hunt him down and feed him to Hakim's baboons, assuming the cook didn't turn him into soup first.

He went up the stairs, keeping the tray as steady as he could in his shaking hands. Just as he was about to step onto the second landing, a British soldier in an officer's uniform came speeding around the corner.

Faisal leaped back, but not before the officer bumped into the tray. The cup fell over on its side and the tray pitched dangerously, threatening to dump all its contents on the stone steps. Faisal spun around, his foot slipping on the stairs. He caught himself by stepping with his other foot on the next step down.

But by them the tray was getting away from him. He had to run down the remaining steps, trying to balance the tray as the teapot and sugar bowl and cup slid away. At the second to last step he jumped, spun around, and thudded his back against the wall. The tea set clattered and slid. The top came off the sugar bowl and clinked against the teacup. Faisal wavered, steadied himself, and let out a sigh of relief to see that nothing had fallen off the tray.

The officer shouted at him. He nodded and tried to look meek. The officer snapped a few more words at him, turned on his heel, and continued down the steps. Faisal stuck his tongue out at him.

That earned him a slap from another officer coming down the steps. The force of the blow nearly made the tea set pitch over.

After giving him a good tongue lashing in English, the officer stormed off. Faisal stood there a minute, letting his heartbeat slow and his breathing get back to normal. Then he rearranged the tea set, brushing away a bit of sugar that had spilled out of the sugar bowl. He took a couple of pinches of sugar for himself to sooth his nerves and set the teacup upright. It had a little chip on the rim. Hopefully Russell Pasha wouldn't notice.

He must be late by this point. They had told him the police commandant and his secretary would only be called away for a few minutes. Faisal climbed the rest of the stairs as fast as he dared, keeping to the center of the steps to avoid getting bumped into again.

Faisal got to the right corridor and saw Russell Pasha's office at the end with the door open. He was in luck. Most of the other doors were closed and there was no one in the hallway at the moment. The only sounds were the clattering of typewriters and the buzz of distant conversation. Faisal hurried to the office.

He paused at the threshold. There were two rooms. The first was a plain little space with a desk covered in piles of paper and a typewriter. The room beyond was much nicer. The floor was covered in carpet and a picture of the English Sultan hung on the wall next to several photos of soldiers. There was a big desk covered with papers and ledgers. A telephone sat in one corner. Beyond the desk was a large window looking out past the walls of the Citadel to the sprawl of the city. Thousands of buildings clustered together, the spires of the mosques rising high above them. Along one wall stood a big wardrobe and some file cabinets.

Faisal set the tea set down on the desk. Taking the letter out of his pocket, he put it on the commandant's chair and glanced down the hall. No one.

This was the only time he could be sure the Apaches couldn't see what he was doing. He needed to leave a message for the Englishman. He was sure to come and investigate his friend's disappearance. But how could he leave a message for him when he couldn't write?

Faisal hesitated. He didn't have much time. What could he do? Draw a picture?

He rushed over to Russell Pasha's desk and found a pencil but no clean paper. The ledgers were all filled with writing and photos of Egyptians. Many of them had bruises on their faces. He tried to open the drawers but they were all locked and he didn't have time to pick them in search of some unused paper. Faisal tried to draw on the stone walls the pencil tip broke without so much as leaving a mark. Stamping his foot, he looked around the room. What could he do?

Then he saw a washbasin in the corner. Next to it stood a pitcher of water, a glass, and a washcloth.

That gave Faisal an idea. He grabbed the cloth and laid it in on the floor where the Englishman would be sure to spot it, but out of sight of the door so no one in the hallway would see what he was doing. Filling the glass with water, he set it on the washcloth, then stuck the pencil in it. Then he took the rest of the water and poured it all around the washcloth.

Just as he was replacing the ewer on the washbasin, he heard the sound of approaching footsteps.

Faisal looked around. The office was at the end of a hall with no way out. He was trapped!

He sped over to the wardrobe and opened it, thanking his luck that the door didn't creak. Several coats and a uniform hung inside. He slipped in among the coats and closed the door behind him, leaving it open a crack so he could see.

Russell Pasha strode into the room. As soon as he entered, he stopped and stared at the clue Faisal had left on the floor. Frowning, Russell Pasha glanced around the room.

Faisal's heart clenched. This was a policeman. Surely he'd see that the wardrobe door was open a bit when before it was closed. What a stupid thing to leave it open!

But Russell Pasha did not see. He moved over to his telephone and picked it up. Just then he paused and stared at the chair where Faisal had left the message.

Putting the telephone back down, Russell Pasha rounded the desk and picked up the message. He opened the envelope and took out the note within.

His eyes went wide and his face paled as he read it.

His hand made a fist, crumpling the note, and he bolted out of the room.

As soon as the sound of his footsteps faded away, Faisal crept out of the wardrobe and peeked down the hallway. No one was in sight.

Time to go. He only hoped the Englishman would figure out his message.

"You did well," Edmond said.

They were back at al-Rawdah Island, living in that strange building that measured the river. Russell Pasha and another European were now their captives. Edmond had told him they were both bad men who had killed many Egyptians.

The Apache leader pulled out a five-piastre coin. Faisal's eyes went wide. Was that for him? Edmond made a fist and balanced the coin on top of it. Then he did something odd. With a flick of his thumb he made the coin spin up into the air. He caught it as it came down and repeated the movement. He had a way of flicking the coin so his thumbnail struck it and made the silver ring like a little bell. Faisal watched, fascinated.

"Want this coin?"

"Yes."

"For your little spell?"

"It's not little. It's very powerful." Faisal wondered if this counted as stolen money or not.

Edmond chuckled. "Well, most people waste their money. The men who follow me waste it on booze and gambling and … other things you'll understand when you're older. I guess a spell is no more wasteful than those things."

He flicked it to him. Faisal caught it.

"How do you do that?" Faisal asked.

Edmond looked surprised. "You don't flick coins here?"

"No. Somebody would grab it."

"I suppose that's right in your case. But would you try to steal a coin from me?"

Faisal shook his head.

"You're young and small and you get picked on. I was like you once. But I learned to fight and I learned to survive. You've done well to last this long, but you need to get together with a group that will watch your back, then you won't have to be afraid anymore."

Faisal didn't say anything. He was afraid, but he had to be afraid. The streets were a scary place. That's why he was so happy to have his little shack on the Englishman's roof. Now he could sleep the whole night through without waking up at every little sound.

"Here, let me show you how to flip a coin."

Edmond moved up beside him and arranged the coin in his hand. "Now just flip your thumb up, like so."

Faisal did as he was instructed. The coin made a little ringing sound and spun in the air. He caught it as it came down.

"Got it right the first time! What a clever boy!"

Faisal grinned at him, basking in the attention.

"Too clever," Hakim said, sitting nearby.

Faisal grew tense.

"Relax," Edmond said with a chuckle. "Ignore Hakim's threats. You are part of our gang now. You have performed your task wonderfully and have already been rewarded. You can be an Apache if you like. You can go far with us."

Faisal nodded, pretending to be eager. "That five piastres sure feels good in my pocket."

Suddenly he had a thought.

"Why kidnap Russell Pasha and not just kill him?" he asked. "Are you hoping someone comes after him? This is a trap, isn't it?"

A trap for the Englishman. Anger simmered inside him. Chief Mohammed would never behave like these people.

What Edmond said next made his anger go away and replaced it with confusion.

"It is. You're very observant. You're a sharp one, Faisal. I might just have to adopt you as my own little Apache."

The words hit Faisal like a camel at full gallop. Adopt him? Did he mean that? Faisal had dreamed of being adopted for as long as he could remember, even back in the days when he still had a supposed father. A real set of parents, or even just one real parent, had been what he had always wanted.

The next instant, Faisal cursed himself for being stupid. This Frenchman would be just as bad as his father. No, worse. When he disobeyed his father, all he got was a slap. If he disobeyed Edmond, he'd get his throat slit.

He was probably lying about the adoption anyway, right?

Edmond grinned at him.

"Let's see you flick the coin again."

Faisal couldn't help but smile back. "All right."

19

Police Sergeant Willard Todd looked like he was fighting an epic battle with panic and losing. He met Augustus at the gate to the Citadel, sweat beading on his face and his eyes bugging out of their sockets.

"Thank you so much for coming at such short notice," he said, sounding out of breath.

"Don't mention it. What's this about a disappearance?"

"Please keep your voice down until we're in private. You'll have to leave your servant here," he said, nodding to Moustafa.

"I trust my assistant implicitly."

Sergeant Todd hesitated a moment, then led them through the gates with quick, long strides. He was practically running.

They entered a large office building across from the barracks. Sergeant Todd led them into an empty meeting room and closed the door.

"The commandant has gone missing!"

"What! When?"

"This morning. His tea hadn't been touched. Some officers saw him running out of the building like it was on fire. One said he clutched a letter in his hand. Sir Thomas ran right out of the Citadel and into the city. A witness there saw him grabbed by a group of European men and bundled into a motorcar."

"Did the witness get the license number?"

"No, it drove off too quickly."

"It's the Apaches, I'll bet my life on it." Then something struck Augustus as odd. "But why did you call me?"

Despite the circumstances, Sergeant Todd could not suppress a smile.

"You have quite the reputation among the men, sir. The khedive's jewels, the murder of that French archaeologist, and several other cases. The commandant speaks quite highly of you when he isn't damning your interference. He suspects you know more about this Apache affair than you're letting on."

Augustus rubbed his jaw. "He's right about that. But I have no idea where these fellows might be."

"There might be a clue in Sir Thomas's office, sir. There's something rather odd up there."

Sergeant Todd led them back into the hallway. "I've made sure no one touched anything, sir."

They headed to the commandant's office. From the door, Augustus could see nothing amiss, but as he stepped into Sir Thomas's office, he stopped abruptly and stared.

A washcloth had been laid on the floor to one side of the door, out of sight of the hallway. On it, near one end, stood a glass of water with a pencil in it.

"Oh, you want to lead me on a bit more, eh? Well, Monsieur Savatier, I will not disappoint you."

Augustus drew his gun and walked around the room with care, keeping an eye out for tripwires or some other sign of a trap.

He found none, and found no other clue than the strange assembly on the floor.

He stared at it for a time, deep in thought. Then he noticed a slight discoloration in the carpet around the washcloth. He bent down and found it was damp. Since Sir Thomas had disappeared more than an hour ago, and the water must have been poured shortly before, the carpet must have been soaked. Nothing stayed damp for long in Cairo. Glancing at the washbasin and ewer, he found them both empty. He turned back and studied the odd message on the floor. This and perhaps that letter Sir Thomas had been holding when he ran out was enough to shake the police commandant into some wild act. He had fled without telling anyone where he was headed or asking for backup.

But why? And what did this message mean? He could come up with nothing. Water under the bridge the note had said. Water in a glass. Water. Water. But what? And why the damn pencil and washcloth?

"You think you are cleverer than me, don't you?" Augustus muttered. "Well, for the moment I will concede the point. But I'll get you. Oh yes, I'll get you."

"What could this mean, boss?" Moustafa asked, gesturing at the arrangement on the floor.

"I have no idea."

"Oh dear, in all the excitement I completely forgot." This came from Sergeant Todd, who stood at the doorway and stared down the hallway with an even more panicked expression than before.

When Augustus peeked down the hallway, he nearly panicked too.

Cordelia and Aunt Pearl walked toward the office, accompanied by an NCO.

Good Lord, this woman is like a bad penny.

He and the sergeant moved a bit down the hallway to meet them, and to keep them from looking inside the office.

"Cordelia! So nice to see you," he said in that superficial friendliness people seemed to find so engaging. "Hello Aunt Pearl. How are things?"

"We were supposed to get a tour of the Citadel from my nephew," Aunt Pearl said, sounding uncharacteristically sober. "It's generally off limits to visitors but of course my nephew can open all doors. But now he's not here! Quite irritating. He's usually so punctual."

"Um, yes. I believe he is detained."

Sergeant Todd nodded eagerly. "Oh yes, quite busy. Don't worry, we'll find him."

"Well, where is he?" Aunt Pearl demanded.

"We can't say for sure," Sergeant Todd said, drawing the words out slowly as he thought them through. "He's engaged in police work."

"Um, yes. Interviewing criminals, one might say," Augustus added.

Cordelia stepped forward, a nauseatingly eager look on her face.

"That's all right, Augustus, you can show us around."

"Um, no. You see, I don't really know the Citadel. Off limits to civilians, as you say."

"I see," Cordelia said, undaunted. "At least we could go to the ramparts. I'm sure it offers a splendid prospect. Can you see the Nile from here?"

"The Nile?" Augustus said, something clicking in his head.

Water. "One moment please. Sergeant Todd, perhaps you could take the ladies downstairs to the canteen for some tea? I'll join you in a minute. I just need to, ah, speak with my assistant."

Augustus hurried back into the office, where Moustafa still stared at the odd arrangement on the floor. Augustus stared too, then pulled out the note the Apaches had left, reading the lines over and over.

"The ruling class turn us into murderers

We should murder them!

Too low. Too high. Perfect. Under the bridge. 100 cm.

The Apaches ruled Paris, and they will rule Cairo!

Will you be RULER or ruled?"

The penultimate line was clear enough from their actions. Several leading figures in the underworld had shown up dead, suggesting a power struggle. The last line and the first two seemed to suggest that they wanted him to join their ranks. Perhaps that's what "under the bridge" meant, as in "water under the bridge"? He had been an officer that grim day as well, but Yves Savatier didn't seem to hold that against him. Perhaps his well-known aversion to the local expatriate community had suggested to the Apaches that they could recruit him, although after the fight on the riverside that invitation most likely had been rescinded.

Then there was this other clue: A washcloth laid out in the middle of the floor. A glass of water with a pencil in it. Water again.

Under the bridge, under the bridge. Water under the bridge. Water too high? Water too low? But a hundred centimeters was perfect, apparently.

A hundred centimeters. A meter. Water. Ruler or ruled.

The answer hit him like a lightning bolt. Of course—measuring water! The Nilometer!

The Nilometer was a stone-lined well on the southern tip of al-Rawdah island in the Nile. Its interior was marked with a ruler for measuring the level of the Nile. Too low and the crops would be bad and famine threatened. Too high and there would be floods and the result would be the same. Every ruler from the first pharaohs measured the level of the Nile. The washcloth was the island, the wet floor was the Nile. The pencil in the glass of water was the measuring column in the Nilometer well!

He grabbed Moustafa by the shoulders.

"The Nilometer! They're summoning us to the Nilometer!"

Augustus quickly outlined his train of thought. At first Moustafa looked doubtful, but as he went on, his assistant grew more and more enthusiastic.

"Yes, that could be it! We should go right now."

Augustus glanced back at Aunt Pearl and Cordelia, who were just rounding the corner to go downstairs. "It's certainly a good excuse to get away from their clutches."

They hurried back to the ladies.

"Terribly sorry," Augustus said brusquely, "must be off. Enjoy your day. Important business. Sergeant Todd, I leave you in charge."

Cordelia looked stricken. "But—"

"Sorry, some other time." Augustus was already heading out the door. "Come, Moustafa, to the Nilometer!"

In his eagerness to be off he didn't notice that Cordelia had heard him, and her expression changed from one of surprise to determination.

20

The Nilometer wasn't much to look at from the outside. The low, round building with a steepled roof looked more like a stubby minaret missing a mosque than the home of an important bit of medieval history. It was one of the oldest buildings in Cairo, dating all the way back to the great Umayyad dynasty more than 1,300 years ago.

That small door he and Mr. Wall watched from a distance was closed, the custodian no doubt having left to attend noon prayers at the little village mosque on the other end of the island. Moustafa should have been there too but he was stuck hunting down murderers. He supposed that was the will of God, but nevertheless he would say a second round of prayers in the evening to compensate. He always seemed to be compensating when he worked for Europeans.

The words of Marcus Simaika came back to him.

"Once we have our freedom we will need trained men like you

to manage our heritage. There could be a place for you in the new order."

Hadn't he sworn he would quit if he got beaten up or shot at again? And here he was with fresh bruises thanks to his second encounter with Vincent.

Moustafa took his mind off that temptation. He saw no point in dreaming of the future when he might not survive the next five minutes.

He wished they had told that sergeant in the Citadel where they were going right away, but Mr. Wall reasoned that a whole troop of police coming over to the island would spook the Apaches into doing something drastic, while the two of them could come over relatively unnoticed. On the way, they had stopped at the house arsenal to grab weapons, and Mr. Wall had also taken a large hooded cloak to hide his features. While the boatman who took them across the water had seen one of his passengers was European, those on the island would not know and hopefully remain off their guard.

On Moustafa's insistence, they placed a call to the Citadel to leave a message for Sergeant Todd saying where they were going. They had enough of a head start that they could hopefully get this done quietly before the blundering police came and started shooting up the entire island.

The question foremost in his mind was—when would they come?

But he had plenty of other questions competing for his attention.

First off, was the custodian really gone or was he subdued somewhere? Or perhaps he was part of the Apaches' growing criminal gang? Few Egyptians came to al-Rawdah Island and no virtually no foreigners. There wasn't even a bridge to it; they had to hire a boatman. It would be a good place to hide out.

"How shall we handle this, boss?" Moustafa asked, his pistol at the ready and a rifle strapped across his back.

"Go up and knock on the door, I suppose." Mr. Wall replied. He gripped a German-model submachine gun he had smuggled from Europe.

"That would be falling into their trap," Moustafa said.

"We already did that when we stepped foot on this island."

Moustafa nodded. Yes, they had. He had known this and yet he had followed Mr. Wall here on this insane mission because he wanted to know the solution to this mystery as much as his boss did. Plus he was hoping to meet that man Vincent again. That little Frenchman thought he could beat him with a few tricky moves and kicks? Well, he had a surprise in store for that fellow!

"All right, Mr. Wall, but let's skirt over to the right where those bushes are. We can get closer without being seen."

A soft step behind them and to the right made them pause. They pressed themselves against the earth and peered through the greenery.

An Egyptian with a rifle moved between the palm trees, peering at the underbrush. They kept still. The figure drew closer. It would only be a matter of moments before he would see them. Moustafa and Mr. Wall lay behind a thicket from which grew a thick palm tree. His boss started to edge to one side of it. Moustafa moved to the other side.

The guard kept moving, drawing closer to Mr. Wall's position.

"I give up, don't shoot," Moustafa said.

The guard spun around, taking a moment to spot him in the thicket. Moustafa raised his hands.

"Don't shoot! I'm standing up now. I am unarmed."

"What are you doing here? Where was that other man with—"

The handle of Mr. Wall's cane took him right in the back of the head and he fell to the ground with a thud.

"Right here, my good fellow," Mr. Wall said.

"What on earth are you two doing there?" a woman's voice called out.

They spun around.

"Cordelia!" Mr. Wall shouted.

The police commandant's sister stood not five paces behind them, a parasol in one hand and a frown upon her face.

"Augustus, I demand an explanation. Why did you abandon us and go gallivanting off with your Soudanese servant? And where is my brother? I heard—"

Her frown turned to an expression of shock when she saw the guns and the body.

"What on Earth—" she began.

She did not get to finish because she was rudely interrupted by a bullet.

It emerged from the doorway to the Nilometer, which had opened a crack. The bullet whizzed right between the three of them to plant itself in the trunk of a palm tree not far from Cordelia.

Mr. Wall spun and fired a burst from his submachine gun. The bullets thudded into the thick wooded door and cracked off the stone frame. Moustafa grabbed Cordelia and dragged her behind a more distant tree. Mr. Wall followed, giving the door another burst to keep whoever hid there quiet.

"To your right!" Cordelia shouted.

Moustafa didn't see the Egyptian with the pistol rise from the underbrush until Mr. Wall was already cutting him apart with a long burst. His boss turned and ran to them.

"Got that one. I don't know about the one behind the door," Mr. Wall said when he made it to them. "There's more coming, I'm sure of it."

Moustafa unslung his rifle as his boss turned to Cordelia.

"How did you get here?" he asked.

"I overheard you saying you were going to al-Rawdah Island. Then I overheard Sergeant Todd speaking with an officer about my brother having gone missing. So I pretended to have a headache, got away from Aunt Pearl, and followed you."

"And straight into danger? Foolish woman!"

"Foolish enough to save your life."

"Well thank you for that but now I have to save yours. Moustafa, take her to the shore, commandeer a boat, and get out of here. I'll keep them busy."

"Alone?"

"Go!"

Moustafa hated to leave him, but they had to get Cordelia out of danger. He grabbed her by the wrist.

"Unhand me!"

Moustafa didn't bother arguing, he simply dragged her along.

"We'll be open to enemy fire if we get out on the water," she said, panting as he ran through the palm grove with her.

"Enemy fire? Did even the women go to the Great War?"

"As a nurse, yes. The Germans shelled my hospital on more than one occasion. We shouldn't go out on the water."

"Don't worry. Mr. Wall will make enough of a racket that they will pay no attention to us. Let's get the first boat we see."

"The boat I came on is just ahead. The boatman was altogether too familiar."

"I will break the hand he touched you with, madam," Moustafa said, his words almost drowned out by a burst of submachine gun fire behind them. At least one rifle thudded in reply.

"He didn't touch me, just sort of wiggled about in my presence."

"Then I will break whatever he wiggled," Moustafa promised.

The shore appeared through the trees. Moustafa stopped and crouched. Cordelia crouched beside him, leaning on her parasol, out of breath.

"Follow me and don't expose yourself," he whispered, letting her go so he could be ready with the rifle.

More shots rang out behind them.

"I'll hide here. You go back and save Augustus," she whispered.

"No."

Moustafa didn't feel like having more of a conversation with this inconvenient Englishwoman than that. He crept forward until he could see the beach. A boat was drawn up on the sand. It wasn't the one they had come on, so it must have been Cordelia's. A man in a faded jellaba sat with his back to him, smoking a cigarette as he gazed out across the river. Taking a final look around, Moustafa rose up, leveled the gun at him, and let out a soft whistle.

The boatman turned around, the cigarette falling out of his mouth as he saw the muzzle gazing at him from barely twenty yards away. Slowly he raised his hands.

"Stay where you are," he told him, then switched to English. "Cordelia, you can come out now."

Cordelia emerged from the underbrush, looking pale.

She was not alone. A European with a smug grin held a pistol to her head.

Vincent.

Moustafa groaned and dropped his rifle.

Just then, the dull thud of an explosion reverberated through the trees.

21

Edmond had just given Faisal some candy when the firing broke out.

They were sitting on one of the lower levels of the Nilometer, near the water, and so the first shots came faintly to their ears.

Edmond shouted to Albert and the silent Egyptian, who were playing cards nearby. They grabbed their guns and hurried up the stairs that spiraled around the well.

"What's happening?" Faisal asked.

"Police," Edmond said, getting up and drawing a pistol. "Or worse. Stay here. If there are any problems, you can go down another level and there's a back exit hidden behind that tapestry hanging down there. You know the one?"

Faisal nodded.

As soon as Edmond hurried up the stairway, Faisal snuck after him. Edmond didn't look back. He was too busy shouting orders in French to the men above.

When Faisal got to the ground floor, he saw Albert and the silent Egyptian taking turns firing out the doorway. They ducked back as a rain of bullets smacked against the wood. A couple broke through, careening off the curved stone walls and flying all around the inside of the building. Faisal screamed as one pinked off the stair right in front of him, spitting up fragments of stone that hit him in the forehead.

His scream made Edmond turn around.

"I told you to stay out of danger!" the Apache leader shouted.

"I want to see what's going on."

Another burst hit the door. Edmond and Faisal threw themselves on the floor.

That wasn't a normal gun, Faisal realized. That sounded like one of those fast guns the soldiers had. The Englishman had one too. Could he be here?

For a minute the firing stopped. Faisal poked his head up over the top of the staircase.

"Are you all right?" he asked Edmond.

"Yes, are you?"

He felt his forehead. No blood. "Yes."

They smiled at each other.

"Go downstairs," Edmond said. More firing crackled through the palm grove outside.

Faisal scurried downstairs. He stopped short when he saw Hakim down there. His two baboons stood right behind him.

The animal trainer glared at him.

"You brought them here."

"Me? How could I?"

Hakim grabbed him by the collar and slammed him against the wall.

"You did. You warned them in the Citadel."

"They wouldn't have believed me. And you had people watching the whole time."

Hakim hesitated. Faisal could tell he was baffled at how Faisal could have warned them, but his suspicious nature assured him that Faisal was the culprit.

Hakim shook him. "Tell me how you did it!"

A shout in French made Hakim turn. Edmond came running down the stairs, rage on his face.

And that saved Edmond's life.

An ear-splitting roar and an explosion. Fragments of the door flew out into the open space above the well, followed by the torn bodies of Albert and Abasi. They plunged into the well below with a splash.

The force of the explosion threw Edmond off the stairs. He landed hard on the floor.

Marius came up from below, limping because of his bandaged foot. Yves came up too. He must have entered through the back passage because Faisal hadn't seen him in the building before.

They nearly got knocked over as the two baboons, screeching in terror from the explosion, scampered down the stairs. Hakim ran after them, shouting for them to come back.

Faisal looked back up at the smoke and dust that obscured the upper floor. A figure emerged out of it, firing as he went.

The Englishman!

Faisal let out a cheer that got drowned out by the roar of the Englishman's fast gun.

Marius took several bullets in the chest and tumbled down the stairs. Yves fired back with a pistol, forcing the Englishman behind a pillar. Edmond leaped up from the floor, grabbed Faisal, and ran down the stairs, practically dragging the boy behind him. Bullets snapped off the stone above their heads.

Why was the Englishman shooting at him?

Then he realized that in his new clothes, the Englishman hadn't recognized him.

Suddenly Edmond didn't need to drag him anymore. He ran just as fast as the Frenchman did.

More shots rang out above. Yves came down behind them, firing as he went. The landings were wide enough and the pillars all around were broad enough that there was plenty of cover. Faisal couldn't see the Englishman anymore.

Yves stopped firing. All Faisal could hear was the ringing in his ears and the splashing of the water below, stirred up by the two bodies that had just fallen into it.

Edmond had dropped his gun when he had fallen, and turned to a nearby table to grab a pistol lying there. Yves started reloading his own pistol.

Thus both were occupied when a strange metal ball came rolling down the stairs. A squawk from Yves told him what he had already figured out—that metal ball needed to go somewhere else.

Faisal gave it a kick, and his heart clenched as he saw it fly over the empty space of the well to hit a pillar on the opposite side and come right back at him.

But it didn't have enough speed, and arced down into the well.

Yves and Edmond had already thrown themselves on the floor. Faisal didn't have time to.

A loud bang echoed through the Nilometer, followed by a plume of water. Faisal jumped back as it drenched him.

Edmond shook the water off himself like a dog and rose laughing.

"Good boy!" he shouted. Faisal grinned.

Wait, why was he taking compliments from the people who

were fighting the Englishman? Everything in his life was getting turned around!

Then he remembered the two prisoners in the level below. Had they been killed? Had he saved his own life only to kill those two Europeans?

Yves peeked up the well shaft and fired a couple of shots before ducking back, chased by the Englishman's bullets. Yves and Edmond exchanged a few words in French. Edmond put a finger to his lips and moved over to the other side of one of the pillars. He pointed to himself and pointed upwards, then pointed to Yves and pointed upwards.

They were going to play a trick on the Englishman! Edmond would fire, and when the Englishman returned fire Yves would get him.

Faisal froze. What could he do? Shout a warning? With all the blasts and shooting going on, everyone's ears rang so much the Englishman would probably not even hear him.

Edmond ducked around the pillar and fired two shots. This was returned by a burst of fire from above. Yves ducked around the other side of the pillar, raising his gun.

Faisal pushed him over the edge. He landed in the water a floor below.

Edmond looked at him. Faisal had expected him to be angry, but he looked more hurt than angry.

He looked disappointed too.

Faisal bit his lip and backed away, unsure what Edmond would do.

But Edmond was too busy with the Englishman. They started trading shots, each protected by their own pillar. Every time Edmond got behind the cover he glanced over at Faisal, keeping an eye on him.

Faisal didn't know what to do. Should he push Edmond into the water too? And where were Hakim and the others?

This was ridiculous. Of course he had to help the Englishman. These people had kidnapped him!

He waited until Edmond started firing again and moved up behind him.

Too slow. He got to Edmond just as he ducked back behind the pillar. They ended up bumping into each other. Edmond grabbed him by the shoulder and shook him.

"What's the matter with you?"

"I-I-"

A burst from upstairs cut off any answer Faisal might give.

"Out with it!" Edmond demanded. "Why did you do that to Yves? No Apache betrays another."

Faisal kicked him in the shin. "I'm not an Apache!"

"You little—"

Edmond grabbed him, raising his pistol like he was going to strike him with the butt of the weapon. Faisal made a desperate decision and threw himself right at the Apache leader. While he was much smaller than Edmond, the surprise and force with which he hit made the man stumble back a couple of steps.

Right into the line of fire.

Edmond and Faisal both flinched. But no fire came.

They looked up at the level above. The Englishman stood there, his weapon gone and his hands raised above his head. He had his back to them.

Then Moustafa and the Englishwoman moved into view, looking grim. Vincent came right behind them, holding a gun to their backs.

When Moustafa recognized Faisal, he gave him a glare more burning than the noonday sun. The Englishman turned and noticed him too, but Faisal couldn't tell what expression he had. It was a curious one, that was soon masked. Faisal decided it would be safer to pretend not to know them.

Edmond pushed him away.

"I'll deal with you later," he said, jabbing a finger at him.

"Sorry," Faisal found himself saying.

Edmond paced up the stairs. Faisal tensed. Was he going to kill the Englishman now?

Then he saw Yves come up the stairs, dripping wet and with murder in his eyes, and he knew that he had as much to worry about as the Englishman did.

22

Augustus supposed he had been in tighter spots before—during the war and in some of his other cases—but he couldn't quite bring a worse situation to mind. He had two guns pointed at him and the younger sister of the police commandant was a fellow prisoner.

Even if he somehow got out of this he'd be a dead man. Or at least an imprisoned one.

And what was Faisal doing here, looking like he had just robbed a clothing shop? The boy had even bathed.

He was still shaking out the cobwebs of his memories. While fighting the Apaches he had been transported back to the front, where he thought he was firing into a crater at a bunch of Germans. An incongruous sound had snapped him out of it—a woman's voice.

Cordelia's voice.

Now why would that have such an effect on him?

The approach of an obviously angry Frenchman brought his thoughts to more immediate matters.

"Edmond Depré, I presume?"

"Indeed. And you are the great Sir Augustus Wall, formerly known as—"

"Enough of that."

Edmond smiled. "So your servant and your sweetheart don't know, eh?"

"He is not my servant, and she is not my sweetheart."

"Perhaps not, but she is the sister of Sir Thomas Russell. Would you like to see him? He's downstairs."

A sharp intake of breath on Cordelia's part showed she had paid attention during her French lessons at school.

"If you've hurt him ..." Augustus said.

Edmond shook his head and grinned. "I haven't, not yet."

He picked up the submachine gun lying nearby and examined it.

"This will prove handy as we expand our territory. A bit of a trick finding ammunition for it, but we've just co-opted a cotton smuggler. I suppose he can smuggle other things too."

A squishing sound coming up the stairs made Augustus and Edmond turn. A dripping-wet Frenchman, no doubt the one that fell of the ledge, came up the stairs, leading Faisal. He had his pistol up to the boy's head.

"Yves Savatier, it's been a long time," Augustus said.

"So you do remember me? The officer corps generally don't remember the ranks." Yves replied in Arabic, instead of the French with which he had been addressed.

"I remember them all."

Yves cocked his head. "Do you? Is that why you take opium every night, so you don't see them?"

"Speak in French," Augustus said.

Yves continued in Arabic. "Why? So the boy won't understand? He knows you, doesn't he? Most likely he led you here."

"Let him go and you can do what you like with me."

Yves grinned and shook his head. "That's not how it works. I was hoping you'd join us. I was hoping you understood."

Something inside him turned. "I do understand. Now let him go."

Yves shook his head again. "I am under no illusions. If I let him go you will kill me. We fought side by side, remember? I know I cannot beat you."

"Get away, Englishman!" Faisal shouted.

"Quiet now. I'll sort it all out," Augustus said.

Yves nodded. "You will. Come downstairs. You'll have another reunion today."

They went downstairs, Yves and Faisal in front, Augustus and the other prisoners behind them, and Edmond and Vincent taking up the rear.

Augustus couldn't help but admire the architecture of this place. He'd only visited once but it was just as fascinating as he remembered it. He didn't recall those chips out of the central pillar, however. Had those been his doing? A pity.

When they got to the bottom floor, just a few inches above the water level, Augustus stopped short and gasped.

Two men stood chained to the wall, both soaked to the skin but otherwise unharmed. One was Sir Thomas. Cordelia rushed for him but Vincent dragged her back.

The other was Captain Fortier.

Yves chuckled. "Yes, you recognize him too, don't you? He's the one we really wanted, not Legrand. We knew Fortier lived incognito somewhere in Alexandria. He had taken on a new name just like you, and we didn't have enough connections in that city to flush him out. Besides, there are richer pickings here. We knew the two were friends, so once Legrand's murder made it into the papers, all we had to do was put a man on the widow's house and eventually he'd come calling."

"Who is this?" Captain Fortier asked in French, staring at Augustus.

The entire conversation had taken place in Arabic, with Yves glancing every now and then at Faisal to make sure he was listening. Now Augustus switched to French.

"I was on a firing squad of yours, Captain Fortier, back when I was a captain in the Oxs and Bucks."

The French veteran stared at the remaining side of Augustus's face and gaped.

"Why it's—"

"That name is long gone."

Captain Fortier paused for a moment, confused, then nodded with understanding. "What happened to you?"

"The same thing that happened to you. The war. You tried to leave it behind too, eh?"

Captain Fortier nodded sadly. "It looks like we never can."

"No we can't," Sir Thomas grumbled.

"How did they get you here?" Augustus asked him. "What was written in that note that made you run off so?"

The police commandant bowed his head. "The war. The past. Nothing I want my sister to hear."

Vincent laughed. "This is quite the reunion of sinners!"

"Keep quiet," Yves told him, then turned to Augustus and addressed him in Arabic. "Would you like to be let go? You and all your friends?"

"At what price?"

"Just kill the captain, that's all I want."

"What! Why?"

Yves's face contorted. For a moment he looked like he would start to cry.

"You know why. He made us murd—"

"Speak in French!"

Yves paused, glanced at Faisal and back at Augustus.

"Why? You don't want him to know?"

"He's seen enough suffering. He doesn't need to see ours."

Yves paused, then switched to French. "Fair enough, but that's not it, is it? I saw how he looked at you when you came sweeping in with your gun blazing. He hero worships you. Oh, it's nice to be a hero, isn't it? They gave us a big parade when the war ended. I marched down the Champs-Élysées as everyone cheered. Girls came out of the crowd and gave us flowers and kisses. Old men bought me drinks every time I stepped into a café. Oh yes, I felt ten feet tall. But I couldn't fool myself for long. I knew what I had done. I had killed German workers so French millionaires could make more millions. I even had to kill one of my own comrades. That's not being a hero. All those kisses tasted like acid and those drinks went down like castor oil. We weren't heroes. The people at home are fools."

"And yet you speak French to me."

Yves shook Faisal. "You think I have anything against this little runt? No, let him continue with his hero worship if you and he live. I'm going to help him. I'm going to make you a hero for real."

"By killing Fortier? Don't be daft."

"It will be a fine lesson in revolution. Edmond has been teaching Faisal. Edmond, too, wants someone to hero worship him. Your little Egyptian boy has been hearing all about class warfare."

"Not that he learned anything," Edmond snapped and glared at the boy. Even though Faisal didn't understand the words, he understood the tone. He hung his head, then looked up at him defiantly.

Augustus turned to the Apache leader. "You've been silent through all this. Aren't you the man in charge?"

Edmond shook his head. "Not in this case. Yves took a blood oath to exact revenge for the death of a fellow Apache. No man can deny him that opportunity."

"And so you imperiled your entire operation just to fulfill that oath?"

"Nothing is more sacred than the sacred oath of the working man."

"What tosh. Getting that sarcophagus into my house was a neat trick, though."

"That was Marius. He was an officer in an engineering regiment, decorated for his service to the nation, but he was a worker at heart. Now he lies dead upstairs."

"I shan't shed a tear," Augustus said. "Oh dear, baboons!"

An Egyptian man had come out from behind a tapestry, revealing a hidden passage. Two baboons loped behind him. It turned out Faisal had been right about that.

The baboons came up and sniffed the newcomers. Cordelia let out a little cry.

"Oh, is the lady afraid of baboons?" Edmond said. "Then I suggest Sir Augustus here had better do as Yves suggests, or those baboons will tear apart that pretty face."

"Watch it, you cad," Augustus said.

Yves gestured with his pistol at the old French captain chained to the wall.

"If you're looking for a cad, look no further than him. Here's the deal, Sir Augustus. Once you let me free when you could have denounced me to Captain Fortier. Now I will give you the same chance. You kill him and you shall all go free."

"Nonsense, you have the police commandant prisoner. As if you'd ever let him slip from your grasp!"

"He's more useful to us alive," Edmond said. "When we let him go safe and sound, but tied naked to the back of a mule and led through the streets of the city, he'll become the laughing stock of the entire Arab world. Better a living fool than a dead martyr."

"Oh, is that how you survived the war? By being a living fool?"

Edmond's face turned red. "I suffered my own war, in a hellhole prison in the Algerian desert."

"Perhaps you shouldn't have been garroting people for their pocket watches."

"Enough of this," Yves said, holding out his pistol. "Edmond, keep your gun aimed at him. Sir Augustus or whatever you call yourself now, take this and shoot Captain Fortier."

The big guns started rumbling in this distance. Augustus caught a whiff of cordite. He took a deep breath. "No."

"If you don't, you will all die, and we'll kill the captain anyway. Kill him, show yourself and your boy what you really are, what I know you to be, and I will let them all go."

Augustus paused.

"You know you want to," Yves said, and his voice was not unkind. "He's what made you what you are today. He's the reason you take opium to sleep at night. He's the reason you've changed your name and hidden yourself away. I saw your face after that execution. You were as sickened as I was. No, more. Because before then you had believed in the war. I was never under any illusions. Take this gun and put your ghosts to rest. Take this gun and set your friends free."

Captain Fortier straightened himself as much as the chains would allow and looked at Augustus with sympathy in his eyes.

"Do it," he said.

Augustus trembled. He blinked his eyes, trying to focus.

"It's the only way," Captain Fortier said. "These men are barbarians, but like all barbarians they have a code they live by. He will keep his promise. Kill me or we all die. It's the only way."

Yves still held the revolver in his outstretched hand. Augustus drew away from it like it was a serpent.

"Any tricks and I'll kill you all," Edmond told him. "If you don't do it, I'll kill you all."

"No, I get Captain Fortier," Yves corrected.

"Of course, comrade," Edmond said, "if the gentleman here doesn't see sense."

One of the baboons shrieked, a sound like metal tearing.

"They can sense blood," the Egyptian said.

As the sound of cannon fire thudded in his ears, Augustus took the gun. He couldn't bring himself to look at any of the others, only Captain Fortier.

"You were a good officer," Fortier said. "You did your duty then when it was a hard thing to do. Do your duty now."

With a shaking hand, Augustus raised the gun. The big guns intensified their bombardment, their low rumble shaking him to his core. The stone walls of the Nilometer began to look like mud. Captain Fortier closed his eyes and began to pray. Instead of the conservative suit he had been wearing, he now had on his uniform.

Augustus cocked the revolver.

23

Moustafa could tell when his boss had one of his attacks, and it was clear he was drifting into one of them right now.

When his mind was off in France, he was capable of anything.

Even shooting that poor old man in chains.

Moustafa had to do something. He didn't believe for a second that these Apaches would be true to their word.

He tensed. Vincent wasn't far behind him. God willing, he could turn around and belt him across that smug jaw before he could fire. And if God had written that they should all die today, at least he could give a good accounting for himself before that happened.

Just as he was preparing to strike, Cordelia spoke up.

"Don't do it, Augustus. Don't give them what they want. I am quite prepared to die rather than see a good Englishman give in to a bunch of Marseille riff raff."

The gun wavered. Faisal glanced at Cordelia and seemed to understand the gist of what she had said.

"Englishman, what are you doing?" Faisal said. "You're in Cairo."

Mr. Wall paused, shook his head, and brought his hand up to his mask.

He lowered his gun.

"I … am in Cairo," he said softly, "and I will not be a murderer a second time."

Yves stepped up to the trembling veteran and took the gun from his hand. He holstered it and gave Mr. Wall a sympathetic look.

"I understand, comrade. I wish you could have seen through the blinders society has put on you, but I understand why you could not." With a sigh he turned to Edmond. "Let's get this finished."

Moustafa spun around, lashing out at Vincent, hoping to hit him square in the jaw and knock him out.

But Vincent was no longer within reach. He had anticipated the movement and took a short hop back, just enough to get out of reach.

The Apache laughed. He wasn't even aiming his gun at Moustafa.

"I'm too quick for you and too clever. Free men always beat slaves."

"What did you call me?" Moustafa growled. He lunged for Vincent again, who nimbly dodged him. This brought them out of the group of people standing before the prisoners, out into the more open landing around the well. Moustafa rushed him, but Vincent veered to the side and ducked the sweep Moustafa made with his arm.

Still laughing, Vincent holstered his pistol and got into a fighting position.

"Think you will be third time lucky, eh? Hold your fire, comrades, I need to teach this slave a lesson."

"I am no slave!" Moustafa roared.

"Anyone who works for the nobility and the police is a slave. You are worse than most. Your country is a colony and you work for your occupiers!"

"I work for my own advancement, and we'll take care of the British before long. But first I'll take care of you!"

Moustafa rushed him. This time Vincent didn't try to back away. Instead he landed one of his expert Savate kicks on Moustafa's thigh. His foot connected with a loud thud but Moustafa barely felt it. Grinning, he swung a meaty fist at Vincent's face. The Frenchman managed to dodge enough that it was only a glancing blow, but it landed with enough force to send him back a couple of steps.

Moustafa rushed him again. Vincent blocked his next punch with his arm, wincing from the impact of the strong man, and kicked him in the thigh again. Just like the last time, it had no visible effect.

Ducking a right hook, Vincent lashed out with his feet again, hitting Moustafa's right thigh and left shin in a rapid one-two kick. Moustafa's grin widened as he stood just as solidly as before. He landed a fist in Vincent's stomach. A normal man would have gone down and spent the next five minutes doubled over and gasping, but Vincent only let out a grunt. It kept him from attacking, however, and Moustafa jabbed at him with his left and his right four times in rapid succession. Vincent blocked all of them, giving ground as he did. He ended up with on the edge of the well with nowhere else to go.

And then the Frenchman recovered enough to fight back.

He swung at Moustafa's face, who blocked it easily enough before discovering that it was merely a feint for a kick to the ribs. Vincent's foot landed a direct hit, and Moustafa felt one of his ribs crack.

Growling, Moustafa lashed out at him. The nimble Frenchman ducked and ended up getting hit on the shoulder, the force of the swing spinning him around.

Moustafa locked him in a bear hug. Vincent groaned, his arms pinned to his sides. He could only move his legs, and kept kicking at Moustafa's shins and instep. The kicks to the feet made Moustafa grit his teeth in pain, but the kicks to the shins did nothing.

Moustafa squeezed harder, expecting a bullet from one of the other Apaches at any second. It did not come. Vincent whipped his head back, butting Moustafa in the face and making him see stars.

"You tricky spawn of a goat!" Moustafa shouted, and slammed him into a nearby pillar. He gave him two hard jabs to the kidneys, lifted him over his head, and tossed him in the water.

Vincent sank like a stone. For a second everyone paused, staring at the rippling surface. Then Vincent came up, sputtering and splashing.

Moustafa belted out a laugh. He knew he was going to die but at least he saw that son of a mangy cur put in his place.

"You think you are the only one who knows how to play dirty tricks?" he taunted Vincent, who splashed about the pool, trying to get a grip on the edge. "I can play them too."

He pulled up his jellaba, making Cordelia yelp and turn away. On his legs were a pair of shin guards, and wrapped around his thighs were thick bundles of cloth.

"I bet you didn't know my boss was once an avid cricket player. His old equipment came in handy!" Moustafa laughed again.

"Well done," Yves said. "I have never seen someone beat Vincent. I hope that means you can die happy."

Yves reached for his gun, but found the holster empty.

Faisal stood beside him with Yves's gun in his hand.

He tossed it to Mr. Wall and the room exploded into violence.

❧ 24 ❧

Everyone had been looking at the fight and it had been easy to slip the gun out of Yves's holster. Edmond and Yves were still staring at Moustafa and they didn't get to react in time as Faisal tossed the pistol to the Englishman.

Edmond saw the movement just as the Englishman caught it. He tried to grab the woman, who stood nearby, but she struck his hand with her parasol and jumped away, ending up right next to Faisal.

That was a mistake, because Hakim let out a whistle and his two baboons lunged for the both of them.

The woman smacked one with the parasol and Faisal dodged the other. Suddenly there was shooting and shouting everywhere, but Faisal didn't have time to pay attention. The baboon sprang for him again and he barely got out of the way in time. Meanwhile the Englishwoman was screaming and jabbing with her parasol like it was a sword, keeping the other baboon at bay.

An especially accurate jab got the baboon right in the eye. It let out a piercing shriek that brought its companion loping over. The Englishwoman didn't see it coming. At the last second, Faisal jumped at it feet first. His brand new sandals hit the side of its head and it staggered, surprise on its brutish face.

Faisal grabbed the woman and dragged her away. He had seen a large chest set against the wall and had an idea.

Before they could make it, the uninjured baboon rushed at them. The Englishwoman jabbed it in the face and it scampered back.

A bullet whizzed right past Faisal's face. He didn't have time to see who shot it or if even they were shooting at him, because just then both baboons prepared to jump at them.

Faisal shoved the Englishwoman aside, opened the chest, and ducked, hoping the chest was empty.

The baboons bashed against the open lid and fell into the chest. Faisal slammed the lid down and sat on it.

The baboons shrieked and banged against the inside of the lid, making it jump and buck. Faisal felt like he was riding an unbroken stallion, and he didn't dare get off.

The Englishwoman rushed over, closed the latch, and stuck her parasol through the hole to secure it.

"Thanks!" Faisal said. She sat down on the chest too, because the baboons hadn't given up trying to smash their way out.

The rest of the fight was still going on. To his immense relief, Faisal saw Karim lying in a pool of blood. The Englishman and Edmond were wrestling. The Englishman had a gun in his hand and Edmond was trying to get it from him. Someone had shot Yves, who leaned against a pillar holding his gut, and Vincent had crawled halfway out of the well, only to get strangled by Moustafa.

The Englishwoman covered her eyes and looked away. Faisal could not look away. Edmond smacked the Englishman's hand and the gun flew into the water. As the Englishman threw a punch at Edmond, the Apache leader jumped back and pulled a tiny pistol with no barrel out of his pocket.

The Englishman chopped at Edmond's gun hand, and the bullet that was aimed at his heart only streaked his side. Edmond fired again, but the gun only made a click. Snarling, he flipped a little spike out to point forwards and jabbed at the Englishman, who managed to get his arm up in time to stop it from hitting his face. Instead the little blade buried itself in his forearm.

Edmond took a quick look around the room. All his companions were down. Moustafa had just dropped Vincent's limp form and turned toward him. The Englishman looked about to spring. A police whistle shrilled upstairs.

Edmond ran.

He ran right through the tapestry covering the hidden passage and disappeared.

Faisal ran after him. He didn't know why.

The passageway was a dank and narrow stone tunnel with a low arch. It sloped upwards and Faisal could see sunlight ahead, partially blocked by Edmond's silhouette.

Edmond reached the end of the tunnel, ducked to the right, and disappeared. Faisal picked up speed.

The tunnel opened up into an area of dense undergrowth. He looked around and saw no sign of Edmond. Shouts and running feet told him the police were almost to him. He peered through the trees and saw them approaching. His sharp ears picked up another sound, a softer sound of someone creeping through the underbrush. Faisal followed it.

He found Edmond hiding in a little hollow made by a swale in the ground covered by a fallen palm tree. The police were almost upon them. They were Egyptian and Nubian, all carrying rifles. A

European officer came huffing up behind them, his red face streaked with sweat.

Faisal turned to them and pointed in a random direction. "He went that way!"

The police nodded and rushed off the way he indicated, the officer still huffing and trying to keep up.

He turned to the hollow. It was empty.

Faisal looked around, feeling suddenly lost. Where had he gone?

Then he saw him several paces away, crouched behind another tree.

Edmond grinned at him, mouthed the words "good boy" and disappeared into the thicket.

Faisal stood there for a moment, then walked back to the secret passage.

Faisal should have enjoyed the ride back on the policeman's motorboat. He had never been on a motorboat before, but he barely noticed.

His mind was so full of thoughts and feelings that it felt like a beehive someone had just thrown a stone at. Why had he helped Edmond get away? It had been a moment's decision and he had gone with the first thing he felt like doing, but was it the right thing?

It wasn't like stealing, which he knew was wrong but did because he had to do it and because it was fun. And it wasn't like saving the woman who was going to take the Englishman away and make him lose his home. That had been the right thing to do even though he didn't want to do it. Helping Edmond had been both right and wrong, and he felt both good and bad about doing it. Edmond had treated him nicely, nicer even than the Englishman. But he was a bad man, and deserved to get caught. Even so, Faisal couldn't bring himself to betray him, and he couldn't quite bring himself to feel guilty about it either. He wondered if he should feel guilty about not feeling guilty.

Good boy, Edmond had said. How often did someone say that to him?

"Did I do well?" Faisal asked the Englishman, who sat in the prow of the boat with the police commandant.

"Not now, Faisal, I need to speak with Sir Thomas."

The Englishwoman put a hand on his shoulder and smiled. She said something to him in her own language.

Faisal frowned back at her.

Just because I saved you doesn't mean I'm not mad at you for stealing the Englishman, he thought.

The woman gave him a confused look and removed her hand.

When he had returned to the Nilometer, she had taken the Englishman's shirt off and was bandaging his wounds. The Englishman had objected and tried to stop her, but she had firmly pushed his hands aside and kept on working on him. Great, she was already taking over.

He stared at the water rushing by the side of the boat, trying to put all his thoughts in order.

At last the Englishman paid some attention to him.

"So what's this get up?" he asked, pointing to his new clothes.

"He's joined them," Moustafa growled. "I told you you shouldn't trust a flea-bitten cur like him. Idris Wakil said a boy had climbed into the house to take the diamonds. What boy do we know who is a good climber?"

"Hakim kidnapped me! He threatened me with the baboons. You're the one who sent me to find him, remember?"

Moustafa glared at him but didn't have a reply. Faisal stuck his tongue out at him. The Nubian lunged for him but the Englishman got between them.

"Enough. I still want an answer to my question."

"They made me work for them. They told me if I didn't, they'd stick me in a cage with those baboons and sell tickets to people who wanted to watch me get eaten alive. I had to spy for them. They wanted me in respectable clothes so I could spy on the Europeans."

"And take bags of diamonds from their houses," Moustafa said.

Faisal gulped.

"What else did you do?" the Englishman asked.

"Nothing."

The two men studied him.

"Nothing!" Faisal repeated.

"Did you go to the Citadel?" the Englishman asked.

Faisal put on a confused face. That face worked pretty good because people always underestimated him. "Why would I do that?"

"Nothing. It's just that someone left a clue there that brought me to the Nilometer."

Faisal felt tempted to admit that. It might get him a bigger reward than the one he was about to ask for, but if he told the Englishman, he would probably tell his friend the police commandant and that would lead to trouble.

"It was Yves," Faisal said.

"Yes, he seemed desperate for a reunion."

Faisal remembered something Yves had said to him the night

before. "He said that he didn't want to fight the war the rest of his life."

The Englishman turned away and looked out over the water. He looked sad. Faisal realized he knew something that might cheer him up.

"I know one of the people they worked with! They, um, mentioned him. His name is Abbas Eldessouky and he lives on Sebil al-Nimir street. He deals in cotton that doesn't have a tax stamp."

"I'll tell Sir Thomas and they'll round him up."

The Englishman fished some coins out of his pocket.

"I suppose you'll want some payment. You did put up a good show back there. We'll just forget what you did under duress. Lord knows I've done worse. How much will it cost me this time?"

Faisal brightened. He only needed five and a half piastres to buy the spell to stop the Englishman from getting married.

"Could I have five and a half piastres?"

"That's a rather specific amount."

"Well, if you want to give me six, that's fine."

The Englishman pulled out some coins and started counting them. Suddenly Faisal remembered something. While he had cast a spell on Mina's marriage and gotten taken care of that greasy old man, Mina's family was still in trouble. They would marry her off soon.

"Actually," Faisal started, then saw the money in the Englishman's hand. Forcing himself to look away from all those bright, shiny coins, he said, "A friend's father hurt his back. It's so bad he can't work any more. Can you get a doctor for him?"

The Englishman cocked his head. "Who is this fellow?"

"He runs the *ful* stand."

"Haven't met the chap."

"He makes very good *ful*. At least he used to."

"Well I wouldn't want to deny the neighborhood gourmands a chance to partake of his culinary excellence."

Faisal blinked.

"That's a yes, Faisal."

"Great!"

"There is no guarantee that a doctor can help him."

"Egyptian magic didn't work, so European medicine will. It's one or the other."

"I wish I shared your faith in modernism."

"What's modernism?"

"A religion that says that everything new is automatically better. I thought the war had killed that belief but I think it's only made it worse."

The Englishman was speaking strangely again. It must have been all that fighting. It made him crazy sometimes.

It didn't matter. He'd get better soon enough, and now Mina's father would get better too. Moustafa was all beaten up but would be all right, and the Englishwoman didn't get her face ripped off by the baboons. The other two Europeans were all right too, and Edmond was sure to get away.

Yes, everyone was fine. Everyone but him.

The Englishwoman was talking to the Englishman. The way she looked at him Faisal could just tell they were going to get married. Women don't look at men like that unless they were going to get married.

She talked to him all the way back to Cairo. Back to the city that would soon offer no home to Faisal.

25

It was several days later, and Sir Thomas had practically forced him to invite himself, Cordelia, and Aunt Pearl to tea. Sir Thomas had done this by a clever ruse. He had invited Augustus to dinner, something he couldn't refuse the man after saving his life, and was thus required to return the favor. Augustus had decided on tea because it was shorter than dinner and he wouldn't have to endure the stares of the diners in some restaurant. Besides, Aunt Pearl was still keen on buying some mementoes. If he had to suffer through their presence, he should at least make some money.

And suffer he did. Because the details of their little outing to al-Rawdah Island had not been shared with Aunt Pearl, they could not discuss the one interesting thing they all had in common. In a brief telephone call, Sir Thomas had made it understood that he would overlook all the sneaking behind his back and he would forget the mention of his wartime deeds, and Augustus knew that came at the price of not ever knowing the contents of the letter the Apaches had put in his office.

He could guess. Sir Thomas had done something in the war he was ashamed of. Who hadn't? Augustus could judge this arrogant, ignorant man for so many things, but not for that. No, never for that.

So instead of talking about what happened in the war or on the island, the conversation remained mind-numbingly dull. Aunt Pearl went into extensive detail about her lineage, none of it particularly interesting. Why did she think that just because her ancestor got clubbed to death by some kilt-wearing rabble she could go on to such tedious length about not only him, but an endless succession of landed gentry and peacetime officers?

Lord, save me from the banality of the English.

But he found no succor. Cordelia practically hung on him, devouring him with those eyes while nattering on about nothing in particular. To give her credit, she had held up well under pressure and had proven her nursing skills had not been forgotten. His wounds were already healing. Unfortunately, she had gone back to being a dull woman of society.

Her brother was even worse, fulminating about how he needed to keep the natives in stricter line.

He wished Zehra were here. Then he could sit back and watch the fireworks between her and Cordelia. That would be fun.

But no, she had politely declined the invitation. Apparently she was too chivalrous to engage in a duel of wits with an unarmed opponent.

Moustafa was also absent, enjoying a well-earned holiday.

Heinrich Schäfer had shown up, but the wily devil had lingered just as long as courtesy required before retiring upstairs to peruse Augustus's library. Being German, none of the English had restrained him. Now the fellow sat comfortably reading while he faced torture alone downstairs. Some friend.

Once Augustus had endured as much as he could take, he excused himself by saying he had to make a telephone call and went to his upstairs sitting room, where he found Heinrich pleasantly buried in an excavation report from the 1890s. This was one of the things he admired about the scholar—he was perfectly aware that there was a tea party going on downstairs, and chose to read by himself anyway. If only Augustus could learn the secret to being left alone!

"Sorry to disturb you," Augustus said as he sat down.

"Not at all. It's your house."

"How goes the writing?"

"Slowly," Heinrich sighed. "At least I've finally settled on a title. I am going to call it *Principles of Egyptian Art*," Heinrich said.

"With the amount of material you're putting into it, shouldn't you call it *Every Last Detail of Egyptian Art*?" Augustus asked with a smile.

"That might scare off readers."

Augustus glanced up at the windows, open now to catch the weak noontime breeze.

"No baboons attack you?"

"Thankfully none. Perhaps I should write a paper on the symbolism of baboons in ancient Egyptian art to commemorate your little adventure."

"Perhaps. Would you like a drink?"

"You already gave me one, thank you."

"Would you like another?" Augustus asked, not wanting to get to the reason why he came up here.

"No, thank you. Is something the matter?"

Augustus shifted uncomfortably in his seat.

"I have a rather delicate matter I need some advice on."

Heinrich put down the excavation report and lit his pipe. "Oh my, this sounds interesting. Would you care to elucidate me?"

"It's an, um, romantic matter."

Heinrich coughed, sending a plume of burning tobacco out of his pipe.

"You? In a romantic affair?" he sputtered as he stamped out the flames on the rug.

"Well, in a manner of speaking, yes. It's more a matter of one party being interested and the other not."

Heinrich sighed. "Now Augustus, we've spoken of this before. Zehra is a fine woman, but she's married."

"Not her. Wait, has she said something to you?" Augustus said, leaning forward anxiously.

"No she has not. Now tell me what's going on," Heinrich said with some impatience as he refilled his pipe.

"It's Sir Thomas's sister. He made me play tour guide to get me off the case. Didn't want to get one-upped again. She's developed an attachment to me."

"What's wrong with that?"

"She's like a little girl who's found a bird with a broken wing. I don't want pity. I want to be left alone."

"So you say. Have you considered the possibility that she's finds you interesting and stimulating company?"

"Perhaps too stimulating," Augustus said. "She almost got torn apart by baboons thanks to me. Even that didn't dissuade her. In fact, it seemed to encourage her. She called me 'most invigorating.'"

"Oh dear, it sounds like a serious case," Heinrich said, puffing on his pipe. "Perhaps reverse psychology would work."

"What's that?"

"A theory by a certain alienist in Vienna—"

"Not Freud again!"

"Yes, Freud. He believes that a sudden change of stance can have the opposite effect on a subject than expected."

"Good Lord, first the Oedipus Complex and now this. That man is going to ruin medical science for a century."

"It might work."

"What? Showing interest at last? It might convince her that she's finally won. Then it will be impossible to shake her."

"Have you tried ignoring her?"

"Yes."

"Have you cancelled appointments at the last minute?"

"At every possible opportunity."

"Have you treated her with your usual brusque and aloof manner?"

"Brusque and aloof? I only treat people the way they deserve to be treated."

"I'll take that as a yes. Have you told her flatly that you are not interested?"

"As far as courtesy allows. And before you make any remarks regarding my social demeanor, I am always courteous to the ladies."

"Too courteous in Zehra's case," Heinrich muttered. "Now then, you have tried every possible manner short of impertinence to rid yourself of the attentions of a kind, intelligent, and lovely young woman and, woe is you, all has failed. You say that she has a bit of a mother/nurse complex, that she likes to take care of the weak and injured."

"To a nauseating degree. It's most humiliating."

"Well, perhaps she has latched onto you because you have withdrawn from society. If you show yourself willing to engage in society, her ardor for you might cool."

"That might make sense in Vienna, but not in the real world."

"It makes quite a bit of sense. You say that every time you have tried to push her away she has renewed her pursuit of you. It may be the pushing away that attracts her. If you pursue her, she will see you like every other man and lose interest."

"Hmmm."

"Think of it," Heinrich said, warming to his subject. "Her brother has surrounded her with feckless socialites and blockheaded officers who drag her to an endless succession of dances and dinner parties. It bores her. She hates to be pursued. She sees that as a sign of weakness in a man. She wants a strong man, one with the will to stand alone. If you act like all the others, she'll soon tire of you."

"You think so?"

"You've tried everything else."

"I don't know ..."

"Give it a try."

"Well, if you think it might work ..."

Heinrich nodded encouragement.

Augustus thought for a moment, shrugged his shoulders, and got up.

"Well, I suppose it's worth a shot."

He returned to the party to find Cordelia watching the doorway through which he had to enter. As soon as he did, her face lit up in a smile.

God save me, he silently moaned.

He sat beside her again and rejoined the conversation. It was so banal that he didn't have to even concentrate on it. At an opportune moment when the others had broken off to talk with each other, he turned to Cordelia and, summoning his courage, began to speak.

"There is, um, a tea dance at Shepheard's this Saturday. I was thinking that you might, um, want to attend."

Cordelia stared at him. Surprise quickly gave way to joy. Augustus' heart sank.

"Why, I'd be delighted!"

Oh dear.

"Oh, you would?"

"Of course! Fancy having a tea dance so early in the year, but it is Egypt after all. Summer all year round," she said and laughed.

"Except when it's hell," Augustus muttered.

"Pardon?"

"Nothing. I, um, Saturday isn't inconvenient, is it? You don't have other plans?"

Cordelia beamed a smile at him.

"None at all."

"Oh. Well, that's that. Oh! I must go back upstairs. I forgot to close the windows. Baboons, you know."

He beat a hasty retreat, almost knocking over the tea service as he did so. He practically bounded up the stairs back to Heinrich.

"She said yes! Now look at the trouble you landed me in, you and your accursed Viennese alienist!"

Heinrich laughed so hard he dropped his excavation report. Augustus jabbed a finger at him.

"Wait. You had planned this all along!"

"Reverse psychology, my friend," the German said between peals of laughter. "It works on men as well as women!"

26

Moustafa arrived at work at the usual hour despite the bullet wound and various bruises. What hurt the most was the nagging lecture Nur had given him.

"Beaten up twice in one week! And for what? Just to please this Englishman?"

"He pays well and allows me access to books."

"And what good will those books and that pay be for me and the children if you wind up dead one of these days?"

Moustafa had no answer to that. He felt grateful he had not told her about Marcus Simaika's job offer. Her nagging would have been endless.

That offer still stuck in his mind. As he rode the streetcar to work he held the Copt's business card in his hand. What would it be like to work for him? A whole new language and era of history to study, a whole new personal library to delve into, plus trips to Sinai and the Western Desert to buy antiquities. Tempting.

Yes, working for Marcus Simaika would be educational, rewarding, and safe.

And dull.

Damn that Englishman! How could he make danger so alluring?

By the time he entered Mr. Wall's antiquities shop, Marcus Simaika's card was safely back in his pocket.

He found his boss going through the morning mail.

"No strange notes from French bandits today, sir?" Moustafa asked.

"Unfortunately not. I suppose we'll have a rest for a time."

"Not a long time, boss."

"Are you implying that I lead a life filled with danger and risk?"

"Yes, boss."

Mr. Wall chuckled and continued to leaf through the mail. He pulled out a letter from the pile.

"Hello, what's this? It's addressed to one George Franklin, care of myself. Moustafa, do you know anything about this?"

Moustafa snatched the letter from his boss's hand.

"It's for me," he said. The return address was from Dr. Lansing at the *Journal of Egyptian Archaeology*. "Yes, it's for me!"

He tore the envelope open, barely able to contain his excitement, and pulled out the note within.

Dear Mr. Franklin,

We were most happy to receive your paper on the Nubian influence on Egyptian monumental art, which we feel is a groundbreaking study in a sadly underdeveloped field of inquiry. We would very much like to publish it in the Spring 1920 issue. Please contact us at your earliest convenience in order to sort out the details. You mentioned in your cover letter that you are frequently traveling and unable to come to our office.

That is quite all right. We will be able to work through all editorial issues via the post.

I did not recognize your name and took the liberty of looking you up in the indices of various journals. It appears this is your first scientific paper. May I congratulate you on such a fine study. You have a most promising career ahead of you.

Kindest regards,

Dr. Jonathan Lansing

Moustafa belted out a laugh that echoed throughout the house.

"What's so funny?" Mr. Wall asked.

It took Moustafa a couple of minutes to control his mirth long enough to tell him. At first Mr. Wall grew angry at how the journal had treated him, but when Moustafa told him he had submitted the paper again by post, this time under a false name, his boss laughed too.

"The fools!" Mr. Wall said. "Serves them right. But weren't you afraid they'd notice it was the same paper?"

Moustafa shook his head, holding his sides and he continued to chuckle. "Not at all. You see, as soon as they saw me, they stopped listening to what I said. They couldn't even remember my name two minutes after I told them."

"Oh dear. I must admit far too many of my countrymen are pig-headed in this regard. Now do you see why I left Europe behind?"

"Ah, but Mr. Wall, you still have the finest archaeological journals. And now I am going to have a paper in one!"

Mr. Wall extended a hand. "Then congratulations are in order."

Moustafa shook his hand.

"Thank you, sir. Coming from you that means a lot," Moustafa said, and meant it.

"So is this George Franklin fellow entirely fictitious?"

"Entirely, Mr. Wall."

"Where did you get the name from?"

That set off another round of laughter. It took some time before Moustafa could reply.

"American history. The name is a combination of George Washington and Benjamin Franklin, two of the Americans who kicked out the English."

"Hmm, you haven't thrown in your lot with the independence crowd, have you? You're not one of those who will 'take care of the British'?"

Moustafa paused as he heard the words he had said in anger at the Nilometer repeated back to him. His laughter stopped. His boss was not a normal European. If Moustafa gave him the answer he wanted to hear, if he said he still supported the British, Mr. Wall would not believe him. But how would he react if he said yes?

And was "yes" even the correct answer?

He remembered the British soldiers firing into the crowd of protestors. He remembered all the insults, great and small, that had been hurled in his direction ever since he had left his village. But he also remembered those Egyptians who had sold out their own country for a bit of money, and all those Egyptians and Soudanese who didn't care about their past, who could never understand why he was fascinated by the deeds of their ancestors. He thought of the Suez Canal and the trams and all the other things the Europeans had built, and he thought of the ignorance and backwardness of the villages.

But most of all, he thought of the people themselves, both European and African, and how only those people who had a nation to call their own held their head high. Even people from small, unimportant countries like Belgium or Greece held their heads high, while those from places far bigger such as the Soudan always ended up as servants no matter what their station.

At last he answered his boss's question. Moustafa knew it was not what Mr. Wall wanted to hear, but it was the only answer he could give.

"We are not ready, but soon we will be, and when that day comes, British rule must end."

"And the British?"

Moustafa paused. "Most will have to go. People like him," Moustafa waved the letter, "will have no place in the nation of Egypt."

"I see," his boss said. His tone sounded guarded.

"Some British can stay," Moustafa added quickly, "as well as other foreigners. Those who respect our ways and obey the new laws."

"Well, I suppose a few of us get to stay then. I couldn't bear the thought of having to be surrounded by English people the rest of my life."

Moustafa smiled. "Don't worry, Mr. Wall. I am sure that in our new nation there will be murders to be solved. You will have a place here."

27

Faisal stood outside the little lean-to of reed mats, listening to the happy conversation within. Mina's father had gone twice to the doctor and was already well enough that he could help out half a day at the *ful* stand. Mina, who was allowed to talk to him again now that Abbas Eldessouky was breaking rocks in a prison mine in the Western Desert, said that his injury was only something called a pinched nerve and that it was a simple thing for a European doctor to fix. The whole family was amazed that the Englishman had heard of their plight and had come to save them. Faisal didn't tell them how that had happened.

While Faisal was happy for Mina, he felt a bit sad for himself. He hadn't been able to get enough honest money for the spell against the Englishman's marriage, and he figured by this time it was too late. The Englishman had saved that Englishwoman and her brother, so there was no way their families wouldn't join now.

So he'd be out on the street soon. The disaster hadn't happened yet, but it was only a matter of time. His heart felt heavy to see that cozy little lean-to and to hear the happy family within. At least he had some money to keep hunger away for a week or so. After that it would be back to his old life.

Faisal accepted his fate. He had been silly to think his life would be any different. At least Mina would be all right.

In his hands was a little paper bird on a string. He had found it at a toy stall in one of the bazaars and bought it with some of his honest money. It had a brown body and black beak just like a real bird, and wings that opened up like a pair of those fans the European ladies used. The wings weren't like a real bird's, more like one of those birds in the stories with all sorts of colors on them. It looked amazing with the wings opened up.

He tiptoed up to the flap that passed for a door in Mina's home and hung the paper bird from the top so she'd see it when she came out in the morning. When he came for a breakfast of *ful* tomorrow he wouldn't say a word.

Faisal went to the end of the Ibn al-Nafis Street and lingered there, spying on the Englishman's house. He had been watching the house for the past few days and hadn't seen any carts coming to bring his wife's dowry with her, or any musicians playing, or chefs bearing trays of food for the feast. In fact, he saw no sign of a wedding at all.

What was going on? Maybe in England the husband went and lived in the wife's home. Europeans did everything the wrong way, so even such a ridiculous thing could be possible.

After a time, he saw the small door set into the main front portal open. The Englishman stepped out, alone. After locking the door behind him, he set off as if for his usual evening stroll, swinging his cane in time with his stride. Faisal grinned as he remembered the surprise on everyone's face when he had turned that cane into a sword to fight a bunch of bullies in this neighborhood.

Faisal looked around, worried. Was the Englishman going to meet his bride? If so, why wasn't he carrying any gifts or bringing his friends and family with him? There weren't even any musicians. Faisal tagged along behind him for a time. After following him for a few blocks, he became more and more convinced that he wasn't going to meet anyone after all. He really did look like he was going for his usual evening stroll.

He couldn't take this suspense anymore. Picking up his pace, he caught up with the Englishman.

"Hello," he said.

"Oh, hello Faisal." The Englishman didn't slow down. That was his way of saying that he didn't want any company.

"Where are you going?" Faisal asked.

"Nowhere interesting."

"Are you meeting anyone?"

"No one I want to meet."

"Are you meeting with that woman?"

"What woman?"

"The ...," Faisal summoned his courage. He had to know. "The Englishwoman you're going to marry."

The Englishman stopped. "What on Earth are you talking about?"

Faisal looked everywhere except at the Englishman. "Um ..."

"You mean Cordelia? You thought I was going to marry her?"

"Well, you took her into your house."

The Englishman's laughter rang out across the street. Faisal felt a bit annoyed. He didn't like being laughed at.

He forgot to be annoyed when the Englishman said, "Of course I'm not going to marry her! I have no intention of getting married."

Faisal resisted the urge to jump up and down and cheer. His mind raced. How could this have happened? He hadn't cast a spell on their marriage, only Mina's.

Then understanding dawned. Because he had stopped Mina's marriage himself by getting that pot-bellied bandit arrested and Mina's father a doctor, the spell had nothing to take effect on and bounced over to work on the Englishman. Khadija umm Mohammed's magic worked every time!

"Good Lord, Faisal, whatever gave you such a peculiar idea?" the Englishman asked.

"Oh, um, street gossip."

"I can't imagine what else people on my street must be saying about me. Ignore it all; it's all wrong."

"So you're not friends with the police commandant?"

"Can't stand the man."

"And you're not moving back to England?"

"Not if I can help it."

"And that woman isn't going to move into your house?"

"Over my dead body."

"Don't say that! It will give the jinn ideas."

"Back to the jinn again. I suppose I'll never win that battle. I did want to thank you for saving Cordelia from the baboons. I would have been in some very hot water if the police commandant's sister got killed on my watch."

Faisal puffed his chest out. "Chief Mohammed protects the innocent and defeats the guilty."

"Indeed. You were a very brave boy to face those baboons. I think you deserve some additional reward."

Faisal perked up. This sounded good.

"Maybe we should ask Tariq ibn Nagy for more information about the Apaches," Faisal suggested. The storyteller usually changed his show every two weeks, and it was getting to be about that time. Maybe the new show would be more useful to the Englishman. Even if it wasn't, it would be sure great to see it.

To his disappointment, the Englishman said, "I don't think so."

"But everyone goes to Tariq ibn Nagy. He's the best!"

"Amusing in his own way, I'm sure. But in England the boys all go to the cinematograph," the Englishman said.

"The what?" Faisal wondered if the Englishman had forgotten how to speak Arabic. That happened sometimes when he saw things that weren't there.

"Moving pictures. Do you know what they are?"

"Of course! The Europeans go to them."

"Yes, but do you know what they are?"

"Pictures. That move." Faisal looked up at him. "Is that right?"

"As far as it goes, yes."

"But that's silly, why would they move the pictures? Then you can't see them right!" Europeans really were strange people.

"No, it's the images that move."

Faisal stared at the Englishman, waiting for him to make sense.

"They take a series of photographs of someone moving, and run them in front of a light really quickly and project them on a wall, and it looks like the person in the picture is moving."

Faisal continued to wait. Usually if you gave him time, the Englishman eventually made sense.

"Here." The Englishman stepped beneath a streetlight and took a notebook and pencil from his pocket. He drew a little man standing on the bottom of the first page. Then he turned the page and drew another little man, this time with his foot a bit forward like he was taking a step. He turned the page and drew another little man with his foot a little further forward. The Englishman continued to draw little men for several pages.

"It's not moving," Faisal said.

"Wait until I'm done."

Faisal felt relieved. The Englishman still understood Arabic. That meant he wasn't gripped by madness at the moment.

After another minute he turned back to the first page and held it in front of Faisal.

"Watch."

Faisal gasped as the Englishman flipped through the pages and the little man looked like he was walking across the bottom of the notebook.

"Now remember, Faisal, this isn't magic—"

"Of course it isn't magic, you silly Englishman."

"Oh, you've finally stopped believing in magic?"

"Europeans can't do magic. That's why they have so many machines."

"This isn't a machine."

"Well, it's not magic, so of course its a machine!"

"Perhaps it would be best just to show you."

"Show me?"

"I have an appointment I am most eager to break, and since I wanted to reward you anyway, I can kill two birds with one stone."

"We're going to hunt birds? It's night time, you silly Englishman!"

"No, I'm going to take you to those moving pictures I told you about. I was supposed to meet Sir Thomas and Cordelia for drinks at the Windsor. A few broken engagements might cool her interest, and as I said you deserve it."

Faisal leaped in the air and spun around. Then he paused.

"Is Moustafa coming?"

"No, he went back home to Giza for the evening."

Good.

The moving pictures were kept inside a big building on one of the main streets. Faisal felt nervous because there were a lot of Europeans and rich Egyptians on the street, plus a lot of fine shops that he wouldn't dare go near if he were alone. When the Englishman went up to a little window next to the front door, he spoke in English to the man sitting behind it. The man behind the window was Egyptian, dressed in a fine red uniform with gold braiding, and he looked at Faisal with open contempt. Faisal was wearing his old jellaba because he had been begging earlier and you couldn't do that in a new jellaba. His had planned to put on his new one to show off to Mina but he hadn't changed yet.

The man at the window said something back to the Englishman. Faisal didn't understand his words, but he understood the meaning well enough.

"Why do you want to bring someone like him in here? People like him don't deserve moving pictures."

That's what the man behind the window was saying.

Faisal slumped his shoulders. He should have known they wouldn't let him in.

The Englishman started getting angry, and he kept repeating the name, "Russell Pasha."

That had an effect on the man behind the window. He took the Englishman's money and gave him two little pieces of paper.

The Englishman turned to Faisal. "We can go in."

Faisal still felt nervous, but not so nervous that he forgot to stick his tongue out at the man behind the window when the Englishman turned his back.

At the door another man in an identical uniform took the pieces of paper and ripped them in half. Faisal groaned. So they had decided not to let them in after all! But then the Englishman motioned for him to enter. The Englishman didn't seem worried at all that the man in the uniform had ripped up their papers. He sure was brave.

As they passed through the door, Faisal stopped and stared. They had entered a big room with green carpet on the floor and pictures on the walls. One was of a man in a ship holding a sword. Another showed some men in big hats riding horses and carrying pistols. Another showed a man and woman who looked like they were about to kiss. The pictures all had big words above them and smaller ones below them. Some of the words were in the European language, while others he recognized as Arabic. He couldn't read any of them, of course, but the pictures were interesting.

He stared at the one with the men on horseback. They were European and rode through a desert. That must be one of the deserts in Europe. He stood in front of it for a minute.

"When do they start to move?" Faisal asked.

The Englishman motioned to a door at the end of the hall. "They move in here."

They entered a big room with long rows of chairs. At the front of the room hung a large white sheet, and below and to one side of the sheet stood a strange musical instrument from Europe called a piano. About half the seats were taken by a mixture of Europeans and Egyptians who dressed like Europeans. The Englishman and Faisal found a couple of seats near the front and sat. A European man sitting in the same row took one look at Faisal and moved to another seat further away.

"Am I allowed to be here?" Faisal asked in a whisper.

"You are because I say so."

Faisal grinned. The Englishman pointed behind them at a hole in the back wall with a funny machine in it. It had a big glass eye and some wheels behind it. An Egyptian man was fiddling with the wheels.

"That's the projector," the Englishman explained. "That's where the moving pictures come from."

"Then why are the seats all facing away from it? You Europeans always get everything backwards!"

The Englishman smiled. "It makes the moving pictures appear on the screen in front of us."

Faisal scratched his head. That didn't make sense, but the Europeans had machines that could fly and go under the water, so why not a machine that could turn a white sheet into a picture?

"When does it start?" he asked, looking around.

"Soon."

"When?"

"I don't know. Soon. Sit still."

After a few minutes, with Faisal asking the Englishman several more times when it was going to start, an old European man sat down at the piano. The lights switched off and Faisal heard a strange rattling coming from the projector. Faisal jumped a little as the sheet suddenly lit up and the piano began to play.

Some words in English appeared on the sheet. Faisal peeked back and saw the projector was shining a bright ray of light toward the sheet, like a really big lantern.

"Eyes front," the Englishman said.

Faisal gasped as a picture appeared on the sheet. It showed the inside of a restaurant, all black and white like normal photographs but this one really did move just like the Englishman said it would!

Faisal was surprised to see that the waiter in the restaurant was a European. Faisal had never heard of a European being a waiter before. He figured that even in Europe the waiters were Egyptian.

He was a funny looking European, though. He had a little square moustache and a round hat too small for his head. He wore a sloppy shirt that hung out of his baggy pants and he waddled around the restaurant with his feet splayed out.

The waiter cleared an empty table of dirty dishes, then waddled over to where a man was still eating and took his dish too. The diner started waving his hands in the air and shouting, but of course Faisal couldn't hear him because even Europeans couldn't make a picture talk. The funny waiter shrugged and dumped the old food from all the other plates onto the man's plate.

Faisal giggled. Then the waiter went into the restaurant's basement where they had a bakery. There were Europeans working down there too. A man kneaded a huge bowl of dough and the waiter with the funny square moustache waddled over to help him. The two got in each other's way and the baker kicked the funny waiter in the rear. Faisal laughed. The waiter kicked the baker back, and soon they started throwing big globs of dough at each other. The man at the piano picked up speed and the music kept time with the two Europeans running around throwing things at each other. Another baker came to stop the fight and they threw him in the bowl of dough.

Faisal laughed and slapped the arm of his chair and drummed his feet on the floor. For once no one told him to be quiet. They couldn't hear him anyway, because the whole audience was laughing—Egyptians, Europeans, everyone. Even the Englishman laughed from time to time, and he hardly ever laughed.

Faisal laughed so long and hard his eyes teared up and his chest started to hurt. Just when he thought he couldn't take it anymore, the pictures stopped moving, the piano fell silent, and the lights came back on.

Faisal wiped his eyes, still giggling. He remembered the fight with the dough and started laughing again. Then there was the time the man with the funny moustache dropped a sack of grain on the baker and squashed him. And the time the funny man got covered in dough and pushed his head up through it like a hippopotamus rising out of the water. After a time, Faisal was able to control himself.

"So what do you think?" the Englishman asked.

"That was great!" Faisal sprang to his feet. "I have to go tell my friends."

"Don't run off. There's more."

"More?" Faisal couldn't believe his luck.

"Yes, the projectionist is only changing the reel."

Faisal had no idea what the Englishman had just said, but if he promised more, that was good enough. He sat back down.

"So you liked it?" the Englishman asked.

"Oh yes. It made me a bit sad, though."

"Sad? You were splitting your sides the entire time."

"I mean sad for Tariq ibn Nagy. Once everyone starts coming to these moving pictures, no one will want to look inside his box anymore."

"Hmm, I suppose you're right."

"Cigarettes! Peanuts! Cigarettes! Peanuts!" A man in a dark red jellaba and matching tarboosh walked up the aisle, calling out his wares that he held in a big tray hanging from a strap around his neck. Augustus called him over.

"Some peanuts for the boy."

Faisal grinned. "How did you know I was hungry?"

"Because you're always hungry." The Englishman handed him a bag of peanuts.

Faisal took the peanuts and looked at them. Then he looked at the Englishman, who was lighting a cigarette.

"Eat up, Chief Mohammed," the Englishman said.

Faisal almost told him then. He almost told him about the little house he had made on the Englishman's roof, and how he had hired himself as the Englishman's bodyguard. He wanted to tell the Englishman that he didn't really live alone like he thought he did but had someone protecting him from jinn and thieves and all the other dangers.

But he sensed that to do so might be pushing his luck. Faisal didn't get much luck, and it would be wise not to get greedy with it.

"You got quiet all of a sudden," the Englishman said.

"I, um, I was wondering what happens next."

"More fun."

Faisal pushed his bag of peanuts toward the Englishman.

"Want one?"

"Thank you."

The piano player returned to his seat, the lights went down, and the projector came to life. The man with the little moustache appeared and caused more chaos in the bakery. Soon Faisal and the Englishman started laughing once more.

HISTORICAL NOTE

While the main characters and story in this novel are fiction, the historical background is as accurate as I could make it. The events of the Egyptian Revolution of 1919 unfolded as they are portrayed here, from the arrest of the independence leaders who were pressuring the British Empire to make good on its promises, to the mass protests and their bloody suppression. This was a key moment in modern Egyptian history and marks the beginnings of an effective independence movement, one that would see completion in the following generation.

A couple of the minor characters are also real, such as Sir Thomas Russell Pasha, Commandant of the Cairo Police. His racist and arrogant attitudes toward the "natives" in my novel are sadly all too accurate. In fact, I think I might have gone a bit easy on him. His personal correspondence from this period makes for appalling reading.

Another real figure is that of Heinrich Schäfer. I am glad to say he finally did finish his *Principles of Egyptian Art* which, while a weighty academic tome, is still one of the most thorough introductions to understanding the art of ancient Egypt almost a hundred years after it was written.

Besides Schäfer's *Principles of Egyptian Art,* two other excellent books that helped with researching this novel are, *Grand Hotels of Egypt in the Golden Age of Travel* and *On the Nile in the Golden Age of Travel,* both by Andrew Humphreys. I also relied on William Edward Lane's classic study, *Manners and Customs of the Modern Egyptians* and the 1929 edition of the *Baedeker's Guide to Egypt and the Sudan.*

Marcus Simaika was an important leader in the Cairo's Coptic community at this time. He founded the Coptic Museum, which still exists today. With the blessings of the Coptic Pope Cyril, he scoured the monasteries and churches of Egypt for old artifacts and manuscripts to add to the museum's collection. Now, a hundred years later, the Coptic Museum is one of the most interesting sights in Cairo, with an impressive collection tracing the history of one of the world's oldest Christian communities. The Nilometer is another historic landmark and worth a trip to al-Rawdah island.

The Apaches are real as well. This Parisian street gang started in the 1880s, taking their name from the famous Native American tribe that was still defying the United States government at that time. The Apache gang survived for more than a generation, committing a string of daring robberies that showed a mixture of bravery, panache, and brutality. Putting the chief of police of Paris in an Old Kingdom sarcophagus would have appealed to their anarchist sensibilities.

The sarcophagus that mysteriously appears in Augustus's showroom is based on one in the Cairo Museum. This Old Kingdom artifact has accession number 48078 if you wish to look it up in the Cairo Museum's collections catalog. Several other artifacts described in the novel are part of the collection as well. One of the benefits of being a writer is that you get to wander around the Cairo Museum looking at ancient Egyptian art and call it "work"!

The Charlie Chaplin film that so entertained Faisal is called *Dough and Dynamite* and came out in 1916. It was playing on my Egyptair flight as I went to Cairo to research this book. Thanks to the airline, I got to start my research early!

Tariq ibn Nagy's magical box is based on one I saw in the Ethnographic Museum in Cairo. In the days before movies became common, Egyptian children were thrilled to watch shows created with pictures and dolls illuminated by differently colored lights, narrated by expert storytellers who once entertained the public on street corners and cafés. Sadly, Faisal's prediction that movies would put people like Tariq ibn Nagy out of business came true, and no storyteller with a magic box has entertained Cairo's children for many years.

The Ethnographic Museum is one of the overlooked delights of Cairo, filled with everyday items and costumes from Cairo's past. In the toy section is the paper bird Faisal gives to Mina. If you want to see the museum, you're in for a bit of work. Located just off Tahrir Square, the building complex where the Ethnographic Museum is located was turned into a police base after the famous protests of 2011. The museum remains open, but to get inside you have to show your passport, walk through a metal detector, sit for some time surrounded by burly policemen, and then get escorted to the museum by a cop carrying a machine gun. No one is going to rob the Ethnographic Museum of its treasures!

Unless, of course, the Apaches return to Cairo. Or the jinn …

ABOUT THE AUTHOR

Sean McLachlan worked for ten years as an archaeologist in Israel, Cyprus, Bulgaria, and the United States before becoming a full-time writer. He is the author of numerous fiction and nonfiction books, which are listed on the following pages. When he's not writing, he enjoys hiking, reading, traveling, and, most of all, teaching his son about the world. He divides his time between Madrid, Oxford, and Cairo.

To find out more about Sean's work and travels, visit him at his blog and feel free to friend him on Goodreads, Twitter, and Facebook.

You might also enjoy his newsletter, *Sean's Travels and Tales,* which comes out every one or two months. Each issue features a short story, a travel article, a coupon for a free or discounted book, and updates on future projects. You can subscribe using this link - http://eepurl.com/bJfiDn. Your email will not be shared with anyone else.

FICTION BY SEAN MCLACHLAN

Tangier Bank Heist: An Interzone Mystery

Right after the war, Tangier was the craziest town in North Africa. Everything was for sale and the price was cheap. The perverts came for the flesh. The addicts came for the drugs. A whole army of hustlers and grifters came for the loose laws and free flow of cash and contraband.

So why was I here? Because it was the only place that would have me. Besides, it was a great place to be a detective. You got cases like in no other place I'd ever been, and I'd been all over. Cases you couldn't believe ever happened. Like when I had to track down the guy who stole the bank.

No, he didn't rob the bank, he stole it.

Here's how it happened . . .

Available in electronic edition! Print edition coming soon!

The Case of the Purloined Pyramid
(The Masked Man of Cairo Book One)

An ancient mystery. A modern murder.

Sir Augustus Wall, a horribly mutilated veteran of the Great War, has left Europe behind to open an antiquities shop in Cairo. But Europe's troubles follow him as a priceless inscription is stolen and those who know its secrets start turning up dead. Teaming up with Egyptology expert Moustafa Ghani, and Faisal, an irritating street urchin he just can't shake, Sir Wall must unravel an ancient secret and face his own dark past.

Available in electronic and print editions!

The Case of the Shifting Sarcophagus
(The Masked Man of Cairo Book Two)

An Old Kingdom coffin. A body from yesterday.

Sir Augustus Wall had seen a lot of death. From the fields of Flanders to the alleys of Cairo, he'd solved several murders and sent many men to their grave. But he's never had a body delivered to his antiquities shop encased in a 5,000 year-old coffin.

Soon he finds himself fighting a vicious street gang bent on causing national mayhem while his assistant, Moustafa Ghani, faces his own enemies in the form of colonial powers determined to ruin him. Throughout all this runs the street urchin Faisal. Ignored as usual, dismissed as usual, he has the most important fight of all.

Available in electronic edition! Print edition coming soon!

Radio Hope (Toxic World Book One)

In a world shattered by war, pollution, and disease…

A gunslinging mother longs to find a safe refuge for her son.

A frustrated revolutionary delivers water to villagers living on a toxic waste dump.

The assistant mayor of humanity's last city hopes he will never have to take command.

One thing gives them the promise of a better future—Radio Hope, a mysterious station that broadcasts vital information about surviving in a blighted world. But when a mad prophet and his army of fanatics march out of the wildlands on a crusade to purify the land with blood and fire, all three will find their lives intertwining, and changing forever.

Available in print and electronic editions!

Refugees from the Righteous Horde (Toxic World Book Two)

When you only have one shot, you better aim true.

In a ravaged world, civilization's last outpost is reeling after fighting off the fanatical warriors of the Righteous Horde. Sheriff Annette Cruz becomes New City's long arm of vengeance as she sets off across the wildlands to take out the cult's leader. All she has is a sniper's rifle with one bullet and a former cultist with his own agenda. Meanwhile, one of the cult's escaped slaves makes a discovery that could tear New City apart…

Refugees from the Righteous Horde continues the Toxic World series started in Radio Hope, an ongoing narrative of humanity's struggle to rebuild the world it ruined.

Available in electronic edition!

We Had Flags (Toxic World Book Three)

A law doesn't work if everyone breaks it.

For forty years, New City has been a bastion of order in a fallen world. One crucial law has maintained the peace: it is illegal to place responsibility for the collapse of civilization on any one group. Anyone found guilty of Blaming is branded and stripped of citizenship.

But when some unwelcome visitors arrive from across the sea, old wounds break open, and no one is safe from Blame.

Available in electronic edition!

The Scavenger (A Toxic World Novelette)

In a world shattered by war, pollution, and disease, a lone scavenger discovers a priceless relic from the Old Times.

The problem is, it's stuck in the middle of the worst wasteland he knows—a contaminated city inhabited by insane chem addicts and vengeful villagers. Only his wits, his gun, and an unlikely ally can get him out alive.

Set in the Toxic World series introduced in the novel *Radio Hope*, this 10,000-word story explores more of the dangers and personalities that make up a post-apocalyptic world that's all too possible.

Available in electronic edition!

Trench Raiders (Trench Raiders Book One)

September 1914: The British Expeditionary Force has the Germans on the run, or so they think.

After a month of bitter fighting, the British are battered,

exhausted, and down to half their strength, yet they've helped save Paris and are pushing towards Berlin. Then the retreating Germans decide to make a stand. Holding a steep slope beside the River Aisne, the entrenched Germans mow down the advancing British with machine gun fire. Soon the British dig in too, and it looks like the war might grind down into deadly stalemate.

Searching through No-Man's Land in the darkness, Private Timothy Crawford of the Oxfordshire and Buckinghamshire Light Infantry finds a chink in the German armor. But can this lowly private, who spends as much time in the battalion guardhouse as he does on the parade ground, convince his commanding officer to risk everything for a chance to break through?

Available in electronic edition!

Digging In (Trench Raiders Book Two)

October 1914: The British line is about to break.

After two months of hard fighting, the British Expeditionary Force is short of men, ammunition, and ideas. With their line stretched to the breaking point, aerial reconnaissance spots German reinforcements massing for the big push. As their trenches are hammered by a German artillery battery, the men of the Oxfordshire and Buckinghamshire Light Infantry come up with a desperate plan—a daring raid behind enemy lines to destroy the enemy guns and give the British a chance to stop the German army from breaking through.

Available in electronic edition!

No Man's Land (Trench Raiders Book Three)

No Man's Land—a hellscape of shell craters and dead bodies. Soldiers have fought over it, charged across it, and bled on it for a year of grueling war, but neither side has dominated it.

Until now.

An elite German raiding party is passing through No Man's Land every night, attacking the British trenches at will. The Oxfordshire and Buckinghamshire Light Infantry need to reassert control over their front lines.

So the exhausted men of Company E decide to set a trap, a nighttime ambush in the middle of No Man's Land, where any mistake can be fatal. But the few surviving veterans are leading recruits who have only been in the trenches for two weeks. Mistakes are inevitable.

Available in electronic edition!

Warpath into Sonora

Arizona 1846

Nantan, a young Apache warrior, is building a name for himself by leading raids against Mexican ranches to impress his war chief, and the chief's lovely daughter. But there is one thing he and all other Apaches fear—a ruthless band of Mexican scalp hunters who slaughter entire villages.

Nantan and his friends have sworn to fight back, but they are inexperienced, and led by a war chief driven mad with a thirst for revenge. Can they track their tribe's worst enemy into unknown territory and defeat them?

Available in electronic edition!

Christmas Truce

Christmas 1914

In the cold, muddy trenches of the Western Front, there is a strange silence. As the members of a crack English trench raiding team enjoy their first day of peace in months, they call out holiday greetings to the men on the German line. Soon both sides are fraternizing in No Man's Land.

But when the English recognize some enemy raiders who only a few days before launched a deadly attack on their position, can they keep the peace through the Christmas truce?

Available in electronic edition!

A Fine Likeness (House Divided Book One)

A Confederate guerrilla and a Union captain discover there's something more dangerous in the woods than each other.

Jimmy Rawlins is a teenage bushwhacker who leads his friends on ambushes of Union patrols. They join infamous guerrilla leader Bloody Bill Anderson on a raid through Missouri, but Jimmy questions his commitment to the cause when he discovers this madman plans to sacrifice a Union prisoner in a hellish ritual to raise the Confederate dead.

Richard Addison is an aging captain of a lackluster Union militia. Depressed over his son's death in battle, a glimpse of Jimmy changes his life. Jimmy and his son look so much alike that Addison becomes obsessed with saving him from Bloody Bill. Captain Addison must wreck his reputation to win this war within a war, while Jimmy must decide whether to betray the Confederacy to stop the evil arising in the woods of Missouri.

Available in electronic edition!

The River of Desperation (House Divided Book Two)

In the waning days of the Civil War, a secret conflict still rages…

Lieutenant Allen Addison of the *USS Essex* is looking forward to the South's defeat so he can build the life he's always wanted. Love and a promising business await him in St. Louis, but he is swept up in a primeval war between the forces of Order and Chaos, a struggle he doesn't understand and can barely believe in. Soon he is fighting to keep a grip on his sanity as he tries to save St. Louis from destruction.

The long-awaited sequel to *A Fine Likeness* continues the story of two opposing forces that threaten to tear the world apart.

Available in electronic edition!

The Last Hotel Room

He came to Tangier to die, but life isn't done with him yet.

Tom Miller has lost his job, his wife, and his dreams. Broke and alone, he ends up in a flophouse in Morocco, ready to end it all. But soon he finds himself tangled in a web of danger and duty as he's pulled into scamming tourists for a crooked cop while trying to help a Syrian refugee boy survive life on the streets. Can a lifelong loser do something good for a change?

A portion of my royalties will go to a charity for Syrian refugees.

Available in electronic and print editions!

The Night the Nazis Came to Dinner and Other Dark Tales

A spectral dinner party goes horribly wrong…

An immortal warrior hopes a final battle will set him free…

A big-game hunter preys on endangered species to supply an illicit restaurant…

A new technology soothes First World guilt…

Here are four dark tales that straddle the boundary between reality and speculation. You better hope they don't come true.

Available in electronic edition!

The Quintessence of Absence

Can a drug-addicted sorcerer sober up long enough to save a kidnapped girl and his own duchy?

In an alternate eighteenth-century Germany where magic is real and paganism never died, Lothar is in the bonds of nepenthe, a powerful drug that gives him ecstatic visions. It has also taken his job, his friends, and his self-respect. Now his old employer has rehired Lothar to find the man's daughter, who is in the grip of her own addiction to nepenthe.

As Lothar digs deeper into the girl's disappearance, he uncovers a plot that threatens the entire Duchy of Anhalt, and finds that the only way to stop it is to face his own weakness.

Available in electronic edition!

HISTORY BOOKS BY SEAN MCLACHLAN

African History

Armies of the Adowa Campaign 1896: The Italian Disaster in Ethiopia (Osprey: 2011)

Wild West History

Apache Warrior vs. US Cavalryman: 1846-86 (Osprey: 2016)

Tombstone—Wyatt Earp, the O.K. Corral, and the Vendetta Ride (Osprey: 2013)

The Last Ride of the James-Younger Gang (Osprey: 2012)

Civil War History

Ride Around Missouri: Shelby's Great Raid 1863 (Osprey: 2011)

American Civil War Guerrilla Tactics (Osprey: 2009)

Missouri History

Outlaw Tales of Missouri (Globe Pequot: 2009)

Missouri: An Illustrated History (Hippocrene: 2008)

It Happened in Missouri (Globe Pequot: 2007)

Medieval History

Medieval Handgonnes: The First Black Powder Infantry Weapons (Osprey: 2010)

Byzantium: An Illustrated History (Hippocrene: 2004)

WRITING BOOKS BY SEAN MCLACHLAN

Writing Secrets of the World's Most Prolific Authors

What does it take to write 100 books? What about 500? Or 1,000?

That may sound like an impossibly high number, but it isn't. Some of the world's most successful authors wrote hundreds of books over the course of highly lucrative careers. Isaac Asimov wrote more than 300 books. Enid Blyton wrote more than 800. Legendary Western writer Lauren Bosworth Paine wrote close to 1,000.

Some wrote even more.

This book examines the techniques and daily habits of more than a dozen of these remarkable writers to show how anyone with the right mindset can massively increase their word count without sacrificing quality. Learn the secrets of working on several projects simultaneously, of reducing the time needed for each book, and how to build the work ethic you need to become more prolific than you ever thought possible.

Made in the USA
Las Vegas, NV
18 April 2023

70785968R00194